New Girl on the Island

Book One of the Island Series

Jonathan Ross

Also by Jonathan Ross

Death in a Carolina Swamp

The Jumbee's Daughter

Scent of Death

For more information about Jonathan Ross and his novels, please visit www.jonathanrossnovels.com

This book is a work of fiction. Names, characters, businesses, organizations, places, events, the island of St. Mark, and incidents either are the product of the author's imagination or are used fictitiously. Any resemblance to actual persons, living or dead, events, or locales is entirely coincidental.

To my friends at the Friday Morning Coffee Group,
solving the world's problems
one cup of coffee at a time.

Acknowledgments

To Sam, Robert, Donna,
Marna, Joye, and Laura,
for their kind editorial assistance;
to Doug O'Connor for sharing his website expertise;
and to my mentor, Kathryn Johnson, for her keen eye for detail
and her her unfailingly diplomatic counsel

CHAPTER 1

Sophie felt the ache return, like yesterday and the day before, creeping into her chest. It would be with her for the rest of the day, she knew. Walking the beach, feeling the sand with her bare feet, hearing the waves, viewing the sandpipers – none of that helped. She might as well have stayed in bed staring at the ceiling.

A low rumble of thunder interrupted her grim thoughts. She blinked. Looked up. Black clouds and lightning, forming an angry squall line, approaching fast. Rain formed a solid gray curtain between cloud and sea. Close by, the ocean turned dark, its waves ponderous. The sand felt oddly warm compared to the oncoming storm's searching fingers of cool wind.

The estate lay a hundred yards farther along. She broke into a trot, recalling stories about dumb people killed by lightning on the beach. Amazingly, only a corner of her mind registered the squall, confirmed its danger, goaded her to shelter. The bulk of her consciousness lay jangled with that ache, caused, she knew by the anguish that kept her awake at night, bedsheets pulled up to her chin.

Sophie replayed snippets of conversation she'd overheard during the past few days, between Cliff Webb – her boyfriend, who owned the estate – and a half dozen flinty-eyed men in black suits, coming early, departing late, and returning again the next morning. The conversations were low-voiced and urgent, and stopped dead when she appeared.

1

Worst of all was Cliff's dismissal, banning her with a stern look and tilt of his head. As if she were a tattered chair in an otherwise well-furnished room.

So different from her usual social standing among guests at the estate – real guests, not these dour men. She had been his partner, the ever-gracious hostess, smoothing ruffled feathers, joining conversations, sharing smiles. These days, she couldn't even grab a snack, because the intruding men commandeered the kitchen.

Their grumbling permeated the house, heard everywhere, even leaking upstairs if she forgot to close the doors. Worse, the grumbling degenerated into sharply-worded arguments, like lightning strikes, followed by rumbles, finally calming again to garrulous chatter.

She felt menace in the air and she finally concluded that these men were not only dangerous, but fearful. Because she knew that fearful men acted loud and brave, mostly loud. They were scared, and that fear crept into her bones, her mind, her chest.

Sometimes she heard not only the tone of conversations but words. Foul, black words. They formed a pattern that told of competition with unnamed others, dirty deals gone sour, chases, threats. And more than once the mention of death. Unpleasant death.

Mid-afternoon, just before her walk on the beach, all the men in black suits departed. Leaving behind two new people, rough men who wore jeans instead of suits. And Cliff remained as well. A different Cliff. Whenever she was alone with him lately, he was brusque, critical. "You ask too many questions," he snarled more than once.

She reached the steps from the beach to the estate, and paused to catch her breath. Ahead, loomed the wide lawn, the pool and the patio, demanding a further sprint to the shelter of the sprawling, Spanish-style structure.

The wind quickened, cold against her sweaty limbs. Thick raindrops fell. Lightning struck, closer now, followed by an immediate snap and growl of thunder. She scooted up the steps. Ran full-out to the patio and dodged inside.

Something caught her eye, and she glanced back through the windows. Strange – one of the chairs was missing from the patio table set. There had been eight chairs when she left, she was sure. Now seven remained. She felt a twinge of anxiety. *It's just a chair*, she chided herself. But the feeling stuck.

Shivering in the air conditioning, she grabbed a towel from the pile on the table beside the door. Dried herself. Outside, lightning and thunder quarreled. Nature's violence. She looked again at the patio, to the empty spot where the heavy iron chair had stood.

She switched on lights, noticed her running shoes by the door where she'd left them. Slipped them on.

So the maid had left early. Another little mystery. Cliff never let her go early. "I want my money's worth," he always said. The maid would have turned the lights on against the dreary storm. Would have greeted Sophie with a smile and a towel. Cliff must have ordered her to leave.

She tiptoed toward the kitchen. Paused in the hall. Listened for voices. Heard only thunder, and the wind-driven rain, striking windows like hordes of pellets.

When she entered the kitchen, an odd scent tickled her nose. Tart, with hints of charcoal and copper. She almost wished the men were there to explain. Almost.

Anyway, even the two rough guys were gone, leaving dirty dishes and beer bottles on the counter. Cliff was gone as well, and she drew a breath. Of relief perhaps. Or maybe regret.

He was the man she had once loved, and she had happily accepted his invitation to move in with him. They hadn't talked much about marriage, but they lived well together and she had dared to dream of kids and laughter in the coming years.

But this past week – no, for many weeks – this vital, intelligent, and once charming man had changed. He had always been private, but when they were alone together he'd let her draw him out.

On his boat or dancing, or even walking the beach, he had seemed to become the real Cliff, the real person inside. They smiled into each other's eyes, held hands, and made love.

There was that smell again.

Acrid. Not exactly a cooking smell. More an odor of burning. Rubber? No, more organic, or maybe metallic. Yes, metallic. Yes, putrid and metallic. She checked the stove and ovens. Both cool. Opened the cupboards. Stepped into the dining room. Then back into the kitchen to open the fridge. But encountered only ordinary kitchen smells.

Sophie looked down a hall at the door to the garage. Felt physically drawn to what lay beyond. She stepped close. A tingle descended her spine.

She reached for the door knob but immediately withdrew her hand. The garage suddenly seemed off limits. More so than the kitchen had been. A private enclave she was forbidden to enter.

Which made no sense, because she'd been in there hundreds of times. Probably, they had gone for dinner and would soon return and reclaim the kitchen. But no, they had already eaten their food, left their dirty dishes.

She extended her hand again and gripped the cold metal of the door knob. Hesitated. Better to be cautious than risk barging in on a meeting and feeling foolish.

With a pounding heart, she pressed her ear to the door.

Voices.

Low voices, insistent, sharp. Was that Cliff? Yes, she recognized the threatening tone, so familiar yet so foreign. She'd never heard him raise his voice before these past weeks.

But now there was another voice – eerily high-pitched, indistinct.

Trembling, she slowly turned the door knob, then pushed the door, planning to open it just wide enough to peek inside. But the door wouldn't open. Strange. Maybe it was jammed. She pressed harder, grasping the door knob to hold the door from swinging fully open.

No go. The door held firm, locked. She brushed her damp hair. Obviously, Cliff and the other men wanted to be left alone.

But she *was* curious.

Of course, there was another way. She could look through the outside window in the garage door. She exited the kitchen and stood on the sidewalk that ran next to the house. Rain poured from the black sky, whipped by wind, overflowed the gutters, clogged downspouts. She was drenched in seconds.

Sophie gritted her teeth. This was her opportunity to discover what these strangers were up to, maybe clear the air with Cliff, let her get on with her life.

She eased along the sidewalk to the door. Leaned down and shaded her eyes to peer inside. All was black. Only then did she remember that she had covered the window with a curtain because the idea of someone looking in at night creeped her out. Darn.

Lightning struck, thunder boomed. Close.

She checked the edges of the curtain and found a small gap on the right side. Again, she peered into the garage, shivering in the splattering rain and frigid wind.

Two ceiling lights illuminated the interior of the garage. Both cars – Cliff's and hers – were gone. The voices were barely audible above the sound of the storm, but the tone was not at all pleasant. She caught cursing in English and Spanish.

Then a hissing sound, like air escaping from an inner tube, but louder. Followed by an entirely different sound, from a person – an intake of breath and a muffled, agonized wail, starting high and strong even though obviously muffled. And keening for an unbearably long time before stopping. She bit her lip to keep from screaming.

The hissing stopped abruptly. Mumbled words passed between Cliff and his tough friends. She adjusted her position.

And gasped at a scene she would take to her grave.

There was the chair from the patio, placed on a plastic mat in the middle of the floor.

5

Bound by his legs, arms, and chest was a man. Muscular build, thick black hair, a rag wrapped around his head and across his mouth. His face was bruised and bloodied, his eyes wide with fear and pain. He emitted a gurgling sound as the hissing resumed. A blowtorch, its flame a luminous blue.

Cliff held the torch!

She swallowed and stared in horror. This man who had made love to her. He knelt in front of the bound man and adjusted the flame with a small knob. He glanced at the two standing men, smiled as if to a couple of friends at a weekend cook-out. He pulled a pair of goggles over his eyes, settled on his haunches and moved the flame close to the bound man's shins, a bloody and blackened mass from previous burning.

Sophie commanded herself to look away, yet she continued to stare.

Flames contacted flesh. God – that was what she had smelled. Smoke rose in a small cloud and the man in the chair jerked convulsively.

Cliff passed the flame back and forth across the bound man's legs. One of the standing men said something and the other laughed.

On the third pass, the bound man heaved his body to the limit of his bonds and abruptly collapsed, leaning forward.

Sophie's stomach heaved and she tasted bile. She covered her mouth with one hand. *Move,* she ordered herself. *Run!* But her body refused to respond.

Cliff shut off the blow torch.

"Muerto," said the standing man who had made the joke.

Sophie knew the Spanish word for 'death' and she shivered.

Cliff stood, shaking his head.

"Too bad. I had more planned for him. He deserved it." He removed his goggles, his face a mask of rage and hatred.

Sophie's entire body shook, revolted at what she witnessed, disgusted with Cliff and the other two. And with herself for not trying to stop the torture. But even as she watched she'd known she couldn't have made a difference. And now she felt dirty, just from having witnessed the horrible act.

She was completely out of her depth. What should she do? *Get as far away as possible!* She backed away from the window, her hand still to her mouth.

At last, her instincts took charge. She patted her pockets, felt car keys and wallet in their waterproof case. In the wallet were four one-hundred-dollar bills. Emergency money for whatever. Maybe a treat, she'd thought. Now it would save her life.

If she moved fast.

Sophie looked down at her soaking beach clothes and running shoes, mentally shrugged, and ran toward the cars, barely aware of her footing on the treacherous, drenched sidewalk.

Her purse was in her bedroom, containing her cell phone. No way to get those, or dry clothes. Certainly no time to call her manager at Sports Training Plus. What would she say? *Sorry, I've got to get out of the country for a while, so I'll miss my appointments this afternoon with the baseball pitcher and the girl training for the summer Olympics.* Nope. No time for that. No time for a clever disguise.

She shot a worried glance at the garage door – still closed – opened the car door and dove in. Reminded herself not to slam the door. She quietly started the engine. Killed the automatic headlights, backed, turned, and eased out of the driveway, onto the road.

South, she thought. The airport. *Gotta get out of here!*

A passing car honked angrily. She flicked on her headlights with a trembling hand. Tears stung her eyes. She'd seen things she never should have. Things Cliff Webb wouldn't want anyone to know. If he could do what she'd seen him do to that man, what might he do to her?

Miami International Airport was just the first step of the plan forming in her head.

She decided it was good she'd left her cell phone. One less way for Cliff to track her. All she needed was cash and a driver's license. She would leave the car unlocked in the airport parking lot. Keys in the ignition. With luck, some punk would steal it and either take it out of state or to a chop shop.

No phone, no car, no credit card trail. Cliff could still track her from airline passenger lists, but he'd have to call in favors. She hoped that would take a day, maybe more.

It was the best she could do.

CHAPTER 2

Richard Drake stepped out of the Red Bay Marina charter boat office feeling good. Damn good. His boat was safely moored, the early afternoon sun warmed his face, and he had a nice backlog of charter parties. Plus, he'd picked up island gossip in the office. The manager said all was quiet – even the drug gangs appeared to be taking a summer break.

As Drake strolled toward the tiki bar, he thought back on bad times, bad places, and how this place was so much better. Yes, the islands were night-and-day different from growing up in the shadow of the Rocky Mountains. Not to mention the dusty gulches of Afghanistan and a half dozen other shit holes around the world where he'd served in Marine Force Recon.

He glanced left to the clubhouse and restaurant, ahead to all the sailboats and motor boats snug in their slips, and over at the palm-thatched tiki bar. During the ten minutes he'd been inside arranging for his next charter party's sail among the Virgin Islands, his buddy, Graham Walters, had taken a seat at the bar. Drake approached the shady enclave. Walters turned and lifted his beer in a toast.

"To the peaceful side of life," he proclaimed with his usual gravitas.

Drake grinned and they shook hands, their eyes meeting and reaffirming their bond as veterans of vicious wars and lost comrades. The bartender placed a cold Heineken on the bar. Drake nodded thanks.

"Nice day for a charter," said Walters. "Got anything in the pipeline?"

"Yeah. Couple of day charters this coming week. We'll explore a few of the British Virgins, find a deserted bay where I'll anchor and take a long walk while they pretend they're the only people on a pristine planet."

Walters sipped his beer. "Sounds like you're into your work."

"Beats combat," Drake said.

"No shit. I feel the same with my cushy job." Walters worked for the St. Thomas Police Department in the Drug Enforcement Task Force. "Most days no one even shoots at me."

"By the way," Walters said. "Word on the street says there's a couple coming our way – guy and a woman – enforcers for a Latin drug cartel. Tough people. They're not visiting for pleasure, that's for sure."

Drake frowned at his beer. "Any hint they might have their sights set on my employer?"

"The judge? Nothing that specific." Walters rubbed his chin. "But your judge *is* trying the case of some Latino drug lord, isn't he?"

Drake laughed. "Drug lord? Man, read a newspaper now and then. He was the damned President of Venezuela. It's a nasty case, the judge tells me. Keep me posted on those two enforcers."

Walters shook his head. "Damn, I knew I shouldn't have told you."

"Yeah?"

"Yeah. You're like a friggin' bulldog any time I get something on my radar."

"Can't be too safe. Man's life at stake."

"You were like that in combat. During your recons."

"You mean all intense? Of course. Haven't we been through this before?"

Walters swigged his beer, shrugged.

"Not more than three dozen times." He looked at Drake, couldn't keep from grinning. "You seem so relaxed in front of your charter parties. You've got the act down pat. Just an island guy, taking them out, showing them a good time. But with anything connected with Judge Santiago, you're on it like stink on shit."

"That's what he pays me for," drawled Drake, grinning.

"Okay, buddie, I'll keep you posted."

"But you're telling me not to make any midnight calls, right?"

"Roger that."

"You promise to let me know anything new?"

"Yep. Scout's honor. Anything happens, I'll call you on your sat phone."

They stared at their beers, a companionable silence which Drake finally broke. "Am I really that much of a pain in the ass?"

"Naw. Truth is, I'd be happy with you covering my six in a combat situation."

"But you *will* keep me informed? Even little stuff?"

"Jesus, Drake." Walters finished his beer, stood and set the bottle on the table with a ten-dollar bill, and grumbled, "Like I said, I'll keep you in the loop."

CHAPTER 3

Sophie had hoped that escaping from the estate and catching a flight out of Miami would be the only scary part. After all, that was where she was most vulnerable. But her anxiety intensified even as the plane took off and Miami disappeared. What would Cliff think when he found she'd gone missing?

He'd know.

Sophie refused the snack and drink offered by the smiling flight attendant. She ignored a polite conversation opener from the lady sitting next to her.

When she furtively surveyed the other passengers, the men appeared to be sizing her up. Not in a sexual way, but as if they were deciding how to kill her. *Maybe in the restroom.* No, too noisy. *Poison her drink.* Nope, she wasn't drinking. *Maybe when she got off the plane.* Yeah. Follow her, catch her alone.

Finally, the captain announced the plane's descent to St. Thomas' Cyril E. King Airport. Sophie swallowed hard. About time.

Getting her luggage took way too long. Everyone moved in slow motion. The minutes dragged and dragged. Still no luggage. Not good. More opportunity for her ex-boyfriend to find her missing and begin the chase. For the tenth time she imagined what he'd do to her.

Kill her, that's what he'd do. He'd tie her up on a frigging iron patio chair with duct tape and roast her legs with that blow torch until she died of pain or a heart attack. Like that guy in the garage.

Now she knew what Cliff did to people who crossed him.

She almost vomited at the thought of being back in his power – those strong arms, big hands. His gentleness seemed so distant. An experience from another life, another person. In recent days, cool arrogance had replaced love. *How did a person change so quickly?* Maybe she'd never truly known him. How had she let herself love a man like that?

Her single piece of luggage appeared on the carousel and inched its way toward her. She'd purchased it at Miami International Airport and filled it with a couple of changes of clothes and toiletries.

She tried to reach for it but could barely move, squished among the other passengers, crabby after their long flights. She lost sight of her suitcase after it passed her by, then saw someone down the line grab it, discover it was not his, and put it back.

It lumbered back toward her again. A man shoved past her, pulled his suitcase off the carousel and shouldered away. She filled the gap he'd made in the crowd. She reached out, grabbed the handle, lost her grip, and felt another hand brush hers.

She almost fainted. *How could he have found me so fast?*

"I'll get it for you, miss," a man said.

Her heart pounded. She nodded thanks but avoided eye contact. Seconds later, her brain had processed the voice: *Not him!* He placed the bag on its wheels, raised the handle, and resumed looking for his own luggage. She gulped a ragged breath.

Outside, it was a zoo. No organization. Cabbies stuffing multiple parties into their cars. Bewildered tourists. Frustrated locals. Hot. Humid.

Sophie scouted out a woman cabbie and told her she wanted the cab for herself and needed to get to the ferry terminal. "Now!" she said firmly, giving her a woman-to-woman look.

The driver nodded. Hoisted Sophie's suitcase into the trunk, slammed the lid, nodded her head toward the passenger door, and took her place behind the wheel. Sophie glanced at the crowd a final time, swallowed hard, and slid inside the cab.

Jeeze. Not even noon and the seats burned through her cotton dress. The seatbelt was lost down the crack at the back of the seat. She didn't care. Get distance between herself and Cliff. That was all she cared about. Disappear. Vaporize!

Suddenly the car was moving, and Sophie reached for the strap hanging over the window. *For God's sake!* The cab was rocketing along at fifty miles per hour down a two-lane road – *on the wrong freaking side!*

"Um," she said, holding on for dear life, "aren't we supposed to drive on the right side of the road?"

The cabbie chuckled politely and replied in the island lilt, "Yah, dat be a surprise to all our visitors on St. Thomas. Don' worry, miss. We drive on the left down here. Island used to be Danish."

"Sorry," Sophie murmured, embarrassed.

"That's okay. Just one of those things 'bout St. Thomas. Another one – when we drive past town, you'll see ferries at the wharf. You don' want them, because they don' go to St. Mark. We be going to Red Hook."

"Where is Red Hook?"

"East end of the island. Not far."

"Thanks." Sophie said sat back, released her grip on the plastic strap, and shut her eyes. Took a deep breath. Tried to relax, be in the moment. Didn't help worth beans.

She'd made her decision late the previous night at Miami airport. Her choices of destinations narrowed down to Hawaii (too easy for trackers to blend in with the tourist population), Alaska (way too cold), or the US Virgin Islands. She set her sights on St. Mark, the smallest, most remote, and least populated of the islands. So claimed the tourist brochure she'd picked up.

She exhaled a pent-up breath, not quite believing what she was doing, how her life had been turned totally inside out. *Such a long way from the University of Florda, toiling for that BS in Applied Physiology and Kinesiology. Too bad I didn't take a course in how to escape a killer boyfriend.* She suddenly missed her clients - teaching them, tracking their progress, sharing their pain and their joy. Especially Susan, so serious. Driven to quality for the the Olympics – Team USA.

A thought occurred to her and she leaned forward so the driver could hear above the noise of hot island air streaming through the open windows.

"There *is* a ferry from Red Hook to St. Mark, isn't there?"

"Oh yes, miss."

They were passing through Charlotte Amalie, the only town on St. Thomas, driving along the waterfront, buildings on the left, harbor on the right, moored cruise ships in the distance up ahead. They passed the low, red fort she'd seen on the cover of the tourist brochure.

The driver turned inland, the road rose among green mountains. Sophie took another deep breath, still not believing she was on the run and had put over a thousand miles between herself and the man she'd once loved.

But now feared.

After half an hour on the winding road, they reached Red Hook, populated by a sprinkling of houses and stores. The ferry terminal consisted of a single-story, green-roofed building, and a pier, against which a blue-and-white ferry was moored, taking on passengers.

Sophie paid the driver, pulled her suitcase inside the terminal, and waited in line to buy a ticket. She scanned the room of milling people in transit between St. Thomas, St. John, and the near-by British Virgin Islands.

She admonished herself. Why on earth was she searching this place for Cliff? That was ridiculous. He was safely behind her for at least a day. *Girl – get a grip.*

Still, she fidgeted in the slow-moving line, anxious to be on the ferry and on her way. In spite of the overhead fans, the terminal was baking. A bead of perspiration trickled down her side. Finally, she reached the ticket window.

"Hi," she said to the agent. "One ticket to St. Mark please."

"She only go once a week."

"Oh?"

"Yah, but you in luck. She go tomorrow morning, bright an' early."

"Tomorrow? But that's too late! I have to be there tonight! How about the boat outside, at the pier? Isn't that going to St. Mark?"

The ticket agent shook his head. "Sorry, miss. Only once a week to St. Mark. That boat's going to St. John. I could sell you a ticket there if you want."

She thought feverishly. *God, if I have to stay overnight, people will see me. They'll remember.* She felt completely vulnerable.

"Miss?"

She looked at the ticket agent. "Yes? Oh…no. I don't want a ticket. Thanks."

At a loss, she turned away. Someone touched her shoulder. Sophie turned, recognizing the middle-aged lady who'd been standing several people behind her.

"Sorry," the lady said, "but I overheard you asking about St. Mark."

"Yes, I need to get there today."

"Well, you can hire a boat to take you."

"Really?" You could just hire a boat? Like a taxi? Is that how people did things down here?

"There's this man, Richard Drake. He lives on St. Mark but he works out of a marina about five minutes from here, by cab. He might take you over to St. Mark in his boat."

Sophie nodded. Was this some sort of an island scam?

"His name is Richard Drake," the lady said, her eyes kind.

"Do you know him?"

"Oh yes. I live on St. John and we've met. He's a charter boat captain. He comes to my little store to buy food. Nice as can be."

"And he's at the marina?"

"Well, he should be. I saw a friend in town this morning who said he saw him there."

Sophie must have looked confused because the lady patted her arm.

"It's a small island, dear."

"Okay."

"Ask the driver to take you to the Red Bay Marina. Tell Richard that Nellie sent you."

She gave Sophie a reassuring pat on her arm, but Sophie didn't feel reassured. She tried to appear confident as she walked to a quiet spot against a wall.

Gathering her thoughts, she gazed at Nellie and the other locals, dressed casually in khaki shorts and patterned island shirts, and at the tourists, dressed in anything from cut-offs to office attire. The tourists sweated. The locals looked completely at ease.

Nellie purchased her ticket to St. John, which was the next island to the east according to the tourist brochure. She gave Sophie a final wave, and Sophie waved back. Knowing she had no other choice, she made her way outside and found a cab.

On the way to the marina, she rubbed her forehead. Jeeze. If this Richard Drake didn't work out, what options did she have? Sleep under a palm tree and catch the ferry the next morning? She had no clue.

One step at a time.

CHAPTER 4

Drake watched Graham Walters saunter away. He was not only his best friend, but a great source of security information, probably the best on St. Thomas, gateway to the US Virgin Islands.

Walters was a competent, no-nosense cop who actually gave a hoot about the people he served. He helped lots of regular folks, from druggies to battered wives. The man looked at justice on a personal level, maybe as a result of his interactions with the locals in Afghanistan. His methods were unorthodox but highly successful, and to say he had street cred was a vast understatement.

Drake looked at the bartender, intending to order another beer, but the man's eyes were on the parking lot. Drake followed the man's gaze, and saw a woman getting out of taxi. She retrieved a single suitcase and walked toward the tiki bar. She entered the shade and removed her sunglasses.

She was about twenty-eight with an athletic figure, mussed blond hair, and emerald eyes. Typical tourist from the States. Drake guessed she was looking for a motel room and her taxi took a wrong turn. Maybe aiming for one of the beachfront hotels along the north coast.

To the bartender she said, "I'm looking for a Mr. Richard Drake. Is he here at the marina?"

"Sure is."

Surprised, Drake turned and smiled. "I'm Richard Drake."

"Hi, Mr. Drake…"

"Richard."

"Oh, okay, hi Richard. My name is Sophie, er…"

He tilted his head, encouraging her to continue.

"Just call me Sophie," she said.

"Welcome to St. Thomas, Sophie."

"Thanks."

She glanced at the bartender. "I'll have an ice tea please."

"Make it two," Drake said.

Sophie seemed jittery and frightened. Her hand shook as she sat on a bar stool next to Drake. The tea arrived.

Drake smiled gently. "How can I help you, Sophie?"

She took a long drink of tea. Drake waited. Figured she was dehydrated. Judging from the suitcase, she'd just arrived by plane or maybe cruise ship, probably hadn't drunk anything for a couple of hours. Not good in the tropics.

She set her glass on the bar. Looked at Drake. "I met this woman at the Red Hook ferry terminal. Sort of, well, heavy set. She said she knew you from St. John and said, 'tell him Nellie sent you.'"

He still didn't have the foggiest idea what this Sophie wanted. He smiled, hoping to encourage her. She gulped the rest of her iced tea and looked him in the eye.

"I need to get to St. Mark."

She was flushed, not from the heat, he was sure, but from thinking about whatever was driving her to reach the island. She could have checked into a motel for the night and caught the morning ferry. Nellie must have told her that. Instead, she tracked him down because she wanted to get there immediately. Or was it a rush not to St. Mark, but more to get off of St. Thomas? Either way, his gut told him this was a woman on the run. Scared shitless was his guess. But of what?

"I need to get there today – now." Her voice quivered. "I understand you live there."

"That's right."

"And you're leaving soon to return to home?"

"After a while," he said, nodding toward dark clouds approaching from the south. "First, I'm going to let that weather blow over."

She kept her eyes on him, didn't even glance at the clouds.

"How long will it take?"

"For the weather or to get to St. Mark?"

"Both, I guess."

"For the weather, if it's a squall, she'll blow over in fifteen minutes. But if it's a storm, it could last all night. Now, in nice weather, I can sail from here to the harbor at St. Mark in…"

"Can't you leave immediately and stay ahead of the bad weather? St. Mark is north, and those clouds are coming from the south. Maybe you could stay ahead of it in your boat."

"Ah, I see you've been looking at the charts."

She shrugged. "What's the problem? If you don't beat the storm, can't your boat handle a little wind and rain?"

Drake eyed his beer. His ice tea. Selected the beer for a good guzzle and reflected how a peaceful day can turn to shit.

"See, lady," he said, an edge to his words, "I'm not in a hurry."

"Why can't you take me now, wait on St. Mark for the weather to clear, and return to St. Thomas?"

Drake waited a beat and drawled, "Two hundred dollars."

"Two hundred! To take me where you're going anyway?"

"For leaving in a hurry and probably getting my pants kicked in a squall. That's my offer. You'd better accept fast, because in another ten minutes it'll be too late. We'll be stuck at the marina."

"But that's not reasonable. I won't take up any space." She looked around at all the motor boats and sailboats rocking gently at their berths along the finger piers. "Where is your boat, anyway? It's a motor boat, right?"

"Sailboat. Just over there." He waved vaguely toward the slips.

"Where? Which one?"

"Well, it doesn't make any difference, because you don't want to pay two hundred dollars. Find someone else to take you. There's the charter office." He pointed at the small building at the head of the marina, adjacent to the slips. "Though they'll charge a lot more, probably the going day rate."

"What's the day rate?"

"About eight hundred dollars, assuming you charter for a week, but for only a single day, maybe three hundred." He shrugged. "I figure you won't eat too much, and since I'm going there anyway, I'll only charge two hundred."

"Okay," she said, raising her hands in surrender. "Two hundred dollars. But we have to leave right now."

He squinted at her.

She leaned into his personal space and whispered, "If you say no, I'll call you a wuss."

"A *wuss*?"

She leaned back. "Yep. A big, bad man who's afraid of a little wind."

Damn. He was looking forward to the cold beer, maybe calling up someone for dinner, sleep on the boat. But he was well and truly hooked into giving this pushy girl a ride to St. Mark. Well, he'd already collected his mail, finalized arrangements at the office for his next charter party, and he was up to date on the security situation. What the hell? Maybe she'd get sea sick. That would be entertaining.

"All right," he said. "But I want my money now."

"Half now, half after we arrive."

She poked around in her purse, pulled out a wallet and extracted a hundred-dollar bill.

"There," she said. "Let's go."

"Jesus," he muttered, folding the bill into his wallet. He grabbed her bag, noticed the claim tag attached to the handle: 'Sophie Cooper.' So, her name *was* Sophie, and he now knew her last name as well. Both no doubt taken from her driver's license by the airline. That added a little legitimacy to his mysterious woman.

After another glance at the weather, he led her down the pier and stopped at CAPRICE, his fifty-four foot cutter, snugly moored at her slip. He stood for a moment, admiring her sleek white hull, then climbed aboard. He swung the suitcase onto the teak deck.

Sophie boarded and looked at the deckhouse, the fittings, and the low safety railings. "This is it?"

"Yep."

She glanced at the dark mass of clouds. Swallowed hard. "Will we be okay?"

He lugged the suitcase below and set it on its side on the salon deck, then returned to the cockpit and started the inboard diesel. As the engine rumbled to life, he stepped back to the pier and released bow, spring, and stern lines, then returned to the boat.

He eased CAPRICE out of the marina and into the three-foot swell, with the wind out of the east at about fifteen knots. Usual for June. Also, seemingly illogical but also usual, was that the surface wind was from one direction and the squall approached from another. The weird stuff that happens in this world.

He looked over at the woman, sitting in the forward port corner of the cockpit bench.

"Yes," he said, "we'll be just fine. We'll raise sails when we're clear of the piers."

She nodded.

He was tempted to ask where she was from, that sort of thing, to help her relax. She was obviously at the end of her tether and the boat's motions had tightened the screw, judging by the worry lines on her forehead. But her eyes showed pluck. He decided to focus on the practical. "You've got a decision to make, Sophie. This squall is going to catch us before we reach St. Mark. You can stay on deck wearing your dress and get soaking wet or you can go below and stay dry."

"How about if I change clothes and borrow some foul weather gear?"

"Good idea. Jackets are hanging in the locker to the left, in the passageway leading forward from the salon. The rain is cold, but you'll be fine with just a top. Maybe you should wear a swim suit. The sun will come out after the squall passes and dry us off pretty fast. Bring me a jacket too, would you?"

"Okay." She disappeared down the stairs.

He wondered why he'd agreed to screw up his plans and take her to St. Mark. God knew it wasn't the money. Maybe his ego got in the way. Pretty girls did that to him. Or maybe it was because she appeared to be a damsel in distress. Girls in distress did that to him as well.

He thought about her now, rummaging through her suitcase as CAPRICE heeled to port on a northwesterly course to work around the west end of Jost Van Dyke. The boat pitched in the swells but the wind steadied out the rolling to a minimum. He sensed Sophie was manipulating him, perhaps by dramatizing her plight. Or maybe she was setting up a scam, against him or someone on the island.

He returned his focus to sailing. They were well away from St. Thomas now and Drake could see the entire wall of foul weather crowding into the gap between St. Thomas and St. John, extending onto either island and looming high. He'd never outrun it.

CHAPTER 5

Sophie sat, wedged into the forward port corner of what Richard called the "cockpit," set at the stern of his sailboat and serving the same purpose as a similar spot toward the back of Cliff's cherished Cigarette Marauder racing boat. It was where the captain steered and a couple of other people could keep him company. She was bundled in bundled in a bright yellow foul weather parka, and wore a pair of shorts that she was sure would soon be sopping wet.

She looked left and felt a pang in her gut. The squall was big and black, and really powerful, judging by those she'd experienced in Florida. It moved from south to north, while their breeze blew from east to west. The squall's wind was ninety degrees to that of the normal breeze. Very odd. Anyway, it made Richard's CAPRICE seem tiny and vulnerable.

Damn, damn, damn. She had screwed up royally. Why in hell couldn't she have waited a few hours, let the squall pass? She could have sipped a beer, chatted with Richard, enjoyed a light salad. Stayed perfectly dry. Oh no, she just had to get going.

The squall approached at an alarming rate. They'd get around the island Richard called 'Jost Van Dyke' okay, but they'd never make St. Mark. She braced herself even more tightly, pressing with feet and holding with hands on various structures and nautical gear. The wind blew from the starboard side, tipping CAPRICE to such an extent that the deck edge dipped into the water.

"Will the boat roll over?" she asked.

"Naw," he said, his eyes darting from the sails to the rigging and off to the south, toward the approaching black mass.

"Well, why not? If you tip a motor boat this far over it'll flip, especially if you take a fast turn. I've seen it happen." She knit her eyebrows in thought for a second and continued, "Also, Hobie Cats and little sailboats capsize all the time. So why can't this boat?"

"She's got a heavy keel," he said absently, his mind obviously elsewhere. "It counterbalances the force of the wind. Of course, a strong gust could break the mast. We're not weatherproof, that's for sure."

She gasped. "Could that happen today?"

"Probably not." He scowled, glancing south again. "But that's one hell of a squall. Be here in just a couple of minutes. It'll make us pitch and roll like a son of a gun."

"Bitch?"

He looked at her, questioning, with his head tilted to one side.

"That's what you meant to say, right?" she asked pertly. "Roll like a bitch? That's what my ex-boyfriend says."

"Just trying to be polite," he grumbled.

A sudden gust reached out from the approaching squall, straining sails and rigging, causing popping noises and making the shrouds hum. The mainsail flapped. The gust subsided and the wind shifted, more from the south now than the east. Drake hauled in the boom and very carefully turned the boat to port. The sail filled and then shook. Up forward, the jib flapped to the starboard side and half filled.

CAPRICE continued to push forward, but with diminished speed. Now she rolled as well as pitched, the motion doing no good to Sophie's stomach, even though she'd had no food since Miami. Damn. She sure didn't need to get sea sick in front of this man.

"Wind strengthening and shifting to boot," Drake said under his breath. "Here it comes."

Wisps of cloud trailed high overhead and then the squall was upon them, pressing, surrounding them with howling wind, pounding seas, and pelting rain. A wave slapped the port side of the boat and water cascaded over both of them. Drake wiped his mouth with the back of his hand and looked at her.

Amazingly, the rain and the ocean water were cold. Especially the rain, now falling in sheets. She pulled the collar of her foul weather parka tight, flipped up the hood and tied the strings. But pulling the draw strings squeezed the hood tight on her drenched hair, pressing water down her back in a shivering stream. Yeah, it would have been better to sip beer and eat an early lunch at the marina.

"Ever been on a sailboat before?" he asked, raising his voice against the howling wind.

"No," she replied, eyes wide.

He nodded to the big, chrome steering wheel. "It's just like driving a car," he said.

"That's what my ex-boyfriend said about his Cigarette boat. But okay, I'll take your word for it."

Why was he telling her this? She held on tight as the boat jounced over a six-foot high swell that appeared out of nowhere. *Damn.* At least her ex-boyfriend knew better than to be out in this kind of weather.

"On second thought," she said, "with sails instead of a motor, isn't your sailboat more like a wind surfer? You know, instead of a car?"

He looked at her with hooded eyes and she could tell he was adjusting his initial judgment of her from "fluff" to something more substantial, even though he was obviously a little pissed at her snarky comeback. Well, now he knew she was familiar with watercraft, if not sailboats.

"Yeah," he said, "more wind surfer than a car. Come here – I want you to keep her on course while I shorten sails."

She stood, keeping her stance wide and her hands braced on rails and bitts and other stuff that offered support as she worked her way to his side behind the wheel. She turned her body forward into the face of the salt spray. The deck jounced beneath her running shoes. Water splashed onto her and ran in chilly rivulets down her legs. And, yep, her shorts were soaked.

The boat slammed into a steep swell, shuddered for a second, then jerked upward, free of the water, heaved down onto the white, foamy top of the wave, and careened down its opposite slope. Wind whined urgently through the rigging. Rain flowed in torrents, driven by the wind, stinging her face and legs.

"What should I do?" She yelled above the noise.

He moved aside, and she stood behind the wheel, gripping with both hands. He leaned close and shouted, "Just keep her on course." He pointed to a compass, gyrating wildly inside a glass dome that was bolted to a pedestal forward of the wheel.

A wave boarded the boat from up forward and washed aft, momentarily submerging the low deckhouse and splashing over the compass. The boat bucked and rose and water cascaded off in foaming sheets. The compass reappeared and she turned the wheel to get back on course. Give or take twenty degrees.

They hit another swell and the whole thing repeated itself. Sophie gripped the wheel, not only to control the boat, but to keep her balance. She felt the rhythm of the storm, its swells, the pulsing gusts, the shrieking wind. She was frightened out of her wits but thrilled at the same time.

Drake moved forward, bent low against the wind and rain, his body moving with the motion of the jerking, pitching boat, methodical, confident, absorbing the motion in a natural way. He reached the mainsail and made adjustments that apparently reduced its area, for she felt a lessening of the heel. But the wind gusted and pressed the boat back over, submerging the deck and continuing until the edge of the sail touched the tormented waves on the downwind side.

Sophie worked the wheel, but not too much, remembering from power boats not to over steer. Drake returned and took the wheel. Sophie moved forward to her corner, giving no more than a quick look at the closed door leading to the protected interior compartment. She could go below and be dry, maybe even wedge herself onto a comfortable bunk.

But she decided to remain on deck. She admitted to being frightened, especially when the wind gusted and the boat lurched against an exceptionally steep swell. But CAPRICE always righted herself, ready and capable to take on the next blast of wind, the next wave.

She glanced at Drake, both hands on the wheel, legs braced, and he caught her eye and smiled. The scene set in her mind's eye. This was who he was, a man who relished the challenge and, she was sure, relished the danger.

Sophie felt the potential for disaster – a broken mast, a wave crushing a deck hatch and flooding the interior, or even losing the keel. There seemed to be no margin for error. She felt that Drake sensed potential disaster as well, his eyes alert, scanning, and his hands adjusting the wheel this way and that, positioning hull and sails to survive the next wave, the next gust, balancing the capabilities of CAPRICE against this brutal onslaught of nature.

This elemental man stood between her and drowning at sea. The wind screamed and the waves pounded and the air turned white with spume as if the whole world had turned crazy. She hung on for dear life.

And suddenly the torment abated, with the strong gusts coming less frequently and with less and less strength. The waves no longer had their tops torn off by the wind, and the swells became less steep. In the span of only a few minutes a patch of blue showed in the sky. Then they were outside the squall, as it marched northward, having done its worst to them.

The wind settled down to a breeze from the east. The sun shone. She could clearly see Jost Van Dyke behind them, and St. Thomas further to the south. Ahead, now itself emerging from the passing squall, she spotted another island up ahead, which had to be St. Mark.

Around them, the sea remained disturbed from the squall, the rollers confused and bumping into each other at odd angles. She scanned the water, amazed that the squall could have such power.

Off the port side she spotted color. Not the deep blue of the sea or the white of foam, but something else. She stared at the spot, but whatever she had seen disappeared behind a large swell. Then it reappeared on the crest of a following swell.

Yes, bright orange. Man made. Only about fifty feet away.

An overturned boat.

And clinging to that was a person, a young girl, very still.

CHAPTER 6

Drake followed Sophie's pointing arm.

"Over there," she yelled. "It's someone on a capsized boat! A girl, I think."

"Take the wheel," he ordered, trotting forward and calling back to her over his shoulder, "Head into the wind, so the sails flap."

Sophie turned the boat east. Drake lowered the mainsail and the jib. Back aft, he took the wheel, turning the bow west, and started the engine.

"I see her," Sophie said, standing with her hand on the boom. She stripped off her foul weather jacket.

Drake gave her the wheel long enough to manhandle the dingy from atop the deckhouse, and lower it into the water. He guided the little boat aft and secured it with a line to the stern rail.

"You can climb into the dinghy," he said, taking the wheel again. "That'll make it easier for you to bring her aboard – lots better than us handing her up directly to CAPRICE from the water. Besides, she may be injured. We'll leave her in the dingy if need be. St. Mark is only a half hour away."

Sophie nodded and scampered over the rail and into the dinghy, keeping her eye on the girl, who disappeared and reappeared, depending on the action of the swells.

Drake slowed CAPRICE to a crawl and approached from the downwind side, with the dinghy trailing directly astern. He kept the bow into the wind and let CAPRICE creep just past the overturned boat. He made alignment corrections with the engine just above idle, a delicate operation in the confused seas, but soon the dinghy lay against the capsized boat.

He looked back and down at the boat and the girl, who moved her head and Drake's heart skipped a beat. The girl was ten-year old Jenny Coxon, the daughter of his best friend on St. Mark. Now Drake's hands felt slippery on the wheel as he maneuvered, maintaining position. Rigging pinged against the mast, something rolled on deck down below.

He recognized the bright orange hull of Jenny's sailboat. Luckily, it had flotation, and remained on the surface. He dared to steal another look at Jenny, who looked pale and drawn from the terrors of the violent squall. Her lips were blue and she was shivering in her t-shirt and shorts. Her eyes opened only once, when Sophie approached and spoke, then fluttered shut. But her little hands clung resolutely to her boat.

Sophie reached over the side of the dinghy and tried to lift Jenny. But Jenny was in no condition to assist, and her dead weight, the motion of the dinghy and overturned sailboat, and the awkward angles made grasping and pulling out of the question. Sophie slipped into the water, alongside Jenny, and put a comforting hand on her shoulder. She spoke and the girl nodded weakly.

Somehow, pulling and pushing, Sophie got her out of the water and lying on top of her boat, which looked stable enough, even though it was capsized. Sophie joined her, legs straddling the boat, and helped Jenny inch sideways to the dinghy. Drake noticed that Jenny's arm hung limp at her side, and she winced as she climbed into the dinghy.

Sophie tied the bow line of the capsized sailboat to the stern of the dinghy and clambered aboard to join Jenny. Drake admired Sophie's strength and determination, bringing the injured girl to safety in the still-wild sea. He tugged at the bow line of the dinghy, maneuvering it up to CAPRICE. He bent down over the transom and hoisted Jenny aboard.

She fell against him, her face against his chest, right arm wrapped tightly around him. He patted her shoulder.

"You're safe now, sweetie," Drake said. She was shivering, and he felt himself shaking with emotion. He muttered a prayer of thanks, a Marine's prayer, sent to the Lord after surviving another battle, with comrades and himself intact.

He kept her wrapped securely in his arms, steadying her against the swells while Sophie scrambled aboard CAPRICE and scooted below decks. He and Jenny didn't speak. Now was not the time for talk or questions. He looked down at her left arm, which appeared unbroken, but probably badly bruised from her ordeal.

Sophie returned from below with a blanket and spoke quietly to Drake. "I'm heating up some broth I found in your cabinet."

She sat down at her usual spot on the cockpit bench and Drake guided Sophie to her. Sophie snuggled onto her lap and into her arms, and Drake wrapped the blanket around the two of them.

Sophie whispered, "I'm Sophie."

"I'm Jenny," the girl whispered.

"Do you want me to tuck you into one of the bunks down below?"

Jenny weakly shook her head. "Here is fine, Miss Sophie. Thanks for rescuing me."

Tears pooled in Sophie's eyes, as if she'd just realized how lucky they had been to have found the child. Drake slipped below and poured the broth into a coffee mug. On deck, he handed the mug to Sophie.

"Watch out, it's still hot."

Jenny looked up at Drake.

"Are we close to St. Mark, Mr. Richard?"

"About a half hour," he said. "Then you'll see your mom and dad and we'll take a look at your arm."

"It hurts, but I'm trying not to cry."

"You're a brave girl."

Sophie tested the temperature of the broth, then asked, "Do you want a sip of warm chicken broth, Jenny?"

"Okay." She moved to get her hands outside the blanket, but winced, and only the right hand came out. She carefully took the cup and sipped.

"Mmm."

Her eyes brightened noticeably, and she lifted her head, again sipping the broth, while gazing at the squall clouds far to the west.

"That was a monster squall!" she declared.

"One of the worst I've seen," Drake said.

Jenny turned to face Sophie. "Are you visiting St. Mark?"

"Yes, for a little while at least."

"You can stay with us if you want."

Sophie looked uncertainly at Drake, who shrugged.

"There aren't any motels or guest houses on the island," he said. "We don't get tourists except for a few who drop anchor for the afternoon and visit the restaurant."

"Well," Sophie said, "you're very kind to invite me. We should check with your mother just to be sure, don't you think?"

Jenny smiled. "She'll say yes."

Drake decided to motor in, not bother with the sails, since they were close to the island. He reflected on the past few minutes. On one hand, he reveled in the man-against-nature challenge. But the high that gave him was tempered by the near-catastrophe with Jenny. She must have been caught at sea and swept away from the island, surprised by the speed of the approaching squall. She was a practical girl and stayed clear of violent weather. She'd been in squalls on CAPRICE and other boats. She knew the danger.

He looked at Sophie and Jenny tucked together. Jenny would be fine, but what about Sophie? Her face had turned pensive as Jenny dozed, and now Sophie looked up at Drake, her eyes again full of uncertainty and fear. Jenny must have sensed her change in mood because she stirred. She patted Sophie's arm.

"Why are you sad, Miss Sophie? I'm safe now."

Sophie blinked and smiled down at her little friend. "I know, sweetie, and I'm very happy."

Jenny smiled, shut her eyes, and melted into sleep.

Drake and Sophie exchanged a look, full of questions, devoid of answers. He felt a pang in his chest, in that spot where he knew someone was in danger but he had no clue how to help. He gazed at the deep blue ocean rollers. The sea was not the only danger in the world.

CHAPTER 7

Drake pointed CAPRICE toward the center of St. Mark, where the harbor lay. They were cruising at four knots, with the dinghy and Jenny's sailboat trailing behind. Sophie and Jenny dozed in the late afternoon sun. The running rigging slapped against the mast. Every now and then the confused sea produced a large swell that poured water over the bow and down the deck.

Sophie's face looked drawn, and Drake again wondered what she was running from. She had shown herself to be resourceful in the rescue – juggling the dingy, the capsized sailboat, and a limp girl with a damaged arm, all in confused seas. Drake admired her athleticism in maneuvering herself and the little girl and had noticed Sophie's lean arms and legs. He wondered what sports she played – swimming, surfing, sailing? Probably all of those.

This woman's grit while rescuing Jenny stood in stark contrast to her flight – from what? Certainly, a danger she that felt was imminent and overwhelming. Was it shame? Fear? Had she broken a law? Time would tell.

Meanwhile, his only concern was that she was not a danger to his friends on the island or to Judge Santiago, whom he had sworn to protect. Between her courage in the squall and her cool skill in the rescue, Drake felt that he had her measure.

She was a strong person faced with an overwhelming problem. He wanted to believe she posed no danger to anyone on the island. He looked at her now, with a trusting Jenny curled up in her lap, and wondered at the ups and downs of life, his own included.

He passed the headlands to right and left, and continued into the harbor, snug and deep, protected on three sides by steep hills that rose to the spine of green mountains that traversed the island from east to west. George Coxon's Boat Works lay to the left, family-owned for generations, and now run by Drake's best friend, the unofficial mayor of the island. Ahead lay the handful of weathered stone buildings, inherited from pirate days when they contained contraband and supplies for seaborne rogues who risked getting hung if they called at any of settled islands.

He ignored the bobbing buoy that marked his mooring spot and permanent anchor, and continued to the weathered concrete pier adjacent to the buildings of the village. The crowd of people, indistinct when he'd been farther out, now came into focus, the men dressed in shorts and brightly patterned shirts, the women in shorts or skirts of blues and greens and reds. The fishermen alone dressed in practical black trousers and dark t-shirts, showing tanned, muscular arms. The kids, in bare feet, for once solemn and still, stood close to their parents. Everyone was there, except of course the rich and famous who lived in their North Side compounds.

George and his wife, Maren, stood toward the front, with their fourteen-year-old son, Michael, holding hands, looking anxious. Every face in the crowd appeared prepared for the worst. They all must have been thinking 'body search' by now.

Drake realized they could not see Jenny because she was low in the cockpit. He felt the urge to stand and shout the good news. But the distance to the pier had narrowed to only two hundred feet. They would arrive in less than a minute. Still, he could feel their tension and he willed the gap between boat and shore to close quickly.

"There!" a kid yelled, jumping up and down, pointing, tugging his father's hand. "I see Jenny. That's her, in the cockpit!"

Drake grinned and waved as CAPRICE's bow bumped the pier. "We've got her!" he yelled.

No one moved for a second, as if in a trance, unable to understand that their ordeal was over, their prayers answered.

Jenny stirred, and Sophie patted her shoulder.

"You're home," Sophie said.

"Your mom and dad and Michael are here, waiting for you," Drake said, embarrassed at the catch in his voice.

Jenny blinked her eyes open. She looked around, untangled herself from the blanket, and stood, shaky on her feet, braced by her right hand on the mainsail boom. She gazed at her parents and brother, and then at the cheering, waving crowd. Tears streamed down her happy face and she shyly waved at everyone in her island world.

The crowd went wild. Kids ran in circles, dogs barked and chased the kids. The fishermen's sun-browned features turned joyful. George and Maren hugged each other and Michael.

Two boys jumped aboard CAPRICE, grabbed mooring lines, and threw them to their friends ashore. The boat was pulled snug against the pier, and a wobbly Jenny clambered ashore, into the arms of her mom, who lifted her and hugged her.

Drake and George locked eyes, and George nodded his thanks. He'd say more, Drake knew, but this was the real deal. A father's deepest thanks. Drake shut off the engine, and he and Sophie joined the jostling throng on the island. Women and men brushed away tears, babbled, and moved close to touch Jenny, give her a smile, a pat, a hug. A few of the kids shyly hugged Sophie and less shyly hugged Drake, who patted each one on the shoulder.

Jenny squirmed away from her mom. "My arm, Mom. I hurt it."

"It's her left arm," Drake said. "You should get Doc to take a look." He waved at Jimmy Franklin, an ex-Navy medic.

"Well, let's have a look," Franklin said, and he knelt and gently felt along Jenny's left hand and elbow and then along her arm.

She tensed when he reached a spot halfway between wrist and elbow.

"There?" he asked.

She bit her lip and nodded.

He touched above and below the sore area and slowly turned her wrist.

"Well, Jenny," he said, just loud enough for her parents to hear, "you don't have a broken arm but you have a pretty big bruise. I'll give you a sling so you can rest your arm for a few days. Don't use it, okay? It needs to heal."

She nodded as he searched through the medical kit he always carried. He pulled out a large square of white cloth, folded it into a triangle, and gently positioned her arm in the fold, pulled the ends to either side of her neck, and tied them in a knot at the back of her neck.

"How's that?" he asked.

"Okay," she said.

"Does it still hurt?'

She nodded shyly.

Franklin looked at Maren. "Give her Tylenol. If that doesn't help, call me and I'll bring along something stronger."

"Thanks, Doc," Maren said.

He smiled. "You're welcome."

The kids crowded around Jenny, peppering her with questions about her dangerous adventure.

George and Maren hugged Drake and Sophie.

"We can't thank you enough," said George.

"Just thank God we were there," Drake said, "and thank God Sophie spotted Jenny's boat. It was right after the squall passed, and the seas were high. The boat was hidden most of the time but Sophie kept tracking it and gave me directions so I could approach. Then she jumped into the sea and somehow managed to get Jenny into the dinghy and up to me on CAPRICE. Not an easy job in those seas."

George and Maren smiled, and Sophie extended her hand. "Hi, I'm Sophie. And it took both of us, plus your daughter's bravery, to get her safely aboard CAPRICE."

"You're very modest," George said. "Well, we sure thank you for saving our daughter. She's a regular fish in the water, but the squall, well, that was too much for her little boat."

Sophie nodded.

Maren gave her another hug and said, "Welcome to St. Mark, Sophie. Oh, I didn't think to ask. Are you on a charter?"

"Um, no," said Sophie. "I was planning to come to St. Mark for a little while. I'm not really into touring right now. I've got sort of a…"

"She needs a little time off," Drake said, his tone confidential. "She was aiming for St. Mark because it's quiet."

"Then it's settled," declared Maren. "You'll be staying as our guest while you're here – for however long you want."

"Thank you, Maren…"

"I found them!" interrupted a girl, tugging on Drake's shirt.

"Oh?" asked Drake, in a puzzled tone.

The girl opened her hand to reveal six individually wrapped chocolate candies. "See? My friends and I found them."

"My gosh," Drake said, kneeling to eye level, ignoring the sniggers of her friends. "And I thought I hid them. I was going to eat all these myself."

"But we *found them*, Mr. Richard," She giggled. "Anyway, they're always in the same place!"

Drake shook his head mournfully. "Okay. You know what they say…"

"Finders keepers, losers weepers," the kids chortled as the girl passed out the loot, one to each kid, including one to Jenny.

Michael Coxon appeared, holding Sophie's suitcase.

She beamed at Drake. "I guess I have a place to stay."

"You sure do. You're in the best of hands. I'll be going now – got some things to do."

CHAPTER 8

Sophie watched Drake depart, then smiled as a woman stepped close and squeezed her hand. The woman spoke in the lilt of the islands, which she'd heard on previous vacations with Cliff. The woman looked into Sophie's eyes, and let go of her hand.

"We are very lucky you came," the woman said. "You saved Little Jenny. She is such an adventurer. She has no fear. Now maybe she realizes the ocean can be a bully."

"It was a strong squall," Sophie said, noticing others gathering around and listening, all grinning in celebration of Jenny's rescue.

"Yes," continued the woman, "and we thank the Lord you were there to save her. You know the sea, yes?"

"Oh yes, I was born near the beach in Florida in a town called Melbourne. I love being in the water – sort of like Jenny, I guess. But I've seen the power of squalls and even a hurricane, and I've learned to respect the ocean."

"Hurricanes," the woman said, her hand to her mouth. "They are the worst. Was that squall today truly bad?"

Sophie nodded. "Yes, I've never been at sea in such weather, with wind, waves, and rain coming at us so strongly. I helped save Jenny, but Richard saved us all. He always knew what to do, no matter what that squall threw at us."

"Ah yes," said a man standing at the edge of the circle of women.

He was dressed in work clothes and his face and hands were tanned dark, his eyes serious. Drake had pointed him out as a fisherman.

"That CAPRICE," the man said, "she is a good boat. She is very tough in the storm. Mr. Richard chose her well – he is a seaman."

"But CAPRICE is not a Tortola sloop, eh?" said George Coxon, smiling and putting an arm around Sophie's shoulder.

The women laughed, and Sophie saw humor also in the fisherman's eyes.

One of the women murmured to Sophie, "George, he is proud of the Tortola sloop, the sailboat of these islands. Maybe because that is what he builds in his boatyard, sometimes for our fishermen, sometimes for museums."

"And don't forget," chimed in the fisherman with a sly grin aimed at George, "your boats are much stronger than the aluminum or the fiberglass boats when it comes to hitting rocks."

"Which you and your friends are good at doing," said his wife with an impish smirk.

The fisherman glanced at George Coxon and shrugged. "My lovely woman."

Coxon nodded solemnly. "Well, we must be going. Sophie is tired from her trip and from the squall. She needs rest, don't you think?"

Everyone said their good-byes to Sophie. George kissed Maren on the cheek and excused himself. He walked west, out of town. Sophie watched him pass by the boatyard, its buildings and half-completed hulls visible along the west side of the harbor.

"He's going into the bush," said Maren, "to find wood for his next boat."

She guided Sophie along the road in the opposite direction, passing through the tiny town.

Michael had retrieved Sophie's suitcase, and he and a quiet Jenny trailed behind Maren and Sophie. At a store labeled "John's Dry Goods," they turned inland and ascended a narrow, blacktopped road that curled into the mountain forest.

"This is our main road," said Maren. "The rich people on North Side built it between the town and the place where the helicopters land. It runs past all of their compounds."

"Were any of them here today?"

"No, they mostly keep to themselves. They come to St. Mark because it's far from the noise of the crowds, and they stay in their homes. Some live here all year round and others just for vacation.

They treat us good and we treat them good. They give us jobs to cook for them, and keep up their houses and gardens, and the money helps our island economy."

They silently trudged up the steep slope. Sophie saw that Maren was in her mid-thirties, slim with blond hair. She wore sandals, a well-cut red skirt, and a white blouse, with gold bracelets and dangly earrings. Her wedding band was plain, accompanied by a diamond engagement ring.

She looked Danish, and she carried herself with grace and dignity that hinted of European roots. She smiled easily and made Sophie feel she was a welcome addition to her family, if only on a temporary basis. Michael had more of a stout, muscular build, similar to his father, and Jenny, she'd noticed earlier, was a willowy stick of a girl, taking after her mom.

With the squall behind her, visions of Cliff reentered Sophie's mind, horrid and unwelcome. She squeezed her eyes shut for a moment and thought of pitch black nothingness, took a deep breath, and opened her eyes, conscious only of the present. She knew the relief was temporary and she dreaded what was to come, both in her mind and in the physical confrontation.

The inevitable confrontation.

The steep hill demanded her attention, and that helped. She looked around. Admired the green foliage. Listened to bird calls and the hum of insects. Heat from the road filtered through the soles of her running shoes, welcome after the chill of the squall.

Ten minutes later, Maren pointed to the right, toward a rough dirt track barely wide enough for a Jeep.

"This is our way," she said.

As they left the paved road, Michael hefted Sophie's suitcase onto a broad shoulder and grinned at her.

"This is a little heavy," he said with an easy smile. "I think you must have pirate gold inside."

"Sorry," she said.

"Oh no," Jenny said, "It's not heavy for Michael. He' strong."

She beamed at her brother and gave his leg a hug. He managed to pat her shoulder and still balance the suitcase. As they trod the uneven surface, thick-trunked trees shaded them.

After another ten minutes the road opened onto a grassy field dotted with trees and flowering tropical plants. Sophie recognized red hibiscus blooms. Three dogs raced to them, barking and wagging tails. They sniffed Maren, who shooed them away, and they surrounded Jenny, who patted them. Then they crowded around Sophie, wagging tails and holding their heads against her leg, letting her pat them.

One looked part German shepherd, the others were complete mutts, with short hair and strong bodies. Finished with their greeting, they bounded toward the house, on the left, built into the top of a ridge that extended from the side of the mountain.

The one-story house was of attractive proportions, constructed of pink-stuccoed masonry. A flight of whitewashed stairs approached the wide front porch. The peaked roof was topped with the usual red corrugated steel of the islands, offset by snow-white rain gutters and downspouts. The front door was flanked by jalousie windows.

"Come," said Maren, smiling modestly, "I will show you."

They climbed the stairs to the porch, stepped over lounging dogs, and entered a spacious great room. Open jalousies let the breeze flow. The walls were massive, at least two feet thick, constructed of stone. The outsides were mortared, the interior surfaces were uncoated, displaying the gray rock joined in neat lines of cement, into which were placed decorative rock chips. Grass matting covered the floor and furnishings were of attractive woods.

Maren said, "That table to the left came from the ship of the person who built the house and started our island colony."

"George's ancestor?" asked Sophie.

"Yes, John Coxon, the English pirate. In the late 1600s he terrorized the Spanish Main. I think all the Spanish colonies in the Caribbean and Mexico breathed a sigh of relief when he retired in 1683. He sought out St. Mark because it was off the beaten path. A little tribe of Mayan Indians lived here already, and they looked at him as a protector from other pirates.

"He married the daughter of their chief, a descendent of two run-away Mayan Indians. There were also a few Arawak Indians and several escaped African slaves. They helped him unload cannons and furniture and supplies from his ship, which he then burned in the middle of the bay. They all lived peacefully, earning money by trading with pirates who found the regular ports too dangerous. Many were wanted men back then, and the English, French, Danish, and other powers hung those they captured."

Michael and Jenny had drifted away. As Maren talked, Sophie gazed at the magnificent table, perhaps mahogany, with seating for ten. She could imagine the pirate Coxon and his men gathered around it, guzzling rum and retelling stories of their conquests. She noticed the other furnishings, set in comfortable arrangements. Bookshelves lined one wall, and etchings of island scenes hung between jalousie windows.

"You know," Maren said, following Sophie's gaze toward two flintlock pistols mounted over the entrance to the adjoining room, "I find it easy to imagine George's ancestor. I always think of him as strong and practical, similar to George, but with a lust for adventure and, well, all the things that pirates used to do in these islands. Anyway, through here is our bedroom."

Maren led the way beneath the crossed pistols, into the master bedroom, with its large bed on a wooden frame, chest of drawers, and the same style of grass matting as in the great room. There were closets, a bathroom to the left, and George's office to the right. Maren pushed open a door to the outside and stepped through. Sophie followed, descending a single stair to the lawn.

Maren pointed uphill to her right. "That is our guest house, where you will stay as long as you wish. Michael has taken your suitcase up there. The house to the left is shared by Michael and Jenny. Our kitchen is on the other side of the main house, separated from the other buildings because of the danger of fire. And way over to the right we keep chickens and pigs for eggs and food. Now you have seen our home."

"Wow! This is magnificent. You have everything you need – even a panoramic view of the Caribbean."

Maren smiled. "I'm glad you see the charm of this place. I'm originally from St. Thomas, but these days I return only to visit family and friends. This is my home." She gave Sophie a hug. "I'm happy you're staying with us. Go to your cottage now, and relax."

CHAPTER 9

Drake needed to walk the island and get the heebie-jeebies out of his system. As he left the crowd and climbed into the mountains, his legs worked hard, his breathing deepened, and the physical labor felt good.

The squall had been much worse than he'd expected, though he should have known better, after one look at its breadth and intense blackness. He'd weathered only one squall worse, and during that one he'd had George's son, Michael, aboard, who was an excellent sailor. But even then they'd nearly lost the mast from a particularly vicious gust. No, squalls were not to be messed with, he chided himself, no matter how demanding your passenger.

But it was discovering, Jenny capsized and at the mercy of the sea, that had truly put Drake on edge. He'd known her since he'd arrived on St. Mark, four years previously. She'd always been scampering around the island and was the ring leader of the little gang of island kids. She had energy, imagination, and people smarts. Everyone adored her.

To see her harmed in any way, and especially to see her in mortal danger, had hit Drake like a gut punch. That Sophie had spotted Jenny was a miracle in those confused seas, and to rescue her had been another miracle. But the biggest miracle was that they'd been there at all. There were no other boats around, and Jenny could have been swept away or slipped into the sea from exhaustion and exposure before the islanders could start their search. Sophie had helped in more ways than one. God, it was a near thing.

Walking the island was not an occasion for him but rather a custom he observed daily when he was not away on a charter. It was part of keeping in shape and helped him maintain a security perimeter for the judge. He wanted to sight coves where people could arrive unseen during the night, and he wanted to spot boats loitering offshore. He couldn't have his eyes on everything – hell, the island was four and a half miles long and full of little nooks and crannies and hidden glens in its mountainous interior – but a daily tour of one part or another acted as a sort of radar for spotting strangers.

He reflected that his other radar was composed of his neighbors – especially the kids – who also roamed about the island and talked about what they saw. The rich and famous folks on the North Side kept to themselves, but his client, Judge Santiago, had his compound up there and they talked among themselves, and provided a third source of intel.

He ascended to a rocky promontory that poked into the sea and provided a magnificent view of the entire South Side. The harbor and town lay to his left, the western reaches of the island to his right, a series of isolated bays and beaches. Hundreds of feet directly below, land met the sea in a place of rocks, coral, sea urchins, and crashing waves, as well as its own pristine beach.

Inland from the beaches, the terrain sloped upward to the mountains, dotted with low trees, bushes, and grass. Peppered through the bushes and trees, as they became tall and dense further inland, were deer, mongoose, and the occasional wild goat. Birds commanded the trees, including colorful parakeets, a flock of which flew overhead, chirping.

Drake turned back to the bush, picked up an animal trail, and worked his way westward. After a quarter of an hour, he emerged from the bush at the peak of the western-most mountain on St. Mark and surveyed the light house.

In days gone by, there was a keeper, and his cottage still remained, attached to the tall tower. The man had long gone, and the light now operated automatically, with a visit once or twice a year by the Coast Guard for maintenance. Drake walked through grass and shrubs to a helo pad, where many of the North Side residents arrived and departed the island. It was a lot quicker trip from the St. Thomas airport than the weekly ferry.

He returned to the bush, and descended to a fertile valley between two mountains, alert to sounds within the foliage – the rush of a shy deer, the flutter of a bird.

The trees grew tall and strong here, for the land had been left alone for centuries. The underbrush had shrunk from the lack of sunlight, and the walking was relatively easy along established animal routes. He had to hunch over, because he was taller than most deer, but that was fine.

As he ranged deeper into the valley, he heard sharp, staccato sounds, no doubt someone chopping with a machete, which was a multi-use tool in the islands. Drake eased toward the noise, purposely shaking branches to announce his arrival. Through the foliage, he saw the shape of a person through the trees. He stopped and waited for a pause in the chopping.

"Hello!" he said.

Someone moved, directly ahead.

CHAPTER 10

Drake stepped into a fifty-foot wide clearing. On the other side in the shade of a tree stood the stocky, muscular form of George Coxon. The man turned, an island machete in his hand, and the shadow made his face look even more serious than usual. Drake grinned – damned if George didn't look totally dangerous. Give him a gold earring and a brace of flintlock pistols and he'd be the picture of a pirate.

Drake had heard the story often enough. The buccaneer had terrorized the Spanish Main, plundered the town of Santa Marta, and even – it was said – abducted the governor and bishop of Santa Maria, taking them to Jamaica. George said there were no records of him after 1683. Coxon family tradition told the rest of the tale.

Drake shook hands with George, noticing the man's high cheekbones, and hints of Arawak and Black in his muscles, his face, his wavy jet-black hair.

"Are you lost in the brush again?" George Coxon asked, his voice grave, eyes teasing.

"Maren sent me to find you," Drake said. "She didn't want you coming home late for dinner, now that you have company."

Coxon shook his head in mock dismay and then his eyes turned serious. He set his machete down and placed both hands on Drake's shoulders.

"Friend, you saved this man's soul today."

Drake felt himself flush. As the recognized leader of the island, he welcomed people who came to him with their problems, stuff they couldn't untangle on their own. Drake knew that George and Maren worked as a team during such times, soothing family grief or resolving hard feelings between people who were usually fast friends.

But the ultimate responsibility lay on George's shoulders, just as the responsibility he took on when he'd reached a personal crossroads in St. Thomas. He had married Maren by then and Michael was a baby. But on St. Mark, George's father was dying, his mother was frail, and the family boat business was in a slump.

Even off the grid, people needed money for the doctor, for food they didn't gather from their little garden, for clothing. So, George Coxon had moved back to St. Mark and assumed the role his father had borne, as had the Coxon men since John, back in the day. George became the island's leader, and a builder of fine boats.

Drake knew he couldn't respond to George's compliment lightly. This wasn't the Marines, where you laughed off death, ignored the close call. Hell, in combat you had no time for emotions. But on St. Mark you had time. You showed respect to your own deep emotions and those of your best friend.

Drake hugged his friend and felt tears in his eyes. Well, heck, he could cry a little out here in the bush. No one could see. They released each other. Yeah, that tough, old descendent of a bad-ass pirate was crying, too.

"She means the world to me, too," Drake said. "I thank God I was there."

"I'm glad it was you."

They stood still, looked up at a flock of chirping parakeets.

"Pretty serious stuff," said Coxon.

"Life is delicate."

"Yeah. Mostly good. Some bad. Always delicate."

Drake sensed that the mood was lightening. He wasn't quite sure until he noticed his friend bend down and pick up his machete. So, what had to be said was said – not with a Marine grunt or casual gesture that ignored the depth of emotion all men feel, but with actual words.

Drake watched Coxon handle the machete as he looked up and around, probably seeking the next tree limb to join those he'd stacked in a neat pile nearby.

"Looking for timber for your next boat?" Drake asked.

"Yeah, another sloop, you know."

"For a collector or a racer or a museum?"

"Hah, well, this one is for Jenny. Don' tell her. She thinks it'll go to a museum or collector. I'm letting her work on it so she gets the feel for the tools. She has the eye and the skill. Anyway, it's a small version, tougher in a storm than her plastic sailboat, eh?"

"It'll be tough if you build it. Pretty lines too."

"Tradition of the Caribbean. Different islands with their different boats, but all tough and, yeah you're right, they all look pretty."

"At least to their builder," said Drake.

Which got a smile out of his friend.

"So, who is this visitor you bring us?" Coxon asked, walking over to a tree and feeling a limb with his left hand.

Drake shared what he knew about Sophie, realizing that she had never mentioned her last name. Coxon had lifted a small saw and a wooden implement in the shape of the letter "L." The two legs of the L were joined by a hinge, and he opened the legs to about sixty degrees, hemmed and hawed, and placed it against the limb he was interested in. Satisfied that the limb had the right shape, he began sawing.

He said over his shoulder, "Isn't it a little strange, her coming out of nowhere, aiming directly for St. Mark?"

"Yeah, I'd say so. At first, I thought she was just another Continental with too much money. After all, when has anyone aimed for St. Mark when they have St. Thomas or St. John? We have a dozen rich people here. St. Thomas has hundreds of rich folks and thousands of well-heeled tourists. So, I'm wondering, when was the last time this happened?"

"Oh, I don't know," George drawled. "I remember John just appeared one day, as if he was washed up with the rising tide."

Drake shook his head, picturing the man who owned the island's only store, selling everything from soap to canned food to blue jeans.

"Yeah, well, you're right, and truth be told, I showed up seeming like I came out of nowhere."

"Yep, hired through your old commanding officer to protect Judge Santiago, using your sailing skills to give charters and keep your ears to the ground for intel."

Drake nodded. To the rest of the island, he had simply shown up one day. Slowly the word got out that he helped protect the judge, but only George knew the rest of the story.

Drake continued, "I get a feeling there's something else going on with Sophie. Maybe she wants to hide from something. But why not hide in the British Virgins? There's more to do, more people, and if she wanted to, she could still drop off the grid."

"She'd need a passport," Coxon said. "Her problem may have come up too quickly for her to get one."

"It bothers me," said Drake.

"Everyone has secrets."

"True, but the question is, what kind of secret? Is it what happened to her or what she plans to do? I know, George, don't look at me that way, and I pretty much figure she's a good person. I know she's attractive and looks innocent, and she sure helped save Jenny in heavy seas. But I have a man to protect, and I have a moral obligation to keep dangerous people off this island."

"Jeeze, Richard. You think she could be an assassin? Aren't you being a little too suspicious?"

"I get paid to be suspicious, although I think you're right, like I said."

"You don't sound convinced."

Drake's mouth quirked into a grin, "I tell you, George, I like her, and I feel we all owe her for helping rescue Jenny. The kids adore her."

"Yeah?"

"I'm still suspicious."

CHAPTER 11

Sophie awoke covered in sweat, the nightmare vivid in her mind. Cliff had come for her in her room in the Coxons' guest house. He'd opened the wooden jalousies and climbed in, having approached through the bush. She'd opened her eyes as he leaned over her, leering, and he'd said, "too bad," then plunged a gleaming hunting knife into her chest.

God, it hurt, even though she was awake and the nightmare should have been over. In disbelief, she looked down at her chest where the knife had stabbed her in her awful dream. Yes, it did hurt. Right there.

But not from the knife.

She had squeezed her bed sheet to herself with her arms folded tightly, hugging so hard that she hurt. She forced her arms to relax, to let them rest at her side, and she drew a deep breath, then another. She stared up at the ceiling beams, turned her head and looked at a water color painting of a palm-fringed beach. She rose, and sipped water from the glass Maren had handed her before her nap.

Nap? My God, had she fallen asleep? She only wanted to rest, but the breeze wafting through the jalousie louvers, the hum of cicadas...

Sophie checked her watch – five o'clock. She'd slept for an hour. She sat up and blinked her eyes, tryed to clear her head. Took another sip of water.

She recalled the stark realism of her nightmare and shivered. What *did* Cliff think about her? Her car was gone, he couldn't contact her by cell phone. By now, he must realize she'd left him.

Because of the timing, he likely assumed she'd witnessed him torturing that man to death. In his mind, she'd become a loose end. The thought of him hunting her, of what he would do if he found her, made Sophie nauseous.

She pulled on her running shoes and left the cottage, took the meandering walkway around the main house and up to the front porch. Maren was sitting, the three dogs snoozing at her feet. She patted the chair next to her.

"So, you did take a nap after all," Maren said, pouring ice tea from a pitcher and handing the glass to Sophie.

Sophie sat, feeling more grounded and confident there beside Maren.

"I did sleep a little," she said. "Your bed is very comfortable."

"Especially after a long trip from the States, and a squall?"

Sophie forced a smile.

Maren examined her face with kind eyes. She sipped her tea and sat back, giving space. They looked over the grassy plot in front of the house, beyond the tree tops and down the mountain to the sea, now a gray-blue in the waning sun.

"I had a nightmare," Sophie said at last, the information slipping out ,almost of its own volition, for she was still in a funk.

"Those are not fun. It may be from the stress of the squall, of saving Jenny. A lot can happen very quickly. Later, you think of how it might have turned out another way, a terrible way."

Sophie nodded absently. "Yes. I relive close calls and they give me the shivers." She faced her new friend. "But, well, I trust you, Maren. May I tell you something in confidence?"

Maren patted Sophie's hand and smiled encouragingly. She could keep a secret, thought Sophie. Maren was that kind of person.

"I'm a woman on the run," Sophie said, blinking away tears of frustration, anger, shame, and fear. She took a deep breath. "I was in love with my boyfriend. I thought he loved me. Maybe, at first, he did. He's a wealthy man. An international businessman, a driven man. He said he loved me, told me I was his girl next door. Totally different and totally better than his two previous wives, both gorgeous European models. We played tennis, swam, took vacations to exotic places. He taught me to drive his power boat and even let me fly his jet plane."

"My goodness, Sophie, you said he was wealthy, but a jet?"

"Oh, yes. He used it for his business trips in the States and Latin America. And he has an oceanfront estate in Palm Beach."

"But – "

"Yes. He has a dark side. Very dark. In businesses that are way over the line of being illegal. I found out little by little, and then more recently I overheard and saw something I shouldn't have. I put two and two together, figured I knew way too much, and I took off."

"But not to Europe or Asia?"

Sophie shook her head. "He has my passport locked in the safe at the estate. I don't know the combination. Did I tell you he's a control freak?"

"You didn't have to. My gosh. So, you came to the furthest place you could find inside the United States."

"Yes, at least to catch my breath."

Maren squeezed Sophie's arm. "You're welcome to stay forever. You're not the only one on St. Mark who's left behind a troubling past."

"Thank you, Maren."

Maren nodded.

After a time, Sophie arose. "I think I'll walk into town."

"Do you want company, or just time to think on your own?"

Sophie smiled. She stooped and patted a slumbering dog. "Maybe just alone this time."

"Okay. Remember, you are completely safe on this island. You shouldn't get lost, but if you do need directions, ask anyone. They all know who you are – you are somewhat of an island hero."

"I didn't realize."

"Well, you are. Have fun. See you soon."

Sophie waved and made her way down the stairs, across the grass, and along the dirt track.

She was thinking of visiting George's boatyard at the west end of the little harbor. But George wasn't there and she didn't want to interrupt the other men, so she decided to simply explore. She strolled slowly down the road that ran in front of the town's four buildings, all built of stone, as were the Coxons' houses.

They stood in a rough row, with a couple of windows along their sides and large, wooden doors hanging open in front and back

– one end facing the harbor, the other facing the road. Looking into the shadowy interior of the first building, she spotted fishing nets, a boat being painted, and nautical gear. The two men painting the boat waved to her as she passed.

The second building housed a bright red Jeep with a pump and a large tank mounted in back. The man leaning on the door grinned as she approached.

"Hi Sophie," he said. "You out takin' a walk?"

"Yes. Getting a little fresh air."

He gestured toward the Jeep. "Well, you're looking at the St. Mark Fire Department. That's our pumper truck, with water and a pump and a hose. She puts out little fires. Don't carry enough water for big ones." He grinned at his little joke.

Sophie was happy for the company and for the friendly chatter. They talked for fifteen minutes, then he excused himself.

"Gotta wash the fire truck," he said. "Fact is, I'm gonna use her to deliver fresh pool water to one of the North Side compounds. The folks had their pool drained and painted. Time to fill 'er up."

They waved, and Sophie continued to the next building, marked with a sign, 'Pirates Rest Bar and Grille.' Inside, it was shadowy, as were the other buildings. The place was attractively, if plainly, built out, with a bar along one side and tables and chairs filling most of the rest of the room. There was a walled-off section, perhaps for the kitchen. A man at the bar nodded to her as she passed.

The sign on the last building read, 'John's Dry Goods.' Underneath, in smaller letters, was printed, 'U.S. Post Office.'

Curious, she entered. She stood just inside the door to let her eyes acclimate to the dim lighting, consisting only of the late afternoon sunlight slanting through the jalousies. Rows of shelves came into focus, all crammed with goods for sale.

From the back of the room a voice interrupted the shadowy silence.

"Ahh. You must be the woman who rescued little Jenny from the sea." The man stood behind a wooden counter, on which stood an ancient cash register and a glass bottle filled with lollypops. He was heavy set, with muscled arms and a welcoming smile. She walked down a narrow aisle and extended her hand.

"Hi. I'm Sophie."

He shook, his hand slightly damp, his grip gentle. His smile made crinkles at the corners of his blue eyes.

"I'm happy to meet you, Sophie. I'm John Parker. Welcome to St. Mark."

"Thanks. You've got quite a store here. There's a little of everything."

"People ask for something and I stock it. Sometimes things sell. Other times, well, they serve as a decoration, I guess." He raised a hinged flap in the counter and joined Sophie, walking her down the aisles. "Here we have canned food, stuff people can't grow in their gardens – vegetables, a few sauces, and over here spices and herbs, though most folks grow the herbs they need for the local dishes. And here are tools, nails, rope."

"And machetes," Sophie said.

"Yes, also called the cutlass, which people around her pronounce 'cutlash,' a cousin to the fighting sword of pirate days. It's handy around the house for opening coconuts, trimming grass or bushes, even repairing furniture."

"And this?" Sophie asked, gazing up at a large bulletin board on which were pinned dozens of pieces of paper with scrawled writing and columns of numbers.

"Ah," John said uneasily, "that is where I keep my customers' financial accounts. If someone can't pay, then they write a note, listing what they picked up and how much it cost. Next week they come back and pay, and take back their note."

"But there are so many…"

He squinted at the forest of notes, his breathing labored, as if the heat and simply standing had tired him out.

"Oh, well, most of these are requests for me to stock new items. See, just these few are IOUs." He sighed. "You can see the problem – I've run out of space. Also, different people tend to request the same things but with other brand names. Look at this – three different brands for tomato sauce."

"You know, Mr. Parker…"

"'John is fine."

"Oh, well, John, I used to work at a little market similar to yours in Florida. It was part of a gas station, and it carried all sorts of stuff, from food to tools, to medicine. We had the same problem. Our regulars would ask us to stock something. At first we did, but it never moved. The original customer probably bought it somewhere else during the time we had it on order, and other customers preferred the brand we already had on the shelves."

"Yep, that's it," Parker said. "So, they don't need another one. What did you do?"

"It turned out there were certain categories of stuff. Cereal was one. All the major cereal companies had their version of types of cereal, like corn flakes. I made a list of the brands and let my regulars vote. We stocked the brand with the most votes. We sympathized with the other customers but, after a few grumps, they bought what we carried and were happy."

"Say, that sounds like a good idea. Tell me, Sophie, did you do the books – the accounting – for this little store of yours?"

"Oh, sure. I was in college, barely twenty-one, but after a year I was promoted to store manager. I ordered stock, put it on the shelves, swept the floors, and took care of the cash register. By the way, I was admiring your cash register. I've never seen a mechanical version. Ours needed electricity."

"Ah, she's a beauty. I've got to oil her now and then, but she's a champ. Well, what I was thinking is – I don't know how long you're planning on staying on our island, but I could sure use your help here in my store. Everyone knows you by now, and you're friendly and know how a little store works."

He walked back behind the counter. He reached up to a shelf and set a three-ring binder down in front of Sophie.

"These are my accounts."

She opened the cover and paged through the book, twice, then let out a deep breath.

John chuckled. "I know. It's hopeless."

"You'd want me to keep accounts and help make stocking decisions?"

"Yes, that's what I'm thinking. I can't pay you much – there's only a small margin of profit after the purchase and shipping costs."

"How about if I come in during your busy times? Then I can help ring up customer purchases, too."

"That'll work just fine. The busy time is after the families eat breakfast. The men leave for work, and the women shop and do errands until they have to get back home to prepare lunch. Most everyone comes home for lunch, you see."

Sophie nodded as he spoke, continuing to walk the aisles, this time with an eye toward duplication, which she found everywhere. She thought about stocking, displays, checking out with the old cash register, and meeting all the people she'd seen when they landed with Jenny. With a smile, she returned to the counter and stuck out her hand.

"You've got yourself a helper, John."

They chatted about this and that and she found he had a gentle way about him, and a sense of humor, as well as an insight to people. He told a few stories of little tricks people played, especially the kids who got bored tagging along with their moms. Some of the little rascals switched the tomato paste over to where the tomato soup was displayed, turned the cereal upside down so the labels were hard to read, stuff like that. He'd cured most of that with the lollipops. The pesky guys got no candy until they quit the tricks.

She laughed at his jokes and listened to his stories, happy she had accepted his offer. She planned to stay on the island for at least a few weeks. Working in the store was a fine way to pass the time and meet people. More and more she was feeling at home on St. Mark – and safe.

After they said their good-byes and she neared the front door, she glanced out and froze in horror. Shaking to her toes, she shrank back into the store, back to where John stood.

All thoughts of having found a safe haven evaporated into the tropical air.

CHAPTER 12

Before visiting his client on the North Side, Drake decided to wait until he checked on Sophie a little more. Talk with her some. He figured she'd be either at the Coxons' or in town. He made his way from where he'd met George, moving toward town and the Coxon home.

It was that quiet part of the afternoon when the wind off the water stopped. Deep in the bush, even the lightest of breezes had disappeared. He sweltered, and soon was dreaming of that first swallow of ice-cold Heineken.

A thought occurred to Drake. Maybe a way to get information about Sophie. He pulled out his satellite phone. He upgraded every two years, and this one was only a month old. He smiled when the display showed, bright and clear. He'd worn the phone on his belt during the squall, and plenty of waves and rain had seeped beneath his foul-weather jacket and soaked the little device.

The Iridium people bragged about its 'military-grade 810' durability. He hadn't a clue what '810' was, but the phone was sure waterproof. He punched in auto-dial for Graham Walters. Yep – got a dial tone. Walters picked up and his gravelly voice came through, loud and clear.

"Holy shit, it's my St. Mark constable."

Drake had to smile. No 'hello' or any preliminaries – the man just jumped into the conversation. He'd made Drake the official Police Department constable on St. Mark a few weeks back and couldn't resist poking fun. Drake played along. No one remembered when the last real crime occurred on the little island.

Probably some kid taking two lollipops instead of one from Uncle John's jar. Drake smiled into the phone.

"Just calling about the bank heist over here," Drake said.

"Bank heist! That's a good one. You don't even have a damned bank on that two-bit chunk of coral you call an island."

"Hell, maybe someone stole all the cash from Uncle John's till. Ever thought about that? It's serious stuff."

"Yeah, I hear you. Did you just call me to screw around or – wait a minute! I heard you got hit by that squall that tore a new asshole through St. John and Jost Van Dyke."

Which was as close as Walters ever got to saying he was glad that his friend survived.

Remembering the vicious wind and waves, Drake turned serious. "It was a bad one, Graham, but CAPRICE pulled through. Didn't even lose my rudder."

"Yeah, like that time off Virgin Gorda?"

"Hmm."

"What's this I hear about Jenny?"

"The little kid was out there in the waves, floating around a few miles south of St. Mark. Her boat capsized and she was hanging onto the hull. Limp as a ragdoll. Scared the living shit out of me."

"But she's okay, right?"

Drake almost laughed at the sympathy in the grizzled Army veteran's voice.

"She hurt her arm," Drake said, his voice softening to reflect his own concern for the girl's safety. "Jimmy Franklin checked her out, said it wasn't broken, just a bad bruise. Fixed her up with a nice white sling."

"I'm glad she's okay. You too, Drake. Hell, if you'd gotten into trouble I'd have had to fill out all the paperwork to assign another constable."

Drake laughed and shook his head.

Walters continued, "So, you're calling about those Latino visitors we're expecting, right?"

"Yeah, just checking in."

"Still getting chatter on the street. Could be drug related. Hell, could even be a terrorist plot against one of the cruise ships. Though I really don't think that's it. We're pretty much off the grid here in the islands. But who knows?"

"Maybe I can find out something from my charter parties. It's amazing the stuff they overhear. By the way, a woman – pretty, late twenties – came up to me at the tiki bar…"

"Is this a joke?"

"No, serious. It was just after you left."

"Okay."

"Anyway, she said she needed a ride to St. Mark. Couldn't stay overnight in St. Thomas for the morning ferry. She was in a real hurry. I told her I didn't want to go, given the look of the weather, but she pushed hard. I told her I'd charge two hundred dollars, which seemed a good way to get rid of her. But she agreed to pay. I don't know what her problem is but she looked frightened about something."

"Or someone?"

"Yeah, could be. She hasn't told me anything and I haven't asked, but I'm more than a little suspicious."

Graham grunted. "Suspicious? You, suspicious of a young lady?"

"Just a gut feeling."

"Let me ask, did you two get along okay?"

"I think you could say that. Plus, she's made a good impression on the islanders."

"Right. And she is attractive?"

"Not exactly a knock-out, but still…"

"So, it's obvious."

"Don't say it."

"Ha, Richard, she's getting under your skin. Of course, something's wrong – you're not in charge."

"Jesus, Walters, I thought you were my friend. This is security shit, not romance."

Walters laughed. "I *am* your friend. That's why I'm telling you. But you've got a point. I'll check around a little."

"Thanks. Her name is Sophie Cooper and she's from Palm Beach, Florida. That's where she was living with her boyfriend. At least, that's what she claims."

"Boyfriend?"

"Ex-boyfriend."

"Then, she could be running from him."

"It's a possibility. Or maybe she broke a law or she's running some kind of scam. She's smart. Capable of acting frightened to gain sympathy."

"Okay, I'll do some checking. I know the police up Palm Beach way, from drug smuggling work. If she has a rap sheet or a sleazy reputation, they'll know."

They hung up as Drake arrived at the west end of town. He didn't expect Sophie to be at the boatyard, so he continued past it and down the street. He looked in at Pirate's Rest Bar and Grille, nestled inside what used to be a warehouse during the Coxon pirate days. It was a single-story stone structure with pink stucco exterior and a pair of massive wooden storm doors, security against pirates and hurricanes.

Popular with the locals and visiting boaters, the bar's owner was Daniel Pearson, descendent of the first mate of pirate John Coxon's crew. He and his pretty Puerto Rican wife, Asunción, ran the place. They lived in an apartment behind the bar.

And there sat Sophie, at one of the wooden tables inside, nursing a Heineken, and wearing a long face. He walked over. She stood up and hugged him. Tight. Not the hug of a sister or a lover, but someone with the shit scared out of her.

He encircled her with his arms. She snuggled close.

They stayed there for a couple of minutes. Daniel Pearson looked over from where he stood behind the bar and mimed drinking a beer. Drake nodded. Finally, Sophie unclasped her arms and stood back. She gave him a shy smile, moved unsteadily to her chair and collapsed into it.

Drake's beer arrived, along with a refill for Sophie. He returned to the bar. She and Drake took long swallows from their bottles. The beer tasted every bit as delicious as Drake had imagined. He set his bottle down the same time Pearson placed two cold ones on the table.

"Thought you'd need another as well," he said.

Drake smiled his thanks and Pearson left them alone. A dog barked outside.

"Hi, Richard," Sophie said, her tone laced with fatigue.

"Hi, Sophie. You don't look very happy for having been crowned the island hero. Has something gone wrong at the Coxons'?"

"Oh, no. They're wonderful. I love them and I feel like I've known them my whole life. Their houses are darling, and they put me up in my own little cottage. I fell asleep, then talked with Maren a little before coming down here to explore."

He looked at her, waiting for her to tell him why in hell she'd glued herself to him as if she were a scared little girl.

She forced a smile, gulped her beer and asked, "Did you know their houses were built before 1700 by a pirate?"

Drake decided not to push her. He'd eventually ask, if she didn't tell him on her own, but he wanted to give her breathing space. He decided a little sea story might help settle her down.

"Yeah, John Coxon, George's ancestor, built the place. Good location, too. It's far enough into the bush that it's isolated from a surprise attack on the town, and high enough to see the harbor and the sea. There's a watch tower further up the mountain behind the house.

"Even has a couple of cannons. In the early days, when piracy was active, John kept the cannons loaded and stationed a lookout on the tower. If a pirate crew did invade the island, there was room inside the tower to shelter the women and children, and the men could spread out on the platform up top with their muskets and the cannons. It was a fine defense."

Sophie kept looking over her shoulder.

Drake decided to cut to the chase.

"What's wrong?" he asked gently. "You look worried."

She looked him in the eye, dropped her gaze, then looked up again. "I saw a man. Jorgue Matazos. A very dangerous man."

CHAPTER 13

Sophie lifted her beer with a shaking hand and set it down immediately, embarrassed.

Drake frowned. "He won't hurt you. I know him. He's a businessman from Colombia. Keeps to himself."

She gestured dismissively. "I'm worried because he saw me and, from the look in his eyes, he recognized me. I met him once at my ex-boyfriend's estate where he was attending a business meeting. I'm afraid he'll tell my ex-boyfriend I'm here. That will lead to serious trouble."

She paused, her eyebrows knitted. Silent.

"You don't have to tell me."

"I don't want you to..."

"Get involved?" he asked.

She nodded.

"No worries. Like I said, old John Coxon chose his home well, up the mountain and along that crooked dirt trail. George could have had it graded and black-topped when they did the main road, but he chose not to. He's never said why – I never asked him – but I think he values his seclusion from unauthorized snoopers.

"He and his friends know every deer track, tree, and termite nest around that house and they are all hunters, some ex-military. Strangers don't know where the Coxon place is, and no one will reveal that sort of information to a visitor, or to Matazos for that matter. As long as you're back there, you're safe."

"Still," she said. "Matazos will tell my ex-boyfriend, and he will either send someone or come himself to settle matters."

"Is he a violent man?"

She lifted her bottle and this time took a drink, the beer tasting stale. Her hand trembled. She looked at Drake, dreading having to tell him and relive those memories. "I'd better start at the beginning. His name is Cliff Webb.

"We met two years ago and I thought we'd fallen in love. I certainly did, but I've begun to wonder about him. He's been married twice, and when we met he'd just ended a messy divorce with his second wife. He said he didn't want a permanent relationship, and I understood. He invited me to live with him and we've been together in his Palm Beach estate for the past year and a half."

Drake nodded, eyes concerned.

Sophie continued, determined to get through. "He's a smart man and well-travelled in Europe and Latin America. He speaks Spanish and French fluently. I guess he's an international broker, putting the right people together for deals.

"It could be grain or factory machines, pretty much anything. He knows the international export-import laws and hires the best lawyers to look after details." She hesitated. "But lately, I've seen and heard things at the estate, one thing in particular. He often invites clients and associates there for parties, and for meetings that turn into parties. After a few drinks, people start talking, always in a sort of code when I'm around, but I've been able to connect the dots. Of course, I know the names of many of his associates, hard men like Matazos"

She stared at Drake. His eyes were sympathetic. He was a good listener. But what could he do to help her – really? She just wished to hell she could dig herself out of this whole mess.

"What I've discovered," she said, choosing her words carefully, "is that he does legitimate business, but often operates way outside the law. Such as arms trading and drug smuggling. He may even be into trafficking immigrants from Latin America into the US.

"The danger of being caught is always present, and he is paranoid about security. I'm amazed I could learn as much as I did, but I guess he saw me as a non-player. Anyway, he's been successful in spite of several close calls with law enforcement. I know he's bribed officials in Colombia and Mexico, and I think he's bribed a US senator."

"You know too much, is that it?"

"Yes."

"This man you saw earlier. Are you sure it's Jorgue Matazos?"

She shrugged. "I'm certain. He was only fifty feet away. I saw him through the front door of John's market. I ducked back into the shadows, but I caught the expression on his face in that split second when our eyes met. He smiled – not in a friendly way, but like he'd made a big score."

"I wonder why he was in town," Drake said thoughtfully. "And won't he think you're here with Cliff?"

"No, because Cliff loves the grand entrance, arriving on a yacht or helicopter, and he'd be looking for Matazos to throw him a big party."

"But you could be here on a solo vacation."

She shook her head. "That's not how it's done with Cliff. He makes the rules. I stick close to home, maybe go shopping with a girlfriend or visit my parents in Melbourne, but never go off on my own overnight."

"And you're thinking that now we've got to keep an eye out for Cliff or one of his men."

"That's about it. I'm terrified."

Drake tapped the table, his forehead wrinkled. "I should share something with you," he said. "I'm a security consultant for a man who has a compound on the North Side. He's an international judge and his name is Ernesto Santiago Valdez. He's sent many important criminals to prison, and is a potential target.

"My sailboat charter business is real, but it's not how I earn my living. I use it as a way to connect with people on the islands, and the people who hire me to take them around. I keep my ear to the ground for strangers, especially strangers who ask questions or are overly interested in visiting St. Mark, which is definitely not on the list of any usual tour of the US and British Virgin Islands."

"So, am I a suspect?" Sophie asked, feeling embarrassed and vulnerable.

"You were for a while."

"Ouch!"

"Of course, you saved Jenny, you appear to be in real danger, and every adult, kid, dog, and probably cat on the island love you."

"Then I'm no longer a suspected assassin or anything?"

"Pretty much."

Her gut lurched, and she blurted angrily, "God, Richard. I trusted you and I thought you trusted me."

He gestured, his eyes sympathetic. "Just bear with me, okay? My job is to be suspicious. I'd be lying if I told you I didn't have to get to know you before, you know, being sure everything was okay."

She winced. Emotionally, she felt dizzy. Where would she be without Richard? He was her rock in a world gone crazy. How could he not trust her in turn? He was in security – couldn't he tell when someone was telling him the truth? She felt stinging tears of frustration.

He waited and then he reached out, put his hand on hers, and said softly, "I'm sorry."

She examined his eyes, his face. She let out a breath and squeezed his hand. Held on tight.

Yeah, her practical side told her to calm down. She had to admit that what he was saying made sense. He'd obviously been trained to suspect first, and trust only when trust had been earned.

Her emotions still roiled inside her chest – God, she had thought she'd earned his trust. Why was everything so complicated?

"Okay, okay," she said, not really feeling it way okay at all.

She mentally kicked herself. *My gosh, Sophie, you have a strong and feeling man on your side, as well as everyone on the island. What more do you want?*

"I got greedy," she said, seeing a flicker of humor in the twitch of his lip.

"I'm greedy too. Give me time, Sophie."

She gave him a little smile and kept holding his hand. Warm, strong, physical proof that there was hope.

She blinked. What did he just say? That he was greedy too?

"To trust me?" she said in a hopeful voice.

"More than that." He flashed a disarming smile, stared at her and didn't look away. She blinked. Her voice came out fluttery but she didn't care. "You're contagious, you know."

"I'll drink to that," he said.

They touched bottles.

"You know," he said. "It's almost dark. The Coxons are probably already eating dinner. Do you want something here? The food is pretty good."

"Okay," she said.

Drake motioned, and Pearson ambled over from behind the bar. They released each other's hands and Sophie smiled inside, feeling warm and safe for this moment.

"You'll be staying for dinner?"

"We will. We'll move to an outside table and enjoy the sunset."

"Of course."

"And I have a question for you, Dan. Did Jorgue Matazos stop by here to make arrangements for that get-together at his place we've been hearing about?"

"Yes, he was here this afternoon. He asked Asunción to make appetizers for the party, which should be in full swing about now. She made him a bunch of her tapas." Pearson gave them a rare grin. "Old Jorgue was steaming because he had to come down personally. Apparently, his staff swarmed to the town earlier today to stand with the Coxons while they waited at the pier, worried about Jenny. That cost a few hours and put him way behind."

He glanced from Drake to Sophie with a puzzled expression.

"Oh, sorry Daniel," Richard said. "This is Sophie, the woman who spotted Jenny at sea and helped bring her in."

Pearson grinned again. "I thought that's who you were, but I didn't recognize you because I neve got to the pier. I had to stay here all afternoon, helping with all the appetizers. It's a real pleasure, Sophie. You saved a very special little girl."

They ordered dinner and changed to a table on the deck, overlooking the harbor, with George's boatyard on the right and John's store along the street to the left. The clouds turned shades of red and yellow and orange and purple.

The food arrived. Drake seemed starved and wolfed down his freshly caught fish, but Sophie found herself again haunted by the specter of Cliff's vengeance. Her appetite vanished and she barely touched her roasted chicken.

Richard must have noticed, because he guided their conversation toward normal parts of life. She tried to focus, and she laughed at his jokes, but her mind wandered.

Should she leave St. Mark and keep running? Maybe buy a forged passport in St. Thomas. She had the money. Get a ride over with Richard. But did she have time? How soon until Cliff got here? Too soon, she suspected.

Another thought came to her, a task undone. "My goodness! I forgot to pay you the other hundred dollars for bringing me here."

"Forget it," he said. "I told you already – you're a friend now, of mine and everyone on the island. I don't charge friends for boat rides."

She began to protest but he turned stern and declared, "It's too late."

She sat back in her chair as an impish thought popped into her head. "Then, how about the hundred I paid you?"

"You mean a refund?"

She grinned.

He shook his head. "Nope. Too late for that too. Back then, we weren't friends."

They laughed together, and Sophie yearned to extend the light mood with this man with another impish thought. She leaned forward and spoke softly. "I've noticed all the houses have jalousie windows."

"Yeah, none of the islanders have glass windows or air conditioning. The weather is mild all year round, and there's usually a breeze."

"Jalousies are your only privacy?" she asked with mock surprise.

"Yup."

"Jeeze, Richard, you can see and hear everything through the louvers, even personal stuff, like arguments – and sex."

"Yeah," he drawled with a gleam in his eye, "I guess I never thought about that. But it doesn't appear to stop anyone."

"From arguments?"

He gave her a look. "You've seen all the kids and babies."

"Well, I'm not going any further with that line of discussion," she said, softening her stern tone with a smirk, "but it's no wonder everyone knows everyone else's business on this island."

"Actually, some people close their storm shutters at night. That's about as private as being in a bank vault. No one overhears them."

"Wouldn't it get too hot?"

"It's pretty warm, but latched shutters keep the Jumbees out."

"Jumbees? "You mean ghosts?"

"Sort of like ghosts, yes."

"My gosh, Richard, the islanders still believe in ghosts?"

"Yes, but don't judge them too harshly."

"Sorry, I just didn't think people still believed in that sort of thing."

"It's different here in the islands. By the way, there's a woman on St. Thomas you may want to meet. She may change your opinion about Jumbees."

"Oh? What's her name?"

"Anika."

"That sounds Scandinavian."

"Yes, she's one of Maren's friends. They're both descendants of the Danes who used to own St. Thomas. But that's for another time. We've got other stuff to figure out right now. We need to keep you safe from Webb."

CHAPTER 14

Drake trudged uphill toward the North Side compounds, his flashlight showing the way in the moonless night. Insects chattered. The leather soles of his hiking boots sounded hollow on the blacktop road. To his right, invisible in the darkness, lay the Atlantic Ocean – St. Mark formed the boundary between the Caribbean to the north, and the Atlantic, to the south. A breeze blew from the sea, gentle, very unlike his thoughts.

Ahead on the right, lights gleamed from the eastern-most compound, its grounds stretching from the road to the rocky northern coast. The compound, with its fancy Mediterranean-style villa, pool, guest house, and manicured garden, was owned by a famous actor who visited once a year. All the lights were on and, as he passed by, Drake heard the hum of the generator, powerful enough for lights, surveillance cameras, refrigerators, even the air conditioner.

He passed the next few compounds, which were lighted as well, for these people brought their civilization to paradise. They kept to themselves, apparently treasuring their privacy, even among their own kind, and only occasionally did they hold parties for each other. Their supplies, including fresh groceries, came on the ferry, and were delivered to their compound.

They paid islanders to garden, maintain their homes, wash their clothes, and cook, although some brought their own cooks. Mostly, they treated the islanders well, and the islanders valued the employment. Over the years, bonds of fondness and loyalty formed.

The presence of two such disparate groups on the tiny island always struck Drake as a perfect opportunity for one or the other to take undue advantage. But there it was – peaceful co-existence. Too bad that wasn't the case between Sophie and her ex-boyfriend, Cliff Webb.

He thought back to dinner with Sophie. She had only nibbled her food, the conversation lagged at the end, and indeed they almost didn't speak at all as he walked her up the mountain and along the track to the Coxon home.

The family had been sitting on the front porch and invited him to stay for a drink, but he said he had something to do and they understood. George pulled up a chair for Sophie. She stooped to pat a dog and sat, appearing at home. She waved to Drake as he turned to go, but even in the dim light of the kerosene lanterns her eyes had looked hollow, her expression forlorn.

Santiago's compound loomed to his right. Drake scuffed his boot and wiggled the light beam to alert the outside guard of his arrival. He avoided aiming the light at the shadows at the base of the compound wall, where the guard usually lurked.

"*Hola*," he said in a low voice. "Soy Ricardo." Best to identify oneself because the guy was armed.

"*Hola, amigo*," drifted from the far corner of the wall. The guard stepped onto the driveway and toward the road, his smile visible in the beam of Drake's flashlight.

He was well-muscled and large-framed, a veteran in the Spanish National Police Corps Grupo Especial de Operaciónes. The GEO's specialties included protecting VIPs such as visiting presidents and, in this case, Santiago, President of the International Criminal Court in The Hague. The same court that had indicted Libyan leader Muammar Gaddafi.

They shook hands and briefly embraced – the Spanish *abrazo* of friends – and Drake continued to the house, built of island stone, with a peaked roof. Inside, Drake followed the man who served as the judge's inside security guard and butler, short and wiry, as dour as the outside guard was friendly.

He was also GEO, and Drake found him to be a little chippy, maybe because he thought the men in his outfit were tougher than those of Marine Recon. Well, that was his choice – too bad he was wrong.

"*Señor* Drake," the man announced, as they entered the great room, airy, plainly furnished, with French doors forming the wall that overlooked the Atlantic.

The ocean remained hidden in inky darkness, but outside lights illuminated a grassy yard, palm trees, and flowering bushes forming a perimeter just inside a nine-foot stone security wall.

Judge Santiago, about fifty-five, heavy set, balding, and distinguished, rose from his chair by the window. He approached Drake and extended his hand. His grip was not as firm as the Americans', not as light as the Latinos', but a single shake that somehow transferred a feeling to Drake of understated strength and, surprisingly, compassion.

"You have had your dinner?" Santiago asked politely.

"Yes, just now, in town."

"Ah yes, you Americans take your evening meal quite early."

Drake nodded. The judge enjoyed ribbing him about the differences in national customs, and the fact that, about the time that Americans went to bed, the Spanish sat down for dinner.

"Well," the judge continued, "perhaps you will join me in a *copa de manzanilla* and a little *manchego* cheese." He grinned with mischief. "That can be your after-dinner dessert and my aperitif."

"That sounds great, sir."

His host nodded in agreement, and a minute later the inside guard arrived, carrying a small silver tray on which perched the drinks, cheese, and slices of typical Spanish bread.

"To peace," toasted Santiago.

"To peace," said Drake.

The wine was a type of sherry, so tart that some people compared it to kerosene. The cheese was hard and bitter. Amazingly, they paired well, and they had become one of Drake's favorite treats.

"So, you come to keep me up to date, am I correct?"

"Yes, sir."

"I can tell you that my cook and housekeeper have both informed me of your dramatic encounter with our afternoon squall and the rescue of little Jenny Coxon. A near thing, true?"

Drake nodded soberly. "It was a bad squall. Luckily, my passenger kept her wits about her – even took the wheel while I reefed the main."

"'Reef the main'?"

"Sorry – it's sailor talk for reducing the area of the sail."

"Ah yes, so you cannot be – I think – 'capsized.'"

Drake nodded. The judge had a way of relaxing him in what could be a formal environment. After all, he was a great man, highly regarded as one of the most knowledgeable and honest of all international judges, or any judges, for that matter. Add to that 'courageous,' because many judges had become targets of kidnap and assassination, often with fatal consequences. But here he was, interested and even humble.

Drake set his glass down, "You know all about Jenny, and I imagine you heard about Sophie, my passenger."

"Oh yes, the heroic Sophie. I feel the island has taken her into their hearts."

"Yes, sir, they have. She's now a guest of George and Maren Coxon..."

"Jenny's parents."

"Yes. And all that's good. But the reason she came here is not good. She's running from a former boyfriend, an international businessman with illegal dealings in Latin America. His name is Cliff Webb."

"Which countries, Richard?"

"Mexico and Colombia, maybe others."

"Colombia." The judge rolled the word around his tongue like a connoisseur tasting a rare wine. "You know that the man whose case I am presently hearing is from the neighbor of Colombia."

Drake nodded. "The ex-President of Venezuela. And it gets more interesting. Webb does business with Jorgue Matazos."

"Yes, very interesting. I watched the sunset from *Señor* Matazos' garden. He gave one of his rare cocktail parties, this one with delicious tapas that I believe were made in town."

"You're correct."

"As you may imagine, *Señor* Matazos does tend to talk in ways that show his importance and connections. He mentioned seeing a visiting woman, who I suspect was Sophie, this afternoon in town."

"Yes, and Sophie recognized him. He's in the same line of business as Cliff Webb and he's even visited Webb's estate in Palm Beach. She's sure Matazos recognized her, and she's afraid he'll tell Webb she's here and Webb will show up – or send someone – with revenge on their mind."

"Because Sophie knows too much?"

"Yes. I called Graham Walters and he'll check into Matazos and Webb. I don't think either is a threat to you, but I want to keep them on my radar, just in case."

The judge nodded and Drake said, "There's something else Graham told me about. A couple, a man and a woman, are headed to St. Thomas. They're enforcers for a drug cartel in Colombia. Graham doesn't know why they're coming. Could be they're on their way someplace else in the islands, or maybe they have business in St. Thomas. He's keeping his ear to the ground. We don't think they have anything to do with you, but I'll track their movements."

The inside guard appeared from the corridor leading to the kitchen and dining room. He coughed discretely.

Santiago nodded to the man and rose. He looked at Richard. "I appreciate your attention to detail. And now, I will hold you no longer. My 'late-night dinner' awaits."

Outside, on the road toward town and toward his cottage, the breeze blew cool, the sky enclosed him in darkness, and Richard felt a chill. Too much was happening, too many coincidences for his liking. He must try to meet Matazos and Webb, and the mysterious couple, and take their measure.

Meanwhile, he'd spend an hour oiling and cleaning the next weapon from the arsenal at his cottage, keeping out the tropical air, avoiding the rust. He cleaned one weapon a night, sometimes, an automatic rifle, sometimes a sniper rifle, but mostly his collection of pistols and knives.

For some reason, into his head crept the motto of Marine Corps Force Reconnaissance – *Celer, Silens, Mortalis* – Swift, Silent, Deadly. That's what he'd be if any of those low-lifes tried anything against Judge Santiago. Or Sophie. Or anyone else on the island.

CHAPTER 15

Cliff Webb counted himself lucky as hell to find the Viking 55C sport fisher on such short notice. Just by chance, the boat was between charters. The St. Thomas charter company said they'd need a day to restock the fridge and bar, but he'd told them all he needed was a full tank of fuel. He'd arranged all this while flying down in his Learjet 70, and congratulated himself that he kept the flight crew on 24-hour stand-by. Very handy for emergencies.

After he took the keys to the boat and cleared St. Thomas harbor, he'd throttled the twin MAN V12 1,550 horsepower engines to the stops and passed the south coast at forty-plus knots, the wake creaming behind, the bow wave flaring port and starboard. The boat was a cow compared to his own Cigarette 50-foot Marauder SS, which he'd cranked up to over a hundred knots.

But, for the job at hand, the sport fisher worked just fine. It even had a huge bed in the master stateroom. He smirked. Yeah, he'd finish up with Sophie, then find a willing woman for a little party.

Now he navigated through the early morning swell in the passage between St. Thomas and St. John, aiming north to St. Mark. He scanned the glass navigation screen, saw his estimated time of arrival was eight twelve.

Shit. Totally too early for Matazos to be out of bed. Well, too bad. Capturing Sophie was a life-or-death priority. Cliff called the Latino on his sat phone. The man answered on the fifth ring.

"*Sí?*"

"Jorgue? Cliff Webb."

"*Dios mío*, Cliff, do you realize the hour? It is eight minutes after seven in the morning. The damned sun has just barely arisen."

"Sorry, Jorgue," Webb said, remembering that the sun had actually arisen at five forty-three. It was daytime for God sake. But he kept his voice sympathetic. "I need to find Sophie. I hope you understand."

"Yes, yes," Matazos muttered. "When do you arrive at my pier?"

"About an hour from now, okay?"

"Yes. I will have a breakfast for us. We can talk."

They disconnected and Webb hoped he hadn't pushed Matazos too far. The man was treacherous, the sort of guy that made Webb's asshole pucker. Matazos' eyes were furtive black pools of hidden schemes, private agendas.

Webb suspected Matazos was always toying with whether or not to put a bullet through his skull. But Webb knew how to deal with such people – simply make sure they profited more with him alive than dead. Webb always had another sweet deal to dangle in front of Matazos. Webb smiled – greed was a wonderful motivator.

But when Webb's train of thought shifted to the purpose of his trip to these dipshit islands, his brow furrowed in anger. The thought of Sophie and the trouble she was putting him through pissed him off. What a waste. Why couldn't women be simple? His two failed marriages should have cured him of long-term relationships with women, but no, he still fell for Sophie.

She was slender and pretty, and reminded him of the girls he'd ached for as a boy. At first it was all bliss, with none of that usual girlie bullshit about constantly buying new clothes, and melt-downs over chipped nail polish.

The fact was, she barely filled a shelf in her spacious walk-in closet in the master suite in his Palm Beach estate, and didn't even paint her nails. A couple of dresses, jeans, and sports outfits, that included a karate gee. And only six pairs of shoes. Also, again unlike his two ex-wives, she was a tigress in bed, and she was good company after sex.

She did have a brain, that was for sure. Once upon a time he even considered bringing her into the business. As a probe – sort of a test of her business sense – he'd asked her a couple of 'theoretical' business questions. He was careful not to give away the breadth and depth of his international dealings, or anything about the use of force.

She'd gotten the point of both questions, came back with clarification questions, and gave him logical and practical opinions. But when he hinted at the darker side of his business, he saw those little muscles around her eyes crinkle in surprise and, yeah, disapproval. So, he backed off. Too bad.

He didn't see the problem with breaking a few laws – or a few of his competitors. Survival of the fittest – isn't that what Darwin said? Anyway, how else can you get ahead? But she obviously disapproved of any dealings outside the law. Holy Mother of Christ! Every business in the world broke the law or they'd go bust.

He admitted that all businesses weren't as far off the reservation as his dealings in Latin America and Europe, but still, all his close competitors were as free-wheeling as he was. Take the Russians, or the Latinos. Hell, Jorgue Matazos, to name someone close to home. That guy must have broken every law in the book during his twenty years in the business.

Webb left St. Thomas in his wake and curved around the west end of Jost Van Dyke. The silhouette of St. Mark stood before him. He set his course to the west end of the island so he could circle around to Matazos' pier on the North Side.

His thoughts drifted back to Sophie. A good girl and great in bed. But she'd heard way too much. Impossible not to have happened, since they spent much time together. Anyway, he couldn't very well keep her locked up every time an associate visited, or shoo her away when the phone rang. No, she was an asset – eye candy, and a demonstration of his power, along with his estate, his cars, his Cigarette boat, and Learjet.

Over the last few months, she'd put all those conversations and names together and was clearly appalled with what she discovered. He'd seen it in her eyes – the condemnation, the fear. He decided that she had enough on him to put his ass behind bars. Or worse, depending on which country charged him. Names, faces, dates and places – she was a walking time bomb. Yep. Her flight from the estate to St. Mark was the final straw, like writing big letters in the sand – she knew, and she knew he knew.

Webb spotted Matazos standing on his pier and his mind returned to the present. Webb eased the boat alongside and they tied up her, bow and stern. On the pier, Matazos gave him a strong *abrazo*, and guided him up the cliff-side stairs. Security looked good, with an eight-foot security wall and cameras aimed into the lawn and garden. He and Matazos skirted a swimming pool and pool house, and settled at a table on the patio.

A sliding glass door opened and a woman carried a tray to the table. She poured coffee and disappeared, then returned, pushing a cart with covered dishes containing eggs, toast, and bacon. Matazos waved her away. The sliding glass door closed and she disappeared inside the house. A seagull cried overhead. Atlantic swells pounded the rocks below.

The men sipped their coffee. Webb took his black and bitter, Matazos added a little sugar.

Matazos gestured to the food and they loaded their plates. Webb was starved. His last meal had been a ham sandwich on his Learjet. There had been no time to stock the plane. He suspected the sandwich had been the pilot's, but what the hell, he could wait. Now, Webb chewed his food with relish. The eggs were just right, not overcooked, and the bacon was crispy. Amazing for this far out in the boonies.

"Good food," Webb said, spooning more eggs onto his plate. "You have an excellent cook."

Matazos made a dismissive gesture. "She's one of the island people. Pretty much what you'd expect. Trainable but very limited ambition." He spread jam on his toast and continued, "You move very fast, *señor*. I just called you yesterday."

"Time is critical." Webb chewed and swallowed. "Sophie ran out on me, and no one does that. I was pissed. Still am."

"I understand. I suspect you are not pleased that she has, perhaps, observed a little too much of your business. She ran, which means she is angry, that is for sure. And when a woman is angry, she is a danger. No?"

Webb sipped his steaming coffee and gazed at the Atlantic, sparkling and blue in the morning sun, and grunted. "Sounds as if you've been there yourself."

Matazos shrugged. "It is a part of life, Cliff. The girls, they come and they go. I provide a small apartment and stipend to my girls who have moved on. The girls know I am watching, and they satisfy themselves that their life is good. I prefer this to having a reputation of my ex-girlfriends disappearing."

"It's too late for that," Webb said, pouring more coffee. "See, she's got morals."

"Ah," said Matazos. "This is not the case with my girls. Morals are not a problem."

"I'll have to kill her."

"It is sad."

"Yeah, we had some good times."

Matazos raised his hands. "Well, it is your business and you must handle it the way you think best." He chewed a bite of toast and let the silence lengthen. At last, he said, "By the way, there's another person on St. Mark you need to know about. His name is Richard Drake and he's a roaming security man for a judge who has a compound here on the North Side. My cook told me that it was Drake who brought Sophie to the island in his sailboat."

Webb looked into his host's eyes, which appeared calculating, and as usual, dangerous. Why was Jorgue telling him this? Certainly, this Drake was not a barrier to him snatching Sophie.

"Richard Drake," said Matazos, "is also a charter boat captain."

"I saw a sailboat in the harbor," Webb said.

"It's his, and chartering is his cover, but everyone knows his real job is to protect Judge Santiago."

"Does he carry?"

"All the time. Probably even when he swims and showers. The man has survived combat."

"And that's how Sophie got here – rode over from St. Thomas on his sailboat?

Matazos nodded. "They spend a lot of time together."

Cliff reddened. "Shit. I'll take out both of them. That'll send a message."

"I hear you. By the way, where you're moored right now is a good place for a quick get-away, or a chase, if you want to go after Drake when he's in his boat. But keep a watch on the weather, because there's no protection from the north."

They'd both finished eating, and pushed away from the table. Webb wiped his mouth with the linen napkin. He felt refreshed. The coffee was kicking in, and he was ready for battle.

"Thanks, Jorge, you've done very well. I owe you big time."

They were silent for a while, Webb weighing the situation, gazing at the sea and sky, both peaceful right now. Recalling his puzzlement when Jorgue was telling him all about Drake, Webb felt one of those little itches he got in the back of his mind, something small but wiggling back there, usually turning out to be important. He couldn't put his finger on what it was. Maybe something that Matazos was holding back from him, maybe a motivation for inviting him that didn't involve Sophie at all. Yeah, that was it. Jorgue had an agenda.

Matazos' sat phone buzzed, and he answered, moving away to stand at the edge of the patio. When he turned back and shrugged apologetically, Webb motioned that he'd show himself out. He made his way through the sliding glass doors and through the house, passed an inside security guard and an outside guard at the gate. They nodded gravely as he passed.

He crossed the road and entered a gap in the foliage that he recognized as a deer track. What the hell – check out this little island. The morning was heating up, birds called and cicadas whined.

He strode along the path, which headed south. He figured it was impossible to get lost. Damn, the island only measured four and a half miles long. Anyway, he wanted to get the lay of the land. Then he'd check to see if there was a bar in the tiny town. Slip the bartender a hundred-dollar bill and learn what he needed to know to set an ambush.

He'd bundle Sophie off to sea, torture her a little just for fun and to learn who she'd talked to. Then weigh her down with an anchor and toss her overboard. Sharks, drawn by the blood, might eat her before she drowned.

Ahead, the path opened onto a grassy knoll. The wind had freshened, and far below white caps speckled the blue sea. He peered left to the mouth of the harbor and saw a sailboat emerge, pitching in the seas, her bow pointed southwest. Damn. That was the security guy's boat.

Webb shaded his eyes and looked hard. There was a guy on deck, handling lines and sails up forward. He looked about six feet tall, stocky, and moving with the efficient grace of a sailor. Once, he turned and seemed to gaze into Webb's eyes. Too far away to gauge his expression, but the movement spoke of an alertness. Good. A worthy opponent.

Back aft, a woman stood, feet wide, her hands on the wheel. Athletic figure and short blond hair, streaming in the wind.

Sophie!

CHAPTER 16

That day at dawn, Drake left his cottage and strode through the deserted village. He entered the bush, moving east, passing into a part of the island he hadn't visited for three days. Maybe he'd spot Sophie's ex-boyfriend, or trespassers planning to rob one of the compounds, or, probably, no one.

He climbed along a winding deer track, rising into the mountains at a measured pace. He took care not to crack twigs in his path, more out of habit than a need for silence or of avoiding trackers. He often paused and listened – again, out of habit.

Sunlight began to penetrate the bush, turning shadows into distinct shapes. A deer bolted at his approach, a lizard ignored him. He passed a large termite nest, brown and lumpy.

His thoughts turned to Sophie. He was attracted to her on several levels, including her calm under deadly pressure, as well as her fitting in to the island community in general, and with the Coxons in particular. Plus, she was pretty and in trouble. He was a sucker for helping a damsel in distress. Sexist? Yes, of course, but he was wired that way. Protect God, country, and women and children.

He paused on a grassy outcropping along the south coast and peered back at the harbor. CAPRICE rocked in the swell, still in partial shadow from the adjacent hills. No one stirred at George's boatyard. A sailboat cut through the gentle swells, her hull creaming the indigo ocean, aiming west of St. Mark.

Drake thought of the young couple who'd booked an afternoon charter. They'd have a good time of it, with a fresh breeze, calm sea, and fine visibility. He'd take them north from St. Thomas, drop anchor in a deserted bay off Jost Van Dyke, and enjoy a picnic lunch with them. They'd all trade life stories and share island gossip.

Maybe he'd learn something of value. That didn't happen often, but tourists noticed things. Like the woman who remarked about a knot of surly young men gathered in an alley very early one morning. She told Drake, and he passed the news on to Walters, who checked it out. Turned out they were local gang members getting set to attack their sleeping rivals.

A breeze ruffled his hair and he felt the first heat of the sun. Time to return or he'd be late getting to St. Thomas for his charter party. He worked his way a little deeper into the mountains and looped back toward town. On the way, he stopped at George's house. He invited Sophie to sail with him and she accepted with a smile.

At his cottage, he changed into shorts and t-shirt. He stopped by the store and picked up mail from a sleepy John Parker, grabbed the picnic lunch from Asunción, and loaded everything into his dinghy, tied at one end of the pier.

Sophie arrived, a little out of breath, wearing white shorts, a light blue blouse, and running shoes. She grinned and waved a piece of paper.

"Maren gave me a list of stuff to pick up. Am I late?"

"No, you're right on time," Drake said, stepping into the dinghy and holding it steady for her to board.

She sat on the small stern bench and he rowed, facing her. She gazed past him at the sea. Her brow creased.

"Don't worry," he said. "There'll be no squalls today. Just nice Caribbean weather."

She smiled. "You read my mind."

"That'll be the day – a man reading a woman's mind?"

She gave him a playful swat.

He pulled easily at the oars, looking over his shoulder from time to time to check that he was on course to CAPRICE. They arrived and boarded the sailboat, her decks damp with morning dew. Sophie had brought a carry bag, and he stowed that and his gear below. He untied from the mooring buoy and motored out of the harbor, becalmed by the hills on three sides. After ten minutes, the boat began to roll and pitch in the swells of the open sea.

He stood and checked for nearby boat traffic. The sea lay empty.

"Take the wheel, would you?" he asked. "Just point her east, into the wind while I raise the sails."

Sophie grinned and stood. "It'll be nice to steer CAPRICE in a gentle breeze."

Drake moved forward and raised the main and the jib, hauling both sails tight. They flapped impatiently in the wind. As he made his way back to the cockpit, he saw Sophie turn the wheel, pointing the bow a point away from the wind. She let the sails fill, then held her course, to the west of Jost Van Dyke. Drake sat and relaxed.

"Pretty good," he said.

She shrugged. "I just filled the mainsail with wind, the way I do on a windsurfer. But you don't have that front sail on a windsurfer."

"The jib," Drake said. "It lets you sail closer into the wind."

"And you adjust to little changes in the wind by hauling in or changing course until the flapping stops?"

"Yep. I better not tell you too much more, or folks will hire you instead of me."

She smirked, then focused on the boat. She asked questions, and paid attention to Drake's responses. She learned about the red yarn tell-tails sewn into the sails that streamed in good wind and flapped in bad, and she trimmed the boat to keep them flat against the sails. For once, she appeared relaxed and at peace.

But the urgency in her voice, when she next spoke, took Drake by surprise.

"I need a passport, Richard. Can I get one in St. Thomas?"

CHAPTER 17

Webb's pulse quickened at the prospect of resolving the Sophie problem. He rushed from the promontory, back through Matazos' house, and boarded the gleaming Viking 55C sport fisher. The diesels rumbled to life. He cast off the lines and accelerated, away from the pier.

The breeze was fresh, the swells about three feet. He pushed the speed to just under twenty knots. Sure, the boat pounded, but what the hell, it was just a rental.

Ten minutes later, he rounded the west end of St. Mark and the Caribbean spread before him, with Jost Van Dyke to the south and St. Thomas beyond. Webb figured Drake was headed for St. Thomas, but he could be bound for one of the British Virgins. Not Jost Van Dyke because it barely had a population, much less an airport. And that's what he feared the most – that Sophie was aiming toward an airport. If she made it, he'd be back to square one. Which was unacceptable. *She must be contained right here.*

Webb pressed the throttle further forward. The speed ramped up nicely, but the pounding increased as well. He maintained his pace for another minute, but there was a loud clatter below. Stuff loose, crashing about. Reluctantly, he backed off the throttle. Bided his time.

Speeding south, he left St. Mark behind and gazed east. Yes, there was Drake's sailboat up ahead, a single mast with main and jib. That told him a lot about the guy. He loved the man-against-nature challenge and the hands-on approach of a sailboat. He wanted to be a part of the process. It wasn't about getting somewhere – it was all about the journey.

To hell with the journey. Except if it was fast. And to hell with nature. Wait for a calm sea and crank up his Cigarette boat to the max. Wind in his face, that was all the nature he needed.

He felt pretty much the same about his plane – get above the clouds and turbulence, then throttle to the max. Get to where you're going. If he wanted sport, he'd watch a damned football game. Relive some of his high school glory days.

Webb vectored toward the sailboat at twenty knots, jouncing over the swells. Soon, he was close enough to see two figures on deck, one a guy, one a girl. He confirmed the girl was Sophie. Couldn't mistake that lithe figure, legs up to her ass, and blond hair. He maneuvered to a parallel course, sixty feet abeam the sailboat, and cut his speed to four knots.

Sophie was looking forward, giving Webb the cold shoulder. What a bitch.

This was his first close look at Drake. He wore khaki shorts, no shoes, no shirt, and a floppy hat. Strong arms and solid features. Stared ahead and occasionally up at the mainsail. A physical sort of guy. Webb had seen plenty of those. He inched to within twenty-five feet of the sailboat, near enough to talk.

He was pissed that Drake ignored him. Sophie, he could understand, but why Drake? It was as if having a big sport fisher come alongside and shadow him was normal. Holy shit! No one within miles, and Webb right next to him. The bastard should say something or give him the finger, or at least look. What the hell?

CHAPTER 18

Drake spotted the sport fisher as it rounded the west end of St. Mark, pointing south. Strangely, the vessel aimed directly at CAPRICE and approached at speed, throwing a high bow wave.

"I think we've got company," he said.

Sophie, her hands on the wheel, had been focused on her course and the trim of the sails. She looked over her shoulder and the color drained from her face.

"It's him," she said in a quivering voice.

Drake stood and moved to her.

"Why don't I take the wheel?" he said quietly.

She made her way forward in the cockpit and sat at her usual corner. With wide eyes she stared at the approaching boat. She drew her legs up and wrapped her arms around her knees. As he approached, she stared over CAPRICE's bow, toward St. Thomas.

The big sport fisher idled twenty-five feet off CAPRICE's port beam. Drake saw only one person aboard, a beefy man seated in the flying bridge, only his chest and head visible. The man leaned on the rail, his left hand on the wheel, eyes hooded. He had a belly, but his hairy arms looked strong.

"You Richard Drake?" he shouted above the grumble of the diesels.

"Who are *you*?" Drake asked. "And keep clear. You're blocking my wind."

"My name is Cliff Webb. Screw your wind. And your boat. You have something of mine."

Drake looked up at him, turned the wheel slightly to straighten out a tell-tail. Webb's face reddened.

"Sophie is taken," Webb declared. "We're together. Heave to and let her board my boat."

"You're married?"

"Look, you little punk! She's my girl. I came down to this dipshit place to bring her home. Come alongside."

Sophie rose, one hand steadied on the boom, her eyes flashing.

"Go away, Clifford! I never want to see you again. Leave me alone."

The two boats continued through the glistening, late-morning swells, their bows rising and falling in rhythm. Drake eyed Sophie, tall and brave, her free hand behind her, shaking.

"It's a personal matter," Webb said to Drake, ignoring Sophie. "Just as good for you to butt out."

"Maybe the lady wants to stay here," Drake drawled.

"I'm warning you."

"Get clear," Drake commanded, his voice suddenly strong.

Webb's face reddened again and he waved his fist.

"Screw you! And screw you, Sophie Cooper!"

Webb inched his boat closer. Waves washed between the two vessels as the distance diminished to ten, five, and then four feet. Drake could almost touch the hull of the sport fisher.

Knowing that to shear off was useless against the superior speed and maneuverability of the sport fisher, Drake maintained his course. The sport fisher masked only a fraction of his wind, enabling CAPRICE to maintain speed.

The waves between the hulls splashed in confusion. The sport fisher's twin diesels rumbled like chained animals. Sophie sat down, hands in her lap, her eyes on the fore deck. Webb dropped onto his seat, checked the distance between boats every few seconds, maintained the tiny four-foot separation.

"Had enough?" he yelled. "I can keep this up all day!"

"Well," Drake said with a flat voice, "it's a free world."

Webb scowled. "I'll be back, you son of a bitch." He veered off, engines screaming at max revolutions, his boat throwing a great bow wave and steep wake.

CHAPTER 19

Sophie watched the motor boat dwindle to a speck on the horizon. Oddly, the speck remained there, on the edge, not totally disappearing. She felt weak with fear and sat still, her mind in turmoil. It struck her that this indigo Caribbean and its lush islands, which were supposed to be a refuge, had become a dangerous place for her.

"I'm scared to death, Richard. I need to get far away from that man and I need a passport as quickly as humanly possible. I have cash. I can pay for a fake passport, but I need it right now."

Drake was silent for a minute. Looked at her once, then at the sails. Adjusted the wheel a fraction.

"I don't blame you," he said at last, his voice gentle. "We could probably get you a fake passport, but that's risky. The last thing you want is to be stopped at a border and sent back to St. Thomas. Or worse, get thrown in jail. I think you can get a valid version quickly, say a couple of days, which is about the same time it'll take to get a fake."

She sat back, surprised. He didn't tell her to stay. In fact, he didn't *tell* her anything. He gave her exactly what she asked for, which in itself was unsettling, because she was in uncharted waters.

He continued, "You'll have to visit the post office on Main Street in Charlotte Amalie to get the forms – no, wait a minute. You may be able to do pretty much the whole thing on the Internet."

"But no one has service on St. Mark."

"Right, but I know someone on St. Thomas we can trust."
She shifted her weight, feeling dizzy. "Who?"
"I think you should visit Anika Stiles."
"Didn't you mention her at dinner last night? The woman who knows about Jumbees?"
"Yeah, that's her. She may not know about passports, but she'll have access to the Internet from where she works, and she's pretty sharp about solving puzzles like this."
"You can Google how to get a passport?"
"That's what I'm thinking. You go to the official government site first to be sure you know what forms and stuff you need, then you search for companies that offer expediting services."
"Should I get a new passport?"
He thought for a moment. "You already have a passport, right?"
"Yes, but it's in Cliff's safe."
"Okay, then say you lost your passport in the squall. That may make the process easier because all you really need to prove is that you are who you say you are. You'll need your driver's license and you may need to get passport photos taken. You can do that in town."
He looked at the sky, then back at her. "Just maybe, you can scan your license and the photos, and send them electronically. If you really get lucky, all you'll need is your scanned driver's license, because the government already has your photo. I think claiming you lost your passport is the best way."
Sophie forced a smile, then turned her head to the sea. She didn't notice the deep blue rollers as they sailed south. Instead, her thoughts turned inward. She reflected on all she had done in the past two years. Her life had been good for a time. She was with a loving, exciting and successful man.
She had begun to think of a career for herself, maybe as an author. She had had several short stories published. But suddenly, life with Cliff turned scary. She pondered a past that was a lie, and her present, full of peril.
They tied up at Richard's marina on St. Thomas well before his noon charter. Sophie found a taxi in front of the marina restaurant. She retraced her route from the previous day. Previous day? It felt as if a year had passed since she'd arrived among the islands. She

sat back and let the scenery whiz by, still uncomfortable driving on the wrong side of the road.

Here she was, returning to the very place she'd left, feeling more vulnerable than ever, with Cliff breathing down her neck, and no inkling of a plan.

Where could she run? Perhaps Spain. She could get by with her rudimentary Spanish. Ride a train south, lose herself in Seville or any of a hundred hilltop villages.

Or she could try France, where she had friends. No, that was a bad idea. She didn't want to involve them, both for her safety and theirs. The taxi bumped over a pothole and she gripped the arm rest.

Well, what about Asia? Or India? No way – she'd be at a complete loss in those places. Better to stay close to home, culturally at least. Maybe fly to England, find a mid-sized town where she wouldn't stand out. Develop a long-term plan. Maybe pose as a travel writer, or get a job. She'd have to change her identity. God, what a mess.

Sophie rubbed her forehead, feeling lost. Cliff had been enraged, and in such a state she knew he was capable of deadly violence. That look he'd given her. He wanted to hurt her, kill her. She had never been this frightened or hopeless.

They descended from the higher ground in the center of the island and entered a teeming Charlotte Amalie, with its narrow, curving streets, old wooden and masonry buildings, and throngs of locals and tourists. The taxi dropped her at a park near the waterfront at the east end of Main Street. The driver pointed to an elegant, old two-story stone building, painted off-white, with blue storm shutters and an arched arcade in front.

"That be the store you want, miss – The Danish Touch. That be a nice store."

Sophie thanked him and paid the fare. She needed a few minutes to prepare what to say to Anika. She entered the park, shady with trees, tropical plants, an old-time band stand, and nice benches. It looked like a quiet place, just right for thinking.

People strolled along the walkways. Toward the harbor, a bustling market was crowded with tourists. She was surrounded by sights and sounds of a normal world.

Where she was an anomaly. A woman in danger.

She unclenched her teeth and forced herself to consider her next steps. Admittedly, she had room for hope. After all, she was free of Clifford for the moment at least, she had plenty of money, and she had ideas for a permanent escape.

St. Mark hadn't worked out, but she was still free. Asking Anika for help was her next step. She decided she should be open, and share her reasons for seeking a new passport. She drew a breath and strode toward The Danish Touch.

But Anika was not there. It was lunch hour.

A sales lady told her the name of the café where Anika usually had lunch, and gave her directions. Sophie returned to the bright sun and rising temperature and strode down Main Street. Past the post office, past the open doors and wafting air conditioning of dozens of modern shops filled with diamonds, watches, and fashionable clothing.

Tourists were everywhere, making a perfect shield behind which Cliff could track her. She knew it was nearly impossible for him to have found her so quickly, but as she walked, she kept a wary eye on everyone in the swirling, babbling crowd.

Sophie found the 'side street' where the sales lady said the café was located, but it was no more than a narrow, shaded alley. Completely empty of people. Perfect place for an ambush. Maybe Cliff had men along with him. They could have kept out of sight during that encounter at sea. God. The palms of her hands started to sweat.

Suddenly, the large potted plants along the length of the alley looked more like hiding places for Cliff's thugs than decorations for shop entrances. One of those entrances must be for the café, though the signs were too shadowed to read. A lady came out of one of the entrances and walked away, toward the waterfront. The alley was again empty. Water dripped next to her. The shadows actually seemed to become murkier.

Get a grip!

She was acting like a fluffy little girl. For gosh sakes, she had a black belt in karate. But she remembered what her instructor told her when she asked how she could possibly defend herself against an attack by a six-foot, three hundred-pound assailant. He had shaken his head and told her, "some guys you just have to shoot."

That was enough. The answer was clear – find a nice café for herself, way out in the open with plenty of people all around. Have lunch, then return and find Anika.

She turned away from the alley. Walked back down Main Street, curved past the post office and Anika's store, onto the waterfront. Found a sandwich shop and ordered lunch. Tables were on a second-floor balcony and there was already a lunch crowd. No Cliff. No furtive looks. No one following her.

Still, she felt exposed and the minutes dragged by.

CHAPTER 20

Webb perched precariously atop the 'tower,' a spindly aluminum framework mounted eight feet above the flying bridge of his Viking sport fisher. The height magnified the boat's motion, which increased when he arrived at the northern end of Pillsbury Sound, the channel between St. Thomas and St John. He suspected the channel amplified the wave pattern, because the rollers were steeper and nastier than when he was up near St. Mark.

He could have sat on the flying bridge, which was a hell of a lot more stable, but up in the tower he could see farther. Which meant he could hang out miles away from that meddler Drake and track him just fine while remaining nearly invisible – just a dot poking up from the horizon.

Drake had bee-lined from St. Mark toward the north-east coast of St. Thomas and was set to make landfall. Webb's challenge was to identify where the bastard was headed. He clambered down the narrow steps of the tower, then to the main deck and into the cabin.

With the engine in neutral, and no one close by, he was safe from collision. But, as always when the propeller stopped, the hull turned parallel to the swells and the vessel rolled like a son of a bitch. He braced himself with feet apart, leaned on the counter, and examined his chart. Yep, Drake was heading into Red Bay Marina.

Webb scrambled back up the tower in his bare feet – easier to grip the deck and the ladder rungs than with deck shoes. He followed the white sails of Drake's boat until it was inside the breakwaters of the marina. Then he throttled up to fifteen knots, descended to the flying bridge, and conned the sport fisher to the east and south until he found another marina, near by but out of sight of Drake and Sophie.

He tied up there, made arrangements to have the fuel topped off, and found a taxi. He ordered the driver to take him to the Red Bay Marina and stop at the entrance. The man, puzzled, did as ordered. They didn't have to wait long before another cab passed them on the way out. Sure enough, Sophie sat in the back seat. Webb grinned and ordered his driver to follow at a distance.

Webb paid off the driver at a park in Charlotte Amalie just in time to see Sophie disappear into a big store called The Danish Touch. Sounded like a Scandinavian whore house. But what the hell. He sat on a bench in the park, behind bushes but with a clear view of the front door of the store. Without the wind in his face he sweated in the tropical heat. He was hungry, too. Matazos' breakfast was history, and the fridge on the boat was empty.

Damn. He sat, stomach growling and sweat trickling down his back. But he had to be there. He wished to hell he could solve the problem once and for all. Catch her in a deserted place and break her neck. Steal her money, make it look like a robbery. His plane was a short taxi ride away and he'd be home for dinner.

He knew that was a pipe dream. Not worth considering with all these gawking tourists packing the streets. Probably the alleys as well. Why weren't they at the beaches? Travel a thousand miles to shop? Would've been cheaper to buy those watches and necklaces at home in Jersey or whatever suburb they called home.

So, what was his plan?

Easy - to see what that traitor was up to. Her ducking into a store was not an issue – couldn't do any harm looking at stuff. But he wanted to see if she visited a lawyer or a travel agent or if she met someone, some friend from the States. That'd tell him what her strategy was and he'd act accordingly.

Not five minutes after entering the store, she walked out, looking puzzled. She turned toward Main Street as if she knew where she was going. Webb followed his prey up and then back down the street, keeping a block away. She didn't duck into any of the stores, didn't even window shop. What the hell? She passed right by The Danish Touch, on to the waterfront, and into a fast food place. She reappeared on its second-floor balcony, carrying a sandwich and drink.

He stayed in the shadows. Made a quick trip to a street vendor and wolfed down a shitty hot dog. Saw a couple of young women walk into The Danish Touch, followed ten minutes later by Sophie. He sat on the same park bench and watched the door. Wondered what in hell the damned bitch was doing, and wished he had a cold beer.

CHAPTER 21

Drake felt hollow inside after Sophie's taxi departed. He liked this woman. She was spunky and had a big heart. No wonder everyone on the island adored her.

But she was in trouble. Sure, she stood up to Webb, straight and tall. That took courage. But courage wasn't enough and a new passport was not the solution. Electronic records could track her down, no matter how far she ran. She needed people to help her, pure and simple, and those she had on St. Mark. Everyone stood behind her. She should stay. After a while, Webb would have no choice but to pack up and leave.

Ironically, Sophie posed no threat to the man. She obviously just wanted to be out of the relationship and lead a peaceful life. She was not the type to seek revenge. It wasn't in her genes. Funny how Webb didn't see that. Well, maybe he did, but his pride had taken over.

At any rate, she was on her way to visit Anika and order a passport. Drake resolved to do his best to keep her safe while she remained on St. Mark. Then say good-bye. Sometimes life sucked.

With twenty minutes on his hands before his charter party was due, he called Graham.

"Well," Walters said, "I phoned my buddy up at Palm Beach and got an earful. He knew about Sophie, because she was Webb's girlfriend, and he ran a background check on her, but she came out clean."

"So, her story checks out," Drake said.

"Sure does, especially the part about Webb being into international crime. Take care, Richard – he's a nasty piece of work. The guy's got three murders tied to his name."

"Sophie didn't mention that. She just said he's violent."

"No shit. Unfortunately, there's not enough evidence to arrest him for the murders, or any of his crimes for that matter. Oh, and you're going to love this – Webb's accomplice in drug smuggling from Colombia is a guy named Jorgue Matazos. Isn't he the asshole who ratted on Sophie?"

"Yeah," said Drake, suddenly feeling very tired. "He lives in one of those compounds on the North Side. Keeps to himself."

"Maybe on St. Mark, but not in Colombia. He's even more violent than Webb. Anyway, that's the scoop. Sophie's good, Matazos and Webb are bad guys."

"Clears it up, I guess."

"Watch your six, good buddy."

CHAPTER 22

When Sophie returned to The Danish Touch, the same sales lady said Anika had come back from lunch. She led the way past displays of sleek wood and burnished metal furniture to a brightly decorated office. A very attractive woman in her mid-twenties sat at a desk littered with catalogues and a flat-screen computer monitor.

Sophie extended her hand. "Hi, I'm Sophie Cooper. I'm a friend of Richard Drake's. He said I could maybe ask you for a favor."

"I'm Anika Stiles, but I guess you knew that already." Anika gestured to a visitor's chair in front of the desk. "How is Richard these days?"

Sophie sat, her heart pounding. "He's okay. He's taking out a charter party today. I'll see him again this evening."

Sophie wished Richard were there, for a little moral support and to save Anika the trouble of figuring out this wasn't a scam. Sophie gave Anika a rueful smile.

"I met him yesterday morning."

Anika blinked.

"He took me to St. Mark," Sophie continued. "On his sailboat, CAPRICE. We raced a squall, but it caught us a few miles from St. Mark. I've lived on the ocean my whole life, and survived plenty of rough weather, but this was the wildest freaking squall I've ever seen. Richard pulled us through and acted as if it was all in a day's work."

"Sounds scary," Anika said, sounding formal, and unconvinced Sophie was who she said she was.

Sophie lowered her voice. No need in everyone passing the open door to the office hearing.

"It was scary, but in a way I didn't care. It was the quickest way to St. Mark. I needed to get there because I thought I could drop off the grid. They don't have the Internet, or phones, or even electricity, except for the people on the North Side."

Sophie knew she was too emotional. Her words tumbled every which way out of her mouth, but she pushed on.

"My ex-boyfriend is after me," she said. "He's a violent man. I didn't know this until recently, but he does lots of illegal things, including murder. I was blown away when I realized all this. Early yesterday morning, I packed a suitcase and aimed for as far away as I could get without a passport."

"That doesn't sound good," Anika said, "the ex-boyfriend part. I once fell in love with a man here on the island, but he turned out to be the worst of the worst. By the way, where are you staying? The last time I was there, St. Mark didn't have a hotel or guest house."

"I'm staying with the Coxons. Maren invited me."

Anika's eyes widened. "You know Maren? How?"

"Well, after the squall, I spotted a little girl hanging onto a capsized sailboat. Richard and I pulled her out of the water and brought her in. She was Jenny…"

Anika's hand went to her mouth.

Sophie gestured, "She's fine. A bruised arm in a sling, but she's back running around with her little gang of friends."

"Well, I'm glad you saved her. And you're in safe hands with the Coxons." She moved the catalogues to one side of her desk. "Now, how can I help you, Sophie?"

CHAPTER 23

Drake said good-bye to the young honeymoon couple. They'd seemed delighted with their Caribbean sailboat excursion and, he suspected, pleased with their hour alone on CAPRICE, anchored in a deserted bay, with him taking a long walk ashore.

Sophie waited for him at the tiki bar, nursing a beer.

"You don't look happy," he said, nodding to the bartender for a beer.

She made a face and smiled, but her eyes looked lost in worry.

"I should be happy," she said. "Anika was kind. She and I checked out passport companies on the Internet and chose one that guaranteed one-day delivery. We ordered a replacement passport..."

"But?"

"I still felt tight and scared inside. I thought getting a passport and flying somewhere far away was the solution to Cliff, but I realize now he'll follow wherever I go, no matter how remote. He'll keep searching and one day he'll show up and..."

Drake put a comforting hand on her shoulder. Sophie drew a breath that turned into a sob. She covered her face. "The thing is, I'm scared." She wiped her eyes with her hands. "I was scared during the squall, but this is different. I can't run away and I can't fight. You saw him – he's as strong as an ox and when he wants something, he always gets it. He's willful, and smart. Not book smart, but cunning, devious, and completely immoral."

She turned to him. "Richard, I'm sure he wants to kill me."

He stood up and leaned close. Gave her a little hug.

"Not today."

He sat again on his bar stool and looked her straight in the eye, underlining his words, his commitment.

She blinked away tears, and said quietly, "You have no idea how comforting it is to hear you say that."

"Well, it's true."

"I think Maren told me you were a Marine?"

He nodded. "Force Recon. And once a Marine, always a Marine. It's a very close group." He looked into her eyes and decided she needed to know more. "Especially if you get into combat. You fight for each other, not the country, not God, not for world peace. It's for your buddies standing next to you."

"God, I've never seen you this serious. Your eyes…"

"You turn into a different person at war. I survived, but I could have taken a bullet just as easily as the next guy. War also makes you humble."

"In a way, you're still at war because you're guarding Judge Santiago, right?"

"Yes."

They were silent for a long time. The sun was low on the horizon. Drake paid their bill and they strolled toward CAPRICE.

She held his hand. When they reached the boat, she faced him. "I came here to say good-bye to you and ask you to say good-bye to the Coxons and to give Maren the things I bought for her. Anika offered to let me stay with her and her husband while I wait for my passport."

"They're good people," Drake managed to say, feeling a pang in his chest, yearning to tell her to stay and fight, but knowing she had to make her own decision.

"Yes, I could tell," she said. "She reminded me of a younger version of Maren."

"And her husband is ex-military. Been in combat. He's a good man."

"Yes, he would have protected me…"

"Would have?"

"I've made my decision," she said, her voice determined. "I'm returning to St. Mark."

CHAPTER 24

On the sail back to St. Mark, Drake kept his eyes peeled for Webb's boat and spotted what appeared to be the top of its tuna tower. It always remained just a bump on the horizon, sometimes visible, but even then, just a suggestion, a hint of what it might be.

Otherwise, the sea was clear except for two sailboats he had just passed, headed south, perhaps to St. Thomas or St. John. They dipped toward the horizon as he continued north. He'd make his moor in the harbor in daylight, but just barely.

He was glad Sophie chose to face Webb. She had appeared comforted when he assured her that he, along with everyone on St. Mark, wanted her to stay. Now she sat at her usual corner in the cockpit, gazing at the ocean, her expression thoughtful. He left her to herself.

Drake navigated around the west end of Jost Van Dyke and angled north and east toward St. Mark. The sailboats disappeared behind the headland of Jost Van Dyke, soon replaced by a motor boat that sped into view from the same headland. She approached at speed and appeared to be Webb's sport fisher.

Had the man stalked them, waiting until the sailboats were out of sight? Drake's gut tightened, concerned that the next confrontation might turn violent. He considered retrieving his pistol from the safe down below, but the sport fisher was eating up the distance too quickly.

Drake glanced at Sophie and she nodded, tense, obviously having spotted the sport fisher and identified it as Webb's. She stared aft, her eyes on the oncoming craft, appearing to steel herself for another encounter.

The boat approached from the starboard beam, upwind, at an angle nearly perpendicular to CAPRICE. She aimed just aft of CAPRICE's mast, her bow wave a crashing waterfall, engines pounding.

Drake held the helm steady until the sport fisher was fifty yards away, then turned the wheel hard over, heeling the boat into the wind, attempting to turn parallel to the Webb's boat so only the sides would collide.

But CAPRICE turned too slowly. Instead of a glancing blow, the bow of the sport fisher sliced into the CAPRICE's hull, splintering fiberglass in an ugly Vee-shaped gash. Drake knew part of that gash continued down the hull and below the water line. There would be flooding, perhaps sufficient to sink his sailboat.

The sails flapped uselessly with their heading into the wind, and CAPRICE's momentum was dragged to a standstill by the sport fisher wedged into her hull. Ironically, the sport fisher filled the gash it created, minimizing flooding.

But only for a few seconds.

Webb threw the big sport fisher into reverse. The engines roared, propellers churned. He backed off, turned, and traced a wide circle around CAPRICE, lining up for another strike.

Drake spun the wheel again, returned to his original course, the sail filled and the boat heeled, her starboard hull rolling high, exposing the gash.

"Look below," he shouted. "See how much water's leaking in."

Sophie scrambled down, lost from sight as Drake switched on the auxiliary engine and bilge pump. He needed speed and he needed to keep the flooding from sinking his boat.

St. Mark was very close and he aimed toward a smooth beach that would offer a haven for him to safely beach his sailboat. He set his course to pass between two rocks, barely poking out of the ocean.

Drake looked back at the sport fisher, her bow marred from the collision, but not torn open. Too bad. The sport fisher lined up for another charge. Its engines roared, the bow wave grew into a white mass, and the boat approached, gaining speed. In a small corner of his mind, Drake wondered what was keeping Sophie.

CAPRICE approached the gap between the rocks. Twenty yards, ten, then the sailboat was abreast the two.

But Webb charged toward them at speed. Couldn't he see the rocks? Well, they were low in the water, and barely broke the surface. Hard to see in the late afternoon light. He obviously hadn't checked the chart. Must have been confident CAPRICE was still in open water.

Drake held his breath.

The sport fisher rumbled on, sliced through rollers, the sound of her engines filling the air.

Suddenly, her engines coughed, paused, and revved up again – but backing instead of charging forward. A wake appeared along the sport fisher's sides and from the bow.

Webb had spotted the danger and had thrown his boat in reverse just yards from the rock between him and CAPRICE. He waved his fist, his eyes bulging with anger as his boat backed off. At a distance of a hundred yards, he stopped the boat, engines idling.

Drake figured the man was now taking the time to check his charts. He'd find the rocks and no doubt would find the wall of coral as well, laying just below the surface, closer to shore, capable of ripping a hull wide open.

Drake headed for one of the two breaks in the coral, his bow pointed toward the pristine beach beyond. Webb maneuvered further west, no doubt aiming for the other break. So he planned to beach the sport fisher and take the fight ashore.

Sophie stuck her head out, frowning. "There's about a foot of water in the boat, more is flooding in."

"Come here, quick."

She scampered up, looked at the sport fisher and at the beach, eyes wide.

Drake felt the boat become sluggish to his rudder commands. She was getting heavy from the flooding and he needed to run her aground before she sank. Then if he could get rid of Webb, he could fill the hole, and pump her dry. He scooted through the gap in the coral and felt the jar of the keel striking the sandy sea floor. Still fifty feet from shore and far from safe.

"Grab your shoes," he commanded. "Good. Now swim to shore. I'll be right there."

He was desperate now. Webb's boat approached the shore, only two hundred yards up the beach from where CAPRICE had grounded. The sport fisher moved forward very slowly, to avoid grounding hard, which could damage the boat or leave her stuck in place. He was a sailor, give him that. Was he also a hunter?

Drake rushed below, grabbed towels, and stuffed them into the gaping hole in the hull next to pillows and a mattress that Sophie had already wedged into place. He pounded them tight with his fist. The patch held – only a trickle of water seeped around the edges.

No time to retrieve his pistol from the safe, but he sacrificed valuable seconds to get his running shoes on. He'd need them.

On deck, he dove into to the water, chilly after the warmth of the day, raced to shore, grabbed Sophie's hand, and they sprinted into the brush.

Through the trees he saw Webb jump from the bow of his boat onto the beach, his face a mask of rage. He gripped a pistol in his right hand.

CHAPTER 25

Webb sprinted down the beach, the sand warm on his bare feet.

Damn Sophie and damn Drake. They had been in his grasp and got away. But he'd chase them down. Solve the Sophie problem for good.

The pistol felt cool in his hand. His adrenalin pumped. He felt the surge of energy. They were dead meat.

Sophie and Drake disappeared into the woods. Cliff marked the spot. He'd catch them. Shoot them. Drag their bodies to his boat and sink them at sea.

He entered the bush and paused. Listened. Heard his prey deeper among the trees and vines. Heading straight to the interior, straight up a mountain. Fine. He was in shape. He'd catch up, easy.

He poured on the steam, twigs and stones biting into the soles of his bare feet.

He ran faster – the quicker he caught them the better – less distance to drag the bodies.

The light was fading but his hunting in the Florida Everglades served him well. He easily identified the path made by generations of deer, along which Sophie and Drake retreated.

He paused again, listened. Considered tearing his shirt and wrapping the pieces around his feet, which had started to throb. He looked at the sole of his right foot. Yeah, it was bleeding. Damn.

He ignored the pain, sprinted upward, toward the faint sounds of someone moving through the bush. Wondered briefly who the fuck Drake was. What had Jorgue said? The guy had been in combat. Well, as what? A spotter? A cook? Shit, maybe he was in combat, maybe even shot someone. But time passes and fighting skills fade. Webb was certain he could take him.

His breathing became labored. Damned mountain. His feet ached and there was sharp pain whenever stones or twigs stabbed him. He gritted his teeth, pressed on, pushing himself hard.

He focused on the trail, paused briefly every minute to listen to his quarry – make sure he was on their track and that they were still together. They were. He could hear two sets of footsteps. He smiled as he trotted up the path.

Webb thought about the encounter, maybe a minute away, for surely they were fatigued and on their last reserves. He'd find them on the path, both of them coughing and puking from their exertion. Too tired to run another step and no place to hide.

He'd approach and savor their humiliation. He'd shoot Drake first – get him out of the mix. A gut shot. Let him feel the agony. Then a double tap to the head.

Then he'd take care of Sophie. There was still enough light, but he'd have to act fast. Maybe put a bullet in her knee to get her attention. Then he'd squat down at her head. Brush her hair back. Pat her shoulder. And ask her who she talked to.

It didn't matter what she said. He was sure she hadn't told a soul. But he wanted to check anyway. Maybe he'd shoot her other knee to encourage her to talk. Put her in hell with agony. And he was the devil.

After she writhed in pain for five minutes, he…

Wait! Why not leave her there? Both knees ruined, bleeding, weeping. What a fine idea! While he dragged numb nuts Drake to his boat, let Sophie suffer. Should be a half hour return trip, but an eternity of anguish for her.

That was the solution. It felt right, he preferred a long and painful death for people who crossed him. Same as that asshole in Colombia. Took him three days to croak. Webb had delivered the agony to that man, glaring into the guy's terrified eyes. Classic.

Funny, he never had an urge to torture deer. He loved the hunt and loved the taste of venison, but he always put the deer down quickly. With people it was different – with them, he always had a serious axe to grind. Plus, torture spawned fear among those tempted to double cross him, which bolstered his grasp on power. Also, he admitted, it made him feel good.

Sophie was no deer. He wanted her to suffer. Satisfy his need for revenge. Unfortunately, he didn't have three days to torment her. But he could let her live while he dragged Drake to the boat and then return and haul her over the rough ground, back down the mountain and along the beach.

Nah. She'd shriek on the way and someone might hear. Besides, dragging her dead body would be easier than if she was alive and thrashing around, grasping every tree and vine on the way to the beach. Okay, so he'd kill her too, after he returned from dragging Drake.

God, his feet ached. He paused and leaned on a tree. Why was he out of breath? He ran every day. Well, almost every day. And he played racket ball. But not every day. Last week? No, not that recently. He levered his right foot up and inspected the sole. He gasped – the flesh was flayed open, like raw hamburger. He had no idea it was that bad. Crap.

He cocked his head. Heard them, fainter now, farther away, and higher. The light was almost gone. The trees and bushes had lost color.

Damn. Damn. Damn.

He used his knife to slice his shirt in two and knotted the pieces around his feet. Trudged back. Lost the path, but he kept walking downhill and found the beach okay. Damned bugs bit his arms and legs. Buzzed around his ears.

When Webb arrived at Matazos' pier, he was in agony from the rocks and twigs digging into his feet. Matazos helped him up the bluff, into the house. Called a doctor friend. The doc was a dour guy. Just laid Webb on his stomach on the kitchen table and slowly pulled all the crap out with surgical pliers.

The guy whistled a little tune and enjoyed his work way too much. Webb didn't give him the satisfaction of asking for a pain pill. He lay still, cursing under his breath. Damn, if the tables could only be turned. He'd love doing that bastard.

The doctor added a dozen stitches, gauze, and tape. Said to use shoes in the future. Well, duh. Matazos ushered the doctor out before Webb could properly pound the shit out of him. The asshole probably had jars bulging with pain pills but his sissy feelings were hurt from Webb swearing at him during his initial examination.

Matazos, remembering Webb's liking for whiskey, passed him a tumbler of the amber liquid. Webb's feet throbbed and still hurt after the second tumbler, but by then he simply didn't give a rat's ass.

He wasn't drunk, not even close. He told Jorgue all that had happened. Jorgue listened, and in the end, responded with a Latino shrug.

"It is unfortunate to lose her," he said, sympathy in his voice, "but you know she's on the island and Drake's boat will be out of commission for days. She is isolated."

Webb shook his head. "It's a small island, but a big damned haystack."

"*Sí*, and she is the needle. The island people, they love this woman. You cannot find her by asking them."

"Pay someone?"

"Not a chance, *amigo*."

"I'll poke around..."

Matazos grinned, his eyes knowing. "Do not be concerned. I have a solution for you."

CHAPTER 26

High above the beach, deep in the bush, Drake paused. Sophie joined him, her breathing deep and regular, her face a sheen of sweat. He gestured for silence, turned downhill, and shut his eyes. Listened for the rustle of undergrowth, the snapped twig, the cry of a startled bird.

He pictured Webb running hard, fueled with rage. He had followed their trail in these dense woods. A man familiar with deer tracks. Perhaps a hunter – of deer or men. Also a man of stamina.

Drake had taken a little-used shortcut that gained him a hundred yards. Still his enemy dogged them, only a minute behind, maybe less. Before, Drake could hear those telltale sounds of movement. Now, only the chirp and squeak of insects. Once a bird, but far away.

Webb must have paused also, but now there was a crunch. He must have resumed the chase. Drake strained to pick out the sounds of pursuit through the hum of insects. Heard one more crunch. Then a cracked twig. The sounds continued, diminished in magnitude. Slow, regular.

Drake whispered, "He's turned around, moving downhill, away from us."

"He gave up? I can't believe that."

Drake shook his head. "For tonight only. A temporary retreat. It's almost dark and he's on unfamiliar ground. Maybe figured we'd ambush him."

"He won't give up," she said, her hand on Drake's shoulder.

Drake nodded.

"I'm afraid you're right. Come on, we've got to go."

He took the lead, anxious to reach the North Side road. Night was at hand, with almost no moon to light their way. Even now, he navigated by touch as much as with sight. He heard her close behind, both of them enveloped by trees, bushes, and the cacophony of small creatures.

They emerged on the road, its black surface just visible. Drake looked left and right, saw no shadows of waiting vehicles. Listened and heard no man-made sounds except for a muffled generator and, further off, the rhythmic bass of music.

He held her hand, and she gripped tight for the first five minutes, then her fingers relaxed a little, but she still held on. They didn't talk. Drake watched and listened and then they walked the road to the trail to the Coxons' and they turned. In five minutes, they entered the clearing. Uphill, the house was lit by kerosene lanterns set along the railing of the front porch.

George and Maren greeted them and brought cold beer. They all sat on the front porch. Drake summarized the tale, wanting to get away, leaving it to Sophie to fill in the blanks. When he was done, George called his son.

"Michael, go up near the road. Keep an eye out. If you see anyone, come back and tell me."

"Okay, Dad."

The boy started to leave, but George lifted his hand.

"You'll be there an hour or so, then I'll come find you. No using that little penlight you carry."

"No problem. I'll leave it in my pocket," Michael looked grown up and serious as he melted into the shadows, making no noise.

"Thanks" said Drake.

"Sophie's one of ours," George said, looking fondly at her. "We'll keep her safe and sound."

Maren and Jenny nodded, their faces pale in the light of the lanterns.

Drake reached out and put his hand on Sophie's knee. He looked her in the eye. "You were courageous today. You stared that man down. Now you need to stay low. Let me look and listen and figure out the next step."

"I'll be here," she said.

Drake didn't see Michael on the way out, but the hair on the back of his neck itched as he approached the main road, and he knew Michael was watching him. Drake turned right and moved upward, keeping eyes and ears open, seeing only a single deer dart cross his path. He reached Santiago's compound just as the judge sat down for dinner.

"Join me," Santiago invited. "I don't know what you have been doing, but you look like you could use food, and a little wine."

Drake strode to the kitchen, nodded to the inside guard, now performing his butler duties at dinner, and quickly washed his hands and brushed the twigs off his shorts.

When he rejoined Santiago, the guard placed bowls of gazpacho at their places. Drake found the soup cool and flavorful, and must have emptied his bowl in record time, because Santiago gave one of his rare smiles.

"You must be very hungry," Santiago said.

"It's been a long day."

The guard removed soup bowls.

"Do you have news for me?" the judge asked, sipping a Rioja wine.

"I hope not for you, sir, but there are things you should know."

Drake recounted the conflict with Webb, this time in detail.

Santiago nodded. "So, Miss Cooper is under threat by Mr. Webb, but you believe she is safe for the time being. And the mysterious couple is getting closer to arriving on St. Thomas." He paused for the guard to place steaming, fragrant plates of *pollo ajillo* in front of them. "What about Mr. Matazos?"

Drake shrugged, spearing a piece of the garlic chicken. "He and Webb are associates, and he's putting Webb up at his compound."

"Do you think there is more to all this than Mr. Webb's search for Miss Cooper?"

"Maybe…"

"We both get these feelings, do we not?"

"There's too much going on, and too much violence," Drake said. "Both Webb and Matazos are killers. I get a bad feeling. They might team up and hold someone hostage and demand that Sophie be given to them."

"After today's events, that sounds possible, maybe even probable."

"But the question now is whether their only focus is Sophie, or are they after something else?"

Santiago took a bite of the garlic chicken, chewed, swallowed, and said, "I only ask this to be sure we have looked from all perspectives. Please forgive me..."

"You think Sophie is working with them?" Drake said.

Santiago shrugged. Drake ate a piece of bread and sipped the tart Rioja, mulling over the idea.

"I started out being suspicious of her," Drake said, his tone thoughtful, "because she wanted to get to St. Mark so badly. Why not another island? But she did have a point, because this is the most distant and isolated of the US Virgin Islands. Then she helped rescue Jenny and when Matazos spotted her she was genuinely scared. Today, she was petrified."

"But stayed calm."

"Yes, she kept her cool. Not easy for a civilian. She kept calm during the squall and the rescue of Jenny as well."

"It is part of her personality. At the same time, you are convinced that her fright was not an act?"

Again Drake paused. Considered. Replayed the events.

"No," he said, "it's no act. She was terrified."

"A partial answer, then. Mr. Webb is after her with malice on his mind. But what of this mysterious couple? We know little about them or of their ultimate destination.

"Which could be another island besides St. Mark."

"Yes."

"But if they come here, or even indicate an interest in the island..."

"My thoughts exactly," Santiago said. "As far as I know, I am the only logical target on the island. No one else is of sufficient political or financial interest to such people as these." His brow furrowed. "I am in the middle of the most disturbing trial of my career. Worse than Gaddafi.

"I am continually amazed at the foul acts of which humans are capable. This man I am trying is fully capable of launching an attack against me. But I choose not to return early to the gloomy Netherlands on the basis of our present information and suspicions. I will remain here for the next few days, as scheduled."

"And we remain vigilant."

CHAPTER 27

The sun shone brightly the next morning, slanting through the shutters of Drake's cottage. He rolled out of bed. His watch said it was seven o'clocl, late for him, but he'd stayed up late the night before. The judge treated him more like a son than a hired security expert. After dinner they'd enjoyed cigars and cognac, shared stories from the bench and from behind an automatic weapon, their respective versions of combat.

He shaved and dressed, and wandered down to the boatyard and watched Jenny, standing astride a partially formed boat rib, her hands gripping an adze. He couldn't believe she was the same wilted and shivering girl he and Sophie had pulled from the sea. Gone was her sling. She used both arms as she swung the ancient tool, shaping the wood. She looked up and he approached.

"You see, Mr. Richard, I'm becoming a boat builder."

"You sure are. I didn't know you could use an adze."

She leaned on the tool, the handle up to her waist, and rested a hand on her hip.

"This is still practice. First, I had to sharpen the adze, which was like sharpening a machete, but it's heavier. Now I get to try it out."

"Sort of a giant wood plane," Drake suggested.

"Yep," she said, gripping the handle and positioning herself again. She raised the head of the tool and, swinging it at her wrist, deliberately shaved the wood, layer by layer, each one even, each one carefully diagonal to the grain.

He waved good-bye, and she grinned, eyes bright.

Seeing her was a welcome interlude to yesterday's collision and chase, and the ongoing tension over security, both for the judge and Sophie. And for any innocent bystanders. God, he thought he'd left the bad guys behind on the battle fields. St. Mark had become his refuge, the perfect medicine to heal the scars of combat.

Until now.

He found George scrunched inside CAPRICE, sawing off sharp edges of shattered fiberglass. Even early in the morning, it was sweaty business. Drake squatted on deck, looking down, frowning at the damage. George turned, eyes serious.

"Pretty rough gash," he said. "Lucky you got it plugged."

"How long to fix it?"

"To cover the hole is easy, a couple of hours, but to do it right, you know, to layer on the fiberglass and feather it in, smooth, then paint…three days."

"Could you make it two? It doesn't have to look perfect, just as long as it's strong and tight. You can make it pretty during the off season."

"Sure. You got a charter coming up?"

"Yeah, day after tomorrow out of St. Thomas. Just for the morning. I'd hate to cancel."

George thought for a minute. Touched the edges of the hole with the tips of his fingers.

"Okay," he said, "I'll push hard, take a few shortcuts. She'll be in the water, ready to sail, day after tomorrow."

"Thanks."

"Sure. You see Jenny?"

Drake nodded. "She has a steady hand and a good eye."

"She loves working outside, sailing outside, swimming outside."

"Sounds like a pattern there."

"She's smart as a whip when it comes to practical stuff. Books don't interest her much and she's bored silly with cooking and mending and house cleaning."

"There's lots of possibilities for an outside person here in the islands."

"I'm thinking the same. Not a bunch of money, but it sure can be a good life."

"No complaints from me, being a charter captain."

"Or me," Coxon said, gripping his saw and eyeing the edges. "It's satisfying, building boats."

Drake wandered to the water's edge where Michael Coxon stood up to his knees in the rippling bay. He looked at Drake.

"Oh, hi Mr. Richard. Just checking a set of ribs."

Drake looked through the water, muddied, but still clear enough to see the curved wooden pieces on the bottom.

"We soak 'em to get the insects out," the boy said.

Drake chatted with him for a couple of minutes, thankful for the friendship of his family, then moved on.

Feeling at loose ends, he wandered through the small town, waved to John at the door to his store, and continued up the hill. Almost without thinking, he found himself at the Coxon home.

Maren and Sophie sat on the front porch, nursing cups of coffee. Drake accepted a cup of the steaming brew and joined them. A morning breeze whispered in the trees.

"How's your boat?" Sophie asked.

"She'll be fine," Drake said. "George will have her fixed by day after tomorrow."

"Oh," Sophie said, sounding disappointed.

"Something wrong?" Drake asked.

"She's got island fever," Maren said kindly.

"Sorry," Sophie said. "Sitting here while Cliff is out there creeps me out. I'm just antsy I guess."

"Tell you what," Drake said. "Why don't we do a little shooting?"

"Shooting? Like deer hunting? I don't think…"

Drake gestured. "No, not that kind of shooting. I mean target practice. Have you ever used a gun?"

"Yes, a pistol."

"Okay, we'll swing by my cottage and pick up a pistol and a couple targets, then we can hike to the west end."

*   *   *

The day warmed as Drake and Sophie walked to his cottage and then westward. They climbed to a promontory and faced the blue Caribbean, letting the wind blow in their faces and muss their hair. Drake set his day pack on the grass and pointed.

The both gazed far below and over a half mile westward, where the beach turned into a formation of rocks, extending into the sea. Waves surged under the rocks and into a hidden chamber, there to build pressure and spew into a white geyser. Drake explained how this 'blow hole' was a favorite hangout for the island kids. Drake spotted Jenny and most of the little gang down there on the black rocks, dressed in shorts and swim suits.

Faint snippets of their yelps and laughter punctuated the hiss of rollers and rumble of the erupting geyser. Three kids squatted near the hole, and shrieked when water shot forth, dousing them. They scampered toward land and sat on a flat rocky shelf, close enough for some of the cooling mist to blow their way but safe from the fierce power of the white water.

Drake smiled. Jenny was in her element, outdoors with her buddies, on the way to recovering from her ordeal. Of course, being ten years old and at home on the sea, maybe she looked at the squall as one more adventure, and not a near brush with death.

Sophie must have caught him smiling.

"She's a special girl, isn't she?"

"Jenny's one of a kind," Drake said. "I hate to think of her all alone in that squall."

Sophie took his arm. "But we saved her, Richard. Now she's safe. Which way to the shooting?" she asked.

He nodded absently.

He did love Jenny, like she was his daughter. A love that almost hurt. She was one of God's good people. He glanced at Sophie, stooping to pick up their little picnic box, and he felt a little of the same pang. She was another of the good ones, and he was growing close to her. She smiled as he gripped his day pack and they aimed back into the bush to their deer track.

The west end of St. Mark was a wild place, pounded by waves, its land populated by desiccated bushes bent low by constant wind. Sophie stood still, her face to the empty north horizon, a place of stolid, marching Atlantic rollers.

"It's so isolated. I feel like I'm on another planet," she said, raising her voice above the roar of crashing waves.

"Yeah, a nice place to sit and think if it wasn't this windy. No one comes here. At least there's no danger of a wild shot hurting anyone. The next land is hundreds of miles away."

"It is lonely."

"That's for sure. There's no beach, no way to fish, and no trees large enough for George to use as ribs for his latest boat or for making charcoal. I come here about once a week for target practice. Never see a soul."

Drake shivered, and not from the cool sea wind. 'Never see a soul' touched a nerve, and he wondered at the words he'd chosen. But indeed, those few words conveyed all too well his feelings about the forlorn western tip of St. Mark. The place set a mood, a dour one at that, and he hoped it didn't rub off on Sophie.

He tied a bulls-eye paper target securely to a wide bush, turned, and guided Sophie fifty feet back from the target, along a path he'd cleared when he chose the location for maintaining his marksmanship.

They set their gear on the ground and Drake retrieved his Glock 19 from his day pack. He hefted the black semi-automatic pistol, its weight and shape familiar in his hand. He ejected the magazine, checked for a full fifteen rounds, and snapped it back in place.

With his feet wide, he faced the target and fired three rounds, the pungent smell of spent ammo quickly whipped away by the wind. He lowered the Glock, noted his group slightly left of center, and fired the remaining rounds, the brass casings clattering to the rocky ground.

As he and Sophie walked forward to inspect his target, Drake grinned with satisfaction – his group was tight inside the center ten-ring. He replaced the target with a new one and they returned to their firing site.

"You said you've shot pistols before?"

She nodded. "Not this kind. I shot my dad's 45 and a couple of Cliff's pistols. I know enough to clear the chamber after firing and never, ever, point a weapon at someone, even if it is 'unloaded.'"

"That's good enough for me." He reloaded the magazine and handed her the pistol.

She aimed downrange, took a breath, let most of it out, and squeezed the trigger. Paused, then emptied the magazine. Walking to the target, Drake shook his head in admiration.

"I'll be darned. You're almost as good a shot as I am. Nice tight group."

"Yeah," she drawled. "Bad day for me. One's outside the ten-ring."

He made a face and she laughed.

"Just joking," she said.

"Well, you're a fine shot," he said, mounting a new target. "What say we back up to seventy-five feet?"

"Suits me."

After they shot all the ammo in friendly competition, and policed the brass casings, they ate lunch, packed by Maren before she'd let them leave. The food was fresh and flavorful, and the beer had stayed ice cold.

Waves crashed and they sat close on a rock overlooking the ocean. Somehow the isolation had turned inviting, friendly. Shooting together had been companionable, their banter fun. Drake smiled for the second time that day.

When they stood and brushed off the dust, she leaned close and kissed him on the cheek.

"Thanks for today," she said.

Making the return hike surprisingly happy for Drake.

CHAPTER 28

Webb stood well up one of the half dozen mountains on this desolate, dip-shit island. Wondered why it couldn't be flat like the Bahamas or the Caymans. He couldn't see a damn thing past twenty yards because of the bush. There were pastures, but few and far between. He wished he had brought more water.

Damned woods were a pain in the ass. No wonder he quit deer hunting. The air lay hot as hell, stagnant under the trees. Even in the little meadows, this late in the afternoon. He wiped sweat from his face. Swatted a mosquito. Crunched a few more paces uphill on the deer track. Gnats buzzed around his head.

He tried unsuccessfully to erase the memory of his setback the previous evening. The image of those two assholes disappearing into the forest made his stomach hurt. God, he had them in his grasp. He could hear them, so close.

He had to admit that asking the locals was a non-starter. Matazos was right. They were thick as thieves. He was an outsider, as was Matazos.

Webb continued, his hands moving branches out of his way. Wondered what Matazos had up his sleeve, his 'solution' to finding Sophie. That guy knew nothing about the island. He only left his compound to catch a helicopter to St. Thomas. Oh yeah, he said he drove to town once to pick up food for a party.

Well, what the hell was his solution? Whatever it was, if Webb accepted, he would be more into the man's debt. Webb hated to owe other people. That's why he'd spent the entire damned morning searching the island by himself.

He could have hired someone from St. Thomas and flown him over in a helo. But he'd have had to rely on Matazos' recommendation, and get even further into the man's debt. Besides, who knew what sort of low-life he'd recommend. Better to go solo.

Webb walked further along the sweaty trail, thinking. He figured Sophie was staying with a local who lived in the bush. Most locals lived in town, but she would know that was too visible. She'd poke her head out one time too many and one of Matazos' guards would see her while he sipped a beer on his day off. They were Colombians and had no island loyalty. They'd give her up in a heartbeat.

But where was she hiding? He'd already tromped around most of the west end of the island. Now he was searching the east end, up and down the mountains. A fold in the land could easily hide the house where she was hiding, as could the trees and bushes.

Damned waste of time. He should be running his business, managing the half dozen active projects he had going. There was a limit to what he could accomplish on the sat phone calling from way down here. Face to face, that's how he liked to   run his business.

But he had to solve the Sophie problem. That damned bitch.

A scent interrupted his train of thought – a scent that was out of place. He stopped. Sniffed the air.

Cooking smells! Could this be where he'd find Sophie? He turned a full circle, eyes searching through the bushes and trees for a hint of man-made structure. White paint. A straight line. But all he saw were natural shapes and colors.

He sniffed again. Yes.

Webb left the deer track at a ninety-degree angle and walked downhill, careful, one step at a time. A dog had begun barking earlier in the morning as he passed above the town. He'd beaten a hasty retreat. Sure didn't need a dog chewing on his leg or alerting the islanders that he was on the prowl.

Now he tread quietly. For once, he was grateful for the lack of a breeze to carry his scent. Though if he stayed too long, his scent could carry, just as the cooking smells had spread, slowly but surely.

He paused and smelled the air, again sensing the wafting hint of cooking. Not stronger – but not weaker. He continued. Off the deer track, the going was slow.

He pushed his way through a row of thorny bushes, arms shielding his eyes. On the other side of the bushes he felt scratches along both arms and a pain on his right shoulder. He touched the spot on his shoulder. Felt a two-inch tear in his shirt and his finger came away with a dab of blood.

A thorn had cut him. Not deep, not even bleeding too much. But it had ripped his shirt. A blue one. A dress shirt – he didn't have time to pack for walking through the jungle. One more reason to hate that bitch.

Far below, a dog barked. Then a human voice. A man. Webb froze. It wasn't far. Maybe a hundred yards, diagonally down the mountain. His heart raced. The good news was he'd likely found a house out in the countryside where Sophie might be hiding.

The bad news was that a dog began barking downhill, out of sight. Two others joined the party, barking like maniacs. What the hell! Hadn't they smelled people before?

Sure, but not strangers, he told himself. Get a grip. Time to boogie. With a muttered string of profanity he turned back to the thorns, swore again and moved to the right a hundred feet, found an opening, and squirmed through. The dogs still yelped. He carefully memorized the look of the thorn thicket, so he could find this place in the future.

He trudged uphill, found the deer track. He broke off a rotten tree limb and placed it crosswise on the track. He planned to return. But now he moved off, continuing as before on the track, letting the dogs win this round.

He looked over his shoulder, concerned he'd see a dog on his trail. He found a stick about four feet long for defense and kept walking, keeping his pace quick. Once, when he looked back, he caught a glimpse of the top of a stone tower. Maybe an abandoned sugar cane mill, which peppered these islands.

Whatever. He kept moving. The barking finally stopped. Either the dogs had gotten bored or he'd moved outside their range of hearing.

Webb broke into a clearing with a view of the sea. He walked through the tall grass to the edge, glanced down at the ocean pounding the shore, rolling swells turning to white spume. Far to his right lay the town, mostly blocked by a rise in the land, but the boatyard was plainly visible. There was Drake's boat, leaning to one side, obviously getting the hole in the hull repaired.

Too bad that bastard turned at the last second.

CHAPTER 29

Drake was worried, and it had nothing to do with CAPRICE. She had sailed well on the trip from St. Mark to St. Thomas, after two days of George's care. Her patch was holding strong and tight.

Nor was he concerned about Sophie, who was due back any minute from her visit to Charlotte Amalie to pick up her new passport. Drake was confident she was safe in the taxi and on the crowded streets of the town.

Finally, he was not worried about the couple he'd taken out that morning, cruising the blue Caribbean, pointing out St. John, Jost Van Dyke, and Tortola. He'd enjoyed their company and was sure they had a good time.

No, what bothered him was what he'd found in the woods above the Coxons' home. After he'd walked Sophie back to the Coxons' following their target practice, he had conducted a detailed security sweep. A hundred yards from where Sophie slept, he found a bit of blue cloth hanging at the end of a branch in a thicket of thorn bushes. He retrieved the cloth and it felt soft and clean to the touch. Un-weathered, and therefore recently lost, tugged from the shirt of someone lurking about.

Further uphill, beyond the thicket, he found a small branch, broken from a tree and placed across a deer track. From the way the branch lay, it had not fallen off the tree from age or rot, or from a collision from a passing deer. It had been broken off by a person. The break had occurred only hours previously.

Someone was there and had marked their position. Had they continued downhill and seen the Coxon houses? Drake didn't know. He did check with George and his family – they had seen no sign of a prowler. The dogs had barked and had taken a while to settle down. Perhaps that indicated the presence of an intruder. Drake shivered at the thought of a man that close to Sophie. He'd believed she was safe, but now he had doubts.

Should he remove the marker? No, the tree with its torn stub was impossible to disguise and it would remain, as effective as the marker. Plus, it was better to leave well enough alone and not let this person know his little trail marker had been discovered.

Someone had come that close, even if they did not get all the way to the houses, and they were sufficiently interested in what they found to leave a marker. Who was it? A wandering local? One of the kids? No, they knew the land, and the nearness of the home, and always stopped in to visit. That was the island way. It had to be Webb, or Matazos, or one of Matazos' men, searching for Sophie's hideaway.

Drake's thoughts were interrupted by a young woman, a Latina in her late twenties, who walked up to his boat.

"Hi," she said, taking off her sunglasses. "I am Maria Ramos. The man in the office said I could find you here. You are Mr. Drake?"

Her English was nearly perfect, with only the musical lilt and a small accent to point to her Latina heritage.

He stood and extended his hand.

"Yes, I'm Richard Drake."

Her grip was firm and she looked him straight in the eye. Not a threatening look, but one that Drake had never experienced from a woman. A hard look, like when a sergeant first greeted a new man in his platoon. A look of evaluation.

Intrigued, Drake joined her on the pier. As she scanned CAPRICE, he noticed that her curvy figure and pretty features clashed with a puffiness in her face. Either she was jet lagged or enjoying too much booze or drugs.

"Nice boat," she said in a tone of authority.

And Drake wondered. She appeared out of nowhere, with no advance notice, but there was something familiar about this woman. Maybe the way she dressed? She wore white slacks and a brightly patterned shirt that marked her as a tourist. She wore lots of jangly gold bracelets, dangly earrings, an engagement diamond ring and gold wedding band. Strappy leather designer sandals. All this was normal, a little flashy, but many women dressed that way, whether Anglos or Latinas.

But something didn't fit.

The eyes. Too knowing. The stance, poised, as if ready. Ready for what? She tried to look relaxed, but this woman was wound tight. She broke the silence.

"I would like to have a charter with you, perhaps a morning or an afternoon. I am here on my honeymoon. The charter is a little surprise for my husband."

"Of course," he said. "Did you check with the agent on my schedule?"

"No." She put on her sunglasses and smiled, and added. "I was told by the charter agent that you managed your own schedule, so I came directly to you."

Which was a lie, a bad guess on her part. A calculated risk. She'd guessed wrong, tipping him off and putting him on alert. He kept his face neutral and wrinkled his brow, pretending to visualize his schedule as he played along with her lie.

But his mind turned elsewhere. It was all about her manner. And this unnecessary lie. His gut insisted she didn't get his name from the charter agent. More likely she never spoke with the agent, never asked about schedule.

She got his name from her boss. The person who hired her and her 'husband' to fly to St. Thomas. Drake knew she was never going to show up for the charter. She didn't care about the other islands or his entertaining company. All she wanted was a face-to-face meeting with him.

Maria Ramos wanted to take his measure.

"I could take you and your husband out the day after tomorrow," he suggested.

"In the morning?"

Again he pondered, but only for a moment. In that brief time he spotted an athletic-looking man leaning against the charter office, back in the shade. Also, he saw Sophie striding returning, carrying her purse and a shopping bag.

"Yes," he said, "Is 9:30 okay for you?"

"That's fine," she said, glancing at Sophie as she approached. Maria extended her hand and they shook. "Thank you Mr. Drake. I look forward to sailing with you. I'm sure my husband will be delighted with my little surprise."

She turned and walked away. She and Sophie passed each other with no sign of recognition, which did not surprise Drake. He wondered if she and her husband were hunting Sophie, but he decided not. Graham had gotten word of the mysterious pair coming before Sophie arrived on the scene. And from his actions, Webb didn't want any help from these two. No, the pair were up to something separate.

"Who was that?" asked Sophie, glanced back at the woman.

Drake looked as well and noticed Maria continue past the tiki bar and to the right, probably to retrieve a rental car or taxi in the restaurant parking lot. The man disappeared behind the charter office. The building blocked his view and he couldn't see whether they met.

"She wanted to arrange a charter," Drake said. "A surprise for her new husband."

He took the shopping bag from Sophie and they boarded CAPRICE. Sophie glanced back down the pier, though Maria had disappeared.

"Strange," Sophie said thoughtfully. "She didn't have that just-married glow. She seemed, well, jaded."

"Maybe it was jet lag," Drake said, figuring it was better not to tell her more. If Maria and her 'husband' were gunning for the judge, Sophie had nothing to worry about. But life wasn't really that simple, Drake admitted.

The problem was, Webb was staying with Matazos and they were associates. The waters could get muddied. Drake planned to tell Sophie if the time came. He smiled at her, pretty in the early afternoon sun.

"Did you get your passport?" he asked.

"Yes, and I had a delightful brunch with Anika. She invited me to visit. They live in an old Danish farm in the country."

Her face clouded.

Drake touched her shoulder.

"That time will come. Soon."

She shook her head, blinked away a tear, and scurried below.

CHAPTER 30

Judge Santiago sat in his chair, cognac in hand, his face serious, posture dignified.

"Do you always assume the worse, Richard?" he asked with the hint of a smile, as if to try to break the tension in the room.

The bodyguard hovered near the kitchen door, asked by Santiago to stay and listen when Drake initially brought up the subject of his meeting with the so-called Maria Ramos.

Drake sipped his cognac, gaining a moment to phrase his reply in a way he hoped would cause Santiago to take the threat seriously. The cognac was of the best quality, typical of his host's fine taste. It was Spanish, of course.

"I spoke with her, sir," Drake said, his tone serious, measured. "We stood close and I read her eyes, dull, empty of emotion. She's a killer."

Santiago nodded, but Drake sensed he was not fully convinced. Drake leaned forward. "Also, she lied to me. She said she talked with the charter agent but she didn't. She said she wanted to go out on a charter but she didn't seem at all interested – didn't ask about where we could go, what the other islands were like. Everyone asks that sort of thing. I'm sure her only motive was to check me out.

"Which means she had to go to the trouble of finding me. She must have been told by whoever hired her that I work security for you and that I am a threat to her success. Why else would she go to the trouble to pretend to set up a charter? It was only to get face to face with me and look me in the eye, see how I moved, whether I looked fit. I am a threat to her only because I am defending you. Sir, you are the target."

"And her husband. You saw him as well?"

Drake nodded. "He was about a hundred yards away, in the shade. He looked lean but I couldn't see his face. That call I made to Graham Walters should get me more information. I'm hoping he can get photos of both of them."

"Did Mr. Walters see them in St. Thomas?"

"One of his men did, at the airport. Saw them getting off a commercial jet that arrived from San Juan. Described them as athletic and serious."

"Athletic?"

"Moving smoothly, gracefully almost."

"I see. And Graham is sure they are assassins, working for a Colombian cartel?"

"He confirmed that today. Said the Colombian police have promised photos and summaries of their past jobs. I'm hoping those summaries will give me insight as to how they operate. Also, I hope to learn whether they only kill people or if they've branched out to kidnapping. That information will help determine our strategy."

Drake glanced at the wiry bodyguard, who gave a slight nod. Drake was sure this was familiar ground to the guard. As a member of Spain's elite Grupo Especial de Operaciónes, the National Police special ops, he appreciated the value of any information on how the two assassins operated. From the man's expression, he was now convinced the couple posed a serious threat to the judge.

Santiago said, "To summarize, you believe that since the woman, Maria, sought you out, there is a threat to me. She found out where to locate you from someone on St. Mark or St. Thomas and wanted to check you out."

"Yes, even though that would warn us that you were a possible target. She gave up the element of surprise. Before our meeting this afternoon, we didn't know their target, or even where the target was located. I think they strongly suspected they were being tracked. I also think they will act quickly, in the next day or two."

"Could they be working for Cliff Webb and going after Sophie?"

Drake shook his head. "Cliff has been doing the searching and the attacking on his own. He was nearly successful in sinking CAPRICE, and he gave us a convincing chase through the woods. Luckily, Sophie's an athlete, or Webb would have caught us – and he was armed."

Santiago gazed out the window at the late afternoon sea.

Drake knew the man realized that it was not far-fetched for a Colombian cartel to be mixed up in an assassination or kidnapping aimed at freeing the ex-president of near-by Venezuela.

"You present a compelling case," Santiago said at last.

Drake drew a breath.

"You look uncomfortable," Santiago said.

"I am. I think you should get off the island now. Go to Spain or to the Hague, or some other place. Get distance between you and these killers."

"You know I don't believe in running."

Drake shrugged. "Judge Santiago, you are the most honest judge on any bench, and the smartest…"

"As well as the most stubborn?"

Drake raised his glass with a grim smile.

They toasted. To what? Drake wondered – the courage to preserve the rule of law, he guessed.

The bodyguard looked even grimmer than usual as Drake passed him on the way to the front door. Outside, he said good-night to the other bodyguard and trudged along the black road, thinking black thoughts.

Protecting Sophie and Judge Santiago – his world had suddenly become very dangerous, very complicated. How could it get any worse?

And he cursed under his breath. His question was answered by the sound of a helicopter, off to the west. On a hunch, he melted into the underbrush, and moved parallel to the road until he was opposite the gate to Matazos' compound. He knew most of the North Side residents preferred to arrive and depart by helo, so a helicopter landing was not unusual. But the timing was – Drake's gut was telling him the helo carried Maria and her husband.

He squatted, the insects sensing the onset of evening and starting their myriad calls. In the still air, he smelled the sharp odor of dirt, mixed with that of tar from the overheated road, twenty feet distant.

From around a bend came the sound of a Jeep, which stopped at Matazos' gate. Drake's heart pounded. Inside he spotted the driver in front and two passengers in back. In the split second when the Jeep was even with him, slowing for the turn to the gate and the driveway beyond, Drake saw the profiles of a man and a woman.

The gate opened, the Jeep entered the curving driveway and disappeared behind a jungle of tropical plants and palm trees. He heard the opening and closing of doors and the faint babble of voices.

He would return to warn Santiago, not that the judge needed to know, but because his bodyguards must be alerted – the enemy had arrived.

CHAPTER 31

Webb stood when Matazos returned through the front door of his house, leading a man and a women dressed in khaki shorts, colorful shirts, and running shoes. Their only apparent luggage were gym bags.

Matazos chatted amiably as he led them into the great room, pointing out exotic plants and gesturing to the picture window and his backyard, darkening with the setting sun.

"Mi casa es su casa," he said, playing the gracious host.

Webb had never seen him this demonstrative and transparently eager to please.

Judging from the look of the guests, this was not a social visit. They smiled mechanically and dutifully looked around the room. But their eyes were cold, and they moved with the grace and poise of predators. Accomplished, efficient, consummate predators. No wonder Matazos looked nervous.

To guess their thoughts or emotions was impossible. As they approached, he noticed that the woman, who initially looked youthful, now appeared worn. But she was lean and muscled.

The trio stopped in the center of the room, close to where Webb stood with his drink in hand. Matazos gestured.

"Cliff, meet Juan and Maria."

Everyone shook hands. The guests murmured pleasantries in colloquial American English with a Latino accent.

Webb reflected, 'Juan and Maria'? Like 'John and Mary,' These were made-up names. Who was Matazos shitting?

131

Matazos must have noticed Webb's frown because he added, "Their working names, of course."

Webb's curiosity spiked. Working names? Why were they here? They looked like enforcers. But was it a coincidence or plan that they arrived during his visit? Whatever, there was no time for conjecture. He had to accept and he had to listen, to learn what Matazos was up to. Understand, check the angles. Be ready to profit.

Matazos gestured to his fully-stocked wet bar. All three chose whiskey, neat. Everyone sat in leather chairs arranged around a coffee table. There was an awkward silence during which Webb felt himself being measured by the couple, and during which time he measured them. He'd heard of such a couple working for a Colombian drug lord with whom he and Matazos often did business.

Webb wondered if he could hire them for a problem client over in Italy. He was sure he could afford them. The question was, would their employer permit such an arrangement? Probably not. The drug lord was an arrogant, self-centered, and a control freak.

Matzos smoothed his hair, the man's 'tell.' Webb had noticed it an hour previously, when his host had answered a call on his sat phone. Perhaps that was the notification that these two had arrived by helo and were on their way to his compound, driven by one of Matazos' guards. He looked like a frightened dog then, and now he'd turned a little gray.

Though to give the man credit, only the most observant onlooker could see the signs of anxiety. Matazos held his drink with a steady hand and gave his visitors calm eye contact, seemingly relaxed.

"First," Matazos said, his tone businesslike, "I want to again welcome my friends from Colombia. You are my guests during your visit to St. Mark. Ask for anything you need and I will make sure it's made available to you."

"We have all we need," said the man, his black eyes resting on Matazos.

Webb had been among Latinos often enough to know an insult when he heard one. Juan should have simply nodded and offered his thanks and stated that he was pleased to be there. But the guy treated Matazos like an inferior, as if working for him was beneath his professional dignity.

Which made Webb think. What the hell was going on? These two killers were there on behalf of the drug lord and they acted like they owned the place, with Matazos their unwanted guest.

Suddenly, Webb knew the answer. Matazos was in trouble with the drug lord. Somehow, he had crossed the man. Hosting his killers and becoming a party to whatever they were plotting was the cost of forgiveness.

Webb almost smirked, realizing Matazos was shitting himself because Plan B was no doubt for them to kill him. There they were, two human piranhas, in his home, sleeping in the next room at night, either one capable of surprising him and slitting his throat.

Yeah, there it was again. The hair gesture. Matazos' glass lay empty. He didn't dare scurry over to the bar for more because that would totally advertise his fear. But to hear him talk...

"I believe we can move forward with our plan. If that is all right with both of you?"

They nodded. Eyes piercing. Faces blank. Webb had to admire them. Scary as hell. Like out of a damned horror movie.

Matazos turned his gaze to Webb, and Webb stiffened. God in heaven, he hoped he wasn't part of whatever scheme the drug lord had cooked up.

"Cliff, my friend," Matazos said, "you also have a role to play."

Cliff felt the urge to excuse himself. To vomit. He forced his face to remain relaxed.

"Not as active a part as Juan and Maria," Matazos said, "but still important to their success."

Matazos smiled, his eyes hard.

Juan stared at Matazos as if he was going to eat him for dinner. Matazos pretended to ignore the man.

"Yes," Matazos continued, "it is fortunate that you have come to visit at this time. A coincidence I realize..."

Webb drew a breath, felt his heart pound. 'Coincidence'? The lying sack of shit. Coincidence, my ass. Or maybe it was. He avoided the temptation to glance at the couple. What a shit storm. Okay, in for a penny...

"I'm pleased to help out," he said, amazed he sounded calm.

"Of course," Matazos said, holding eye contact as if sending a message. Of what? To remind Webb of his debt? Shit – one phone call saying Sophie was on the island. For that he was pressing for a big favor? Unbelievable.

Silence grew in the room. Way too much tension. Webb sat very still. Attentive to his surroundings. The pounding surf down beyond the garden. The hum of air conditioning. The slight rasp as Matazos took his next breath.

"What will happen," Matazos said, "is much larger than catching up with a naughty girlfriend."

Webb nodded. Felt sweat in his arm pits.

"The good news," Matazos said, maintaining his gaze on Webb, "is that your role is only to divert attention from what Juan and Maria must do."

"Of course," murmured Webb.

So, the drug lord needed Matazos, and Matazos needed Webb. Supposedly for a small diversion. Fat chance. Things had a way of turning to shit. Webb wondered what the mission was.

Maybe something simple. Assassinate one of the rich people who had insulted the drug lord in an unforgivable way – a public slur that demanded visible retribution.

The enforcers remained silent, their movements reptilian, their lidded stares all encompassing.

"Good," said Matazos, rubbing his hands together. "Now if you will excuse me, I must make a call to a client. I will be gone only a few minutes."

Matazos departed down a hall, his footsteps clunking on the tile floor, his office door shutting. A lock thrown with a metallic click.

Juan leaned forward and gazed at Webb. "Why are you here on the island at this particular time?"

Which Webb understood to mean something along the lines of, 'Are you a spy sent here to screw up our mission? Will I have to kill you also?'

A reasonable question, because that damned Matazos had called his presence on St. Mark a coincidence. In their business there were no coincidences. Not among the major players. Things happened because of intent, not by chance. To Juan, that meant Webb's timing related to his intent, which must be to interfere with their mission.

Webb felt Juan's stare, like a needle pricking at his flesh. The asshole was probably calculating how to kill him right there in Matazos' great room. Wondering if he could avoid staining the carpets or damaging the furniture. Probably deciding a single bullet would do. Yeah, signal Maria to invite him to the bar for a refill and shoot him from behind. Maria would make sure Webb fell backward and not into the expensive bottles of booze and all the crystal glasses.

Webb sipped his whiskey, organed his thoughts, and said, "In the past two weeks, my girlfriend overheard too many conversations. Business conversations. She put two and two together and concluded that my business has a, shall we say, dangerous part to it. She may also have witnessed an interrogation."

"She knows too much?" said Maria.

Webb nodded. "The interrogation went south. He died."

"You are concerned she witnessed this death," Maria said thoughtfully. "That is much more dangerous than bits and pieces of conversation. I now understand. You will kill her?"

"Yes."

"That is the only solution," she said in a knowing tone.

"Do you need help?" Juan asked.

Maria's eyes glowed. She licked her lower lip.

"No, I'm fine." But an idea formed in his head. Something that could help him find Sophie, and at the same time, convince these two that his reason for being on the island was to eliminate Sophie and not to ruin their mission.

Juan asked, "You will kill her in such a way that the authorities do not become suspicious?"

He seemed concerned, probably because he didn't want to get caught in the net thrown by police descending on the island if Sophie's death looked like foul play.

"She's stuck on the island," Webb said, pleased with his idea. "It can't be that hard to arrange an accident. Maybe she'll fall off a precipice. Maybe she'll just disappear."

Juan looked into the distance for a long time and then said, "I assume she is hiding. Perhaps Maria and I could be of assistance."

Damn, Webb thought. *Just what I was about to suggest. I couldn't have scripted this! Of course, Juan figures if I refuse, then*

Sophie was an excuse for me being here. But if I follow through with his line of thinking, then I'm only here for Sophie. Webb paused, as if thinking, then spoke with confidence.

"I have a suspicion she's staying with friends out in the country – the Coxons. She helped save their daughter from drowning at sea. I got close to a house I think is theirs, but the dogs started barking. I had to leave."

Juan nodded. "This is a small island, *sí*, but sometimes it is not so easy to find someone who wants to remain hidden."

"Damn, Cliff," Matazos blurted, entering the room and crossing to the bar. "Have you tried Google Earth?"

All eyes turned to the host, who poured himself a scotch, turned, and signaled for them to follow back down the hall. He led them into his office, which surprised Webb. On the other hand, he must keep the sensitive stuff in a safe, and must assume the killers could enter at will anyway, during the night.

They gathered around his large, cluttered desk, on which stood a wide-screen monitor. He opened Google Earth, tapped in 'St. Mark, USVI,' and they watched the screen zoom in to the island.

"I thought you were off the grid," Webb said, admiring the detail of the picture, wondering why in hell he hadn't thought of this before he spent hours rummaging through the bush, sweating his ass off and swatting mosquitos.

"The island is off the grid, but I am very much attached. Otherwise I could not run my affairs. Now, where do you think the Coxons live?"

Webb pointed to the screen. "The place I found was toward the east end of the island."

"Hmm," Matazos said, "Here's a couple of buildings. Path back to the main road. Could be right here."

Juan gestured at a round object above the buildings and Matazos zoomed in.

"Looks like a tower," Matazos said. "They're all over the place on the islands. Used for the sugar cane."

"Or a watch tower," suggested Juan.

"Could be," Matazos said.

"I think," Juan said thoughtfully, "Maria and I could locate this woman."

Webb nodded absently, pulse quickening. If anyone could track Sophie it was these two. He didn't trust them worth a damn, and they still didn't know for sure if this place was where the Coxons lived, or even if Sophie was their guest.

This did look like where he'd been. It might be their house, but just as likely it was someone else's place. There could be a dozen houses scattered around under the trees, invisible to Google Earth. Plus, he couldn't just walk in and grab her. There might be other family members, employees, household staff...who knew? And they could be armed. But he was moving too fast. First, he needed to know where she lived. He looked at Juan.

"What do you suggest?"

Juan spread his hands, palms up. "It is simple. Maria and I have lived our whole lives in the jungle of Colombia. Since we could carry a gun we have been guerrillas, warriors against the corrupt government."

"Until you began working for your present boss? Isn't he based in a city?"

"That is correct. Still, we prefer operating in *el campo*, the countryside." He grinned, his eyes hard. "We are completely at home in the bush. We will find this woman and tell you where to ambush her. Rest assured."

Webb nodded in agreement. That would solve his problem of finding the bitch. The rest he could take care of himself. Squeeze her for information, then kill her. End of the Sophie problem.

Matazos ushered them all back to the living room and they sat.

"You will interrogate her?" asked Maria. Changing the subject, as if giving Webb time to reflect on whether to accept Juan's offer. She was a clever woman. Subtle. Therefore, dangerous in her own way.

"Yes," said Webb, "I need to find out what she knows about my business. Before I kill her."

Matazos nodded. "I attended several parties at your Florida estate. Sophie circulated, a gracious hostess, and she could overhear. I know people talked too much about my business as well."

"And the business of my boss, I am sure," said Juan. "He is very jealous of his privacy."

Matazos said, "She could be a threat to all of us. You see, Cliff? Your girlfriend has made herself a thorn in our side."

Three sets of eyes glared at Webb, daring him to disagree, and his mouth went dry. All of a sudden, the control he thought he had gained evaporated.

Questions tumbled through his mind. Had Matazos schemed for Sophie to come here? Was this couple sent to interrogate her? Was that their true mission? Most importantly, did they view him as a security risk? Well, they could screw themselves.

"You're right," he said. "When I interrogate her, I'll find out what she knows – about all of our businesses."

"That is not sufficient," said Maria. "We must go further. I must conduct the interrogation. I am well versed in the art, especially with women. She will tell me everything."

"But first," Juan said quietly, "we need to find her."

Webb nodded as if considering – they'd backed him into a corner. There was only one answer if he were to retain any control over the situation. Hell, whatever he said, those two would be out combing the island. Better if he stayed close to them. So he looked into the two pairs of black eyes and nodded.

"Yes, we need to find her. Quickly. She may take off again."

"You accept my offer?"

"It is a generous offer," Webb said. "I accept. I must go with you, of course. I know Sophie and her tricks."

Maria started to say something but stopped, Juan's eyes on her.

"What you say makes sense," Juan said. "The three of us will search, beginning with those buildings we saw on the screen."

"You're certain you can find them?" Webb asked.

"Yes," Juan said. "We will not simply follow the trail from the road. That is what the Coxon people will expect. That is constraining ourselves to their ground, their home territory. Who knows what they will have waiting for us? We will follow the mountain contour. That way we will soon locate the houses, and can approach from the direction we choose, not from a predetermined trail."

Webb nodded. Made sense.

Maria stirred. "After we have her, I will take charge of the interrogation."

Which served Webb just fine. He nodded and she smiled, a dangerous smile, just like Juan's.

Webb wondered whether part of their plan was to cut his throat out there in the bush. He figured they had no reason to, since he was a known associate of Matazos. Still, he looked forward to being done with all these people.

He sat back in his chair. Allowed himself a sip of his scotch, and reflected. It was a win-win situation. Let them do the dirty work. Pissed as he was, he didn't relish beating Sophie to a pulp for names and places. Or ruining her gorgeous legs with a blow torch. But he needed to remain in control during the questioning. The last thing he wanted was for these three to learn something about him that was none of their concern.

"That's okay with me," he said. "But I must be present."

"You have the stomach for this?" asked Maria.

"It's okay," said Matazos, playing the peacemaker.

Maria shrugged. "As you wish. But you will remain behind her, silent, and out of her vision. She must not know you are there."

Webb nodded. He'd stop Maria if she started asking stuff that was out of bounds.

Juan asked casually, "The interrogation is, how do you say, 'terminal?'"

"By the time I am finished," Maria hissed, "she will not *want* to live. Her ability to speak will remain, but the rest of her will be ruined beyond repair."

CHAPTER 32

Drake walked home in the dark after his meeting with Santiago, frustrated that the judge still did not take the threat seriously enough to leave the island. Well, the judge was in charge.

Drake shook his head. Maybe he took life too seriously, attempting to mold events to his end. Perhaps he'd seen too much combat, where if you didn't take everything seriously, you'd end up in a body bag. He hoped Santiago's bodyguards knew their profession.

In his cottage, emotions in turmoil, Drake called Graham Walters. The policeman was still in his office and answered on the first ring.

"Heard you got company," Walters said.

"Man and a woman, like your contact at the airport described. Latinos – lean and mean. The woman visited me while I was buffing up CAPRICE at the pier in St. Thomas. Her partner stayed back in the shadows. They choppered to the island this evening. I saw them enter the Matazos compound. So here we are with Matazos, Webb, and two assassins."

"What's the judge think? He must have been in threatening situations before."

Drake let out a frustrated breath. "He agrees they may be after him, but he won't consider leaving the island."

"I'll bet his guards are licking their chops over the idea of a little action."

"Yep."

"On my side, Frank Ames, my man at the airport, got a couple of fuzzy pictures that match the file photos the Colombian police finally sent me. Ames said they just had carry-on luggage, which means they'll need arms."

"Matazos will help them," Drake said. "He and his guards probably have a small armory."

"Yeah. I'll copy the Colombian police file and it'll be at the charter office on St. Thomas, in their safe, as usual."

"Anything I should know about right now?" Drake asked. "Maybe a description of their tactics, what weapons they prefer?"

"They're versatile – served as enforcers, assassins, and escorted a couple of high-risk drug shipments. Nothing in the file about tactics or weapon preferences. I'd guess small arms and knives."

"Right. Maybe a stun grenade for intrusion into the judge's house?"

"Could be. Do you need backup?"

"We could sure use a special forces team."

"I hear you. They'd come from Puerto Rico or Florida. Take two days to run the paperwork for permission."

"Too long," Drake said, feeling frustrated. "I get the feeling they want to be in and out. Spend tonight and tomorrow on recon, and attack tomorrow night or dawn the next day. Then leave."

"I'll start the ball rolling anyway – we might get lucky. Also, I'll alert the boys in my shop and give the Coast Guard a heads up. We can move fast if the shit hits the fan."

They hung up. Drake opened his safe. Considered what weapons he'd carry on his next recon to Matazos' compound. After a moment's thought, he decided who he could call on to help him out.

CHAPTER 33

"We should depart now," Juan said in his quiet voice. He and Maria rose, eyes on Webb.

To hell with it, Webb thought as he stood up. Dinner can wait. It was evening, fully dark outside.

He followed them to the front door, curious as to what gear they would take. But out they went, Juan lifting his hand in a good-bye to Matazos, who looked after them with hooded eyes. Damn it! Webb thought. Everyone was suspicious of everyone else. Maybe Juan and Maria trusted each other. Or not. The front-yard guard watched them pass through the gate.

"Don't you want a machete?" Webb asked Juan as the three of them crossed the road and entered the bush on the other side.

"No," Juan said, turning on a flashlight with just enough illumination to see the next five feet of brush. "We disturb nothing, leave no trace. You follow me. Maria will come last. We are your eyes and ears. We must remain silent. Cough very quietly if you must say something and we will stop and get close. Then we talk in a whisper."

"How about I tap your shoulder?" Webb asked as they turned east on a faint animal track he would have passed unnoticed. These guys might just be as good as they said they were.

Juan gave him a look. "Never, ever touch me."

"Or me," echoed Maria.

Webb had partnered with lots of paranoid people, but these two took the cake. He left about ten feet of space between himself and Juan, not wanting to bump into the man if he suddenly stopped. He noticed the sheath knife at Juan's waist. Reached down and touched his own, which he'd worn during his search of these woods. Wondered for a moment why Juan didn't let him guide them to where he'd been earlier that day.

Pride, he figured. The guy wanted to spin the yarn that he was king of the trackers. Gringos had pride, but nothing compared to the Latinos, at least the men. Everyone was super touchy. 'Don't ever touch me.' Christ, he sounded like a little kid.

But the man moved like a cat, guiding his feet to miss all the twigs. Something Webb found impossible to do. They were impossible to see in the darkening evening light, often turning off his flashlight. Juan moved like a ghost. Creepy.

So did Maria. He glanced back once, met her hard obsidian eyes for a split second, glittering from her own flashlight's dull illumination, and returned his gaze to the front. Yeah, she moved like a cat as well. Not like him and his buddies out hunting in the Florida woods. They bantered and joked every foot of the way. Of course, they got real quiet when they were actually hunting. Not even a burp or fart. Maybe the assassins considered getting to the target house was a walk through enemy territory. Probably did. Okay, let's live and learn a little.

He settled down, tried to watch for sticks, and maybe didn't step on quite as many. But the light was bad, only snatches from one or the other flashlights. He didn't know if there'd be a bright moon that night. Hell, its light wouldn't help anyway, because of the brush cover over the tracks.

He kept his mouth shut and followed the slinking figure of Juan. Shortened the distance to six feet for better visibility of the path and branches that could swat his face. He focused like hell so he could stop if Juan stopped. Didn't want to test what would happen if he *did* touch the guy.

After forty minutes Juan led them off the deer track, through the bush, and onto the track that Webb had followed several hours previously.

Webb pointed to the branch he'd placed as a marker. Juan nodded. Maria paused ten paces back, looking into the woods where they'd come from. Webb got the jitters with those two being so uptight. Damn, they were in the US of A. No narco cops or federales, or whatever were hunting them. Why act like that?

Juan came close, gestured at Maria, and she joined them. "Food," he said. "Do you smell it?"

Webb nodded. Maria as well.

Webb whispered, "There are dogs down the hill."

"You both stay here," Juan said. "Move apart and off this path. Sit. Remain alert. I will return from downhill."

Webb worked his way uphill and sat, watching Juan edge down toward where the smells were coming from. Felt for a breeze against his cheek, his neck. But the air was still. He reached out in front and to the sides, touched branches, attempting to memorize the foliage between himself and the path, twenty feet distant.

Time stretched out. He almost nodded off twice in the darkness. Kept himself from swatting the mosquitos – just brushed them away silently. It was much like sitting in a duck blind, trying to remain alert. Except he was too hot instead of too cold, and had no booze and junk food to while away the time.

He heard a low sound, like a whistle turned into a whisper. Heard it again. Then his whispered name. Good. Juan had returned and wanted to talk.

They gathered as before, heads close.

"I got to the houses. There are four. One large, and the others smaller. One of the small ones is a kitchen, with cooking smells. The others were dark, and I think they were sleeping houses. People talked, but I could not see them or hear their words. I felt the dogs' presence, heard them a little, but never saw them. To move closer would have brought them out, I am sure."

"Did you see Sophie?"

"No. I saw no one," Juan said with impatience. "Only heard."

"What now?" Maria asked.

"We move west a little and then downhill to intersect their trail to the road. We remain alert to other houses along the way that do not show up in the satellite photos of Google Earth."

Webb looked around. There was absolutely nothing to see. Just black. As if reading his mind, Juan spoke.

"I will take the lead. *Señor* Webb, you will hold my belt. Maria will hold yours. I do not want to risk using even the low-beam visibility of our flashlights."

Juan led the way with confidence. They found the path and moved silently. At the intersection with the blacktop road, they had another conference.

"Now we know what is here," Juan whispered. "I believe this is the place where you will find Sophie. There are no smells from other houses, no lights, no voices or dogs. That was the only home out there. It is close to the town, and a logical place. You, *señor*, come tomorrow morning, not too early, but before lunch time. Sophie will go into town with others, but she may return alone. Lay in ambush at this path. Stay low so others miss you. Look for Sophie."

Which all sounded dandy to Webb, except that she might well not walk the path alone. What if she was escorted? What if she didn't leave the house that day at all? Somehow those appeared to be dumb questions, so he whispered his assent.

CHAPTER 34

Sophie was pleased with her morning the following day. George and Michael had escorted her to the store on their way to the boatyard, and there she had helped John, who seemed more of an uncle than a boss.

Mostly, she spent time with the women who came to shop. It was a small-town atmosphere, where everyone knew everyone else, and they chatted and traded island news. Along the way, Sophie got a feel for their buying patterns, which was important when deciding what to stock and what to special order.

Business was brisk, and Sophie began to sort out who was who, and to learn names. Some women were more open than others, but she understood that people shared their personality in layers and she determined to wait before she formed any opinions. She was thankful she could talk with Maren about such things.

Now, as she walked up the road with Michael in the growing heat of the late morning, she looked forward to lunch with Maren. For once, Sophie had tidbits of news for her host – little things like a child's new tooth and also the big news of a new pregnancy.

Michael was a quiet person, Sophie discovered, but alone with him and asking questions about boat building, she succeeded in putting him at ease. When she asked him about future his plans, he responded easily.

"I may go somewhere for school, or I may join the Navy for a few years, but this island is my home. I guess I'll take over the boatyard when Dad retires, but I hope that's a long way off. He has a lot of boatbuilding in his head – it'll take me lots more years to learn. Boatbuilding looks simple, but to make a boat that is strong and behaves well in the sea, with the mast and sail and rudder all in balance, is not easy."

They had reached the path to the Coxon home. Sophie turned to Michael.

"I can go from here," she said. She was grateful for the Coxon men's thoughtfulness, but a little chagrinned that they felt she had to be protected quite so much. After all, if she met Cliff on the street, she could just outrun him and duck into the bar, the store, or the boatyard. He wouldn't dare do anything with witnesses present. She was pleased when Michael smiled down at her.

"Okay, Miss Sophie. You just send someone to get me if you want to go out again. I'll come."

She touched his shoulder.

"Thanks, Michael, but today I think I'll stay with your mom. Maybe I can help on one of her projects, perhaps in the garden."

Sophie entered the tree-shaded path, still harboring the morning's cool air. The path, and the home at its end, were like a delightful step backward in time and she relished an existence where she could pause and pass news back and forth, admittedly slower than with a Twitter or e-mail, but immensely full of the feelings of human contact. Information was only a part of the conversation – the sharing of emotions was just as important. Joy, anger, along with subtler feelings, all helping to forge a growing trust and intimacy among friends.

She found she was utterly alone now, as if no one else existed. Leaves rustled high overhead, causing splotches of sunlight to appear and shake and disappear on the dirt track. The smell of earth and flowers wafted to her. Little birds sang as they darted about. She looked ahead, to where the track took a turn, looping into a switchback as it ascended the mountain.

She remembered a shortcut that Jenny had shown her, a dim route, not even a deer track. A gnarled tree on her left marked the entrance, and on a whim she entered the trackless woods, happy at experiencing a mini-adventure of stepping off the tried-and-true path.

She knew all she had to do was walk straight uphill and she'd join the track again, but still, the woods around her appeared wilder and more exotic. She found her mind clear of all but that moment in time, conscious only of her physical exertion, the challenge of weaving through virgin brush.

After five minutes, she began to wonder when she'd meet the track. And after ten minutes, she stopped cold. Stood still in the woods. Looked back, forward, and all around. Everything appeared curiously the same. She shivered and a spooky scene from 'Alice in Wonderland' popped into her head. How could she be lost? Had she turned at the wrong place, mistaken that tree for another one Jenny had shown her?

She frowned. Yes, she must have turned too early and missed joining the track above, which didn't loop back that far. She faced downhill. Should she return to the original track? That was the simplest solution. But also unsatisfactory – a boring end to a delightful adventure.

The woods offered no clue as to where the Coxon home was located. She figured it was to the right of her march up the mountain, but had she already gone too far? She could be above the houses, even the tower, and if she walked to the right she could end up at the eastern tip of the island. It could take hours and hours to find her way to the house, and meanwhile the Coxons would worry. Muttering under her breath, she turned straight downhill and retraced her steps.

As she pushed branches away from her face and placed her feet carefully to avoid slipping, she got a creepy feeling that she was being watched. She paused and looked all around, through the underbrush, sometimes seeing only ten feet, other times seeing past trees and bushes for dozens of feet. Now the noises in the woods – the snaps, plops, and brushing – sounded furtive, and she felt a chill.

She was surprised that the woods through which she retraced her steps seemed untouched by her passing. No tracks appeared on the leafy ground, no broken twigs. No bread-crumb trail.

Jeeze, get a grip!

Feeling impatient with herself, she moved onward and reached the track. She stood on the familiar ground, her wistful, adventurous mood gone, replaced by a growling stomach.

She brushed a leaf off her shorts and noticed movement out of the corner of her eye. Something up the hill, where she had just walked.

Colors that didn't belong there.

She heard rustling, and was convinced a person was descending toward her through thick foliage. One of the bushes parted.

CHAPTER 35

Drake munched a ham sandwich and sipped a Heineken at a table in the shadowed interior of Pirate's Rest Bar and Grille, alone with his thoughts. Starting with that Latino couple. The assassins. They were after the judge, pure and simple. No one else on the island came close to being a potential target.

What threat could they pose against Drake and the judge's two Grupo Especial de Operaciónes guards? The assassins were among the best in the business according to Graham's intel. If it was a fight in the jungle, the assassins would win, hands down. But this was a fight on the GEO guys' fortified home turf – Drake's as well, for he had studied the defenses of the judge's compound. His conclusion was that the judge was safe from attack.

The rub was that Drake had two people to defend – the judge and Sophie. In separate locations, facing different threats. Drake could defend either with confidence, but not both at the same time. The solution was obvious – get Sophie or the judge out of harm's way. Then he'd defend the other. Divide and conquer.

The judge had refused to leave the island. How about Sophie? Could he convince her to stay in St. Thomas with Anika and her husband for a few days? Doubtful. Sophie was as stubborn as the judge. Okay, how about letting the judge stay on the island but at a hidden, defendable location?

And it came to him – the Coxon tower.

Built in the pirate days, and kept up by the Coxons through the generations as a tribute to their pirate ancestor who settled the island with his cutthroat crew. Drake ate the last of his sandwich, gulped the last of his beer. Slipped a five-dollar bill under the bottle and waved to Daniel on his way out.

Daniel's eyes widened – he seemed surprised at the smile and the look of determination that replaced Drake's reticent manner a half hour previously. 'A man on a mission,' Drake's first sergeant had always said when Drake came up with an idea of how to defend a position against superior enemy numbers. Now, he was definitely a man on a mission as he aimed for the judge's compound, remaining in the bush in the hope of staying out of sight of Matazos' guards and the assassins, who may be out on the prowl.

The judge was in a corner of the manicured backyard of his compound, leaning over a raised box that held his precious herbs. As he rose to greet Drake, he looked like a Spanish peasant, dressed in baggy black pants, a loose white shirt, and wide-brimmed hat. They shook hands, and the judge looked at Drake with dark, curious eyes. Neither man spoke for a second, the air empty except for the chirp of a bird, the muted thump of Atlantic swells against the rocks below.

The judge finally smiled and gestured to his herbs. He poked the soil gently in three places.

"Yes," he said, brushing black bits of dirt from his finger, "the bed is a little dry, just as my herbs prefer."

Drake knew the drill. A little chatter before getting down to business, what Graham called 'the social shit,' but a cherished ritual for the judge. He came from an old and aristocratic family in Spain. Very formal.

"Rosemary, thyme, sage, and – my favorite – oregano, grow here and are quite happy." The judge grinned. "You have tasted these many times in the food my cook and my guard prepare."

He wiped his hands on a rag, replaced it on a hook attached to the herb box, and gestured toward the shaded patio. They sat at a table, and the inside guard set glasses of ice tea at their places. He withdrew toward the house where he had a view of the backyard, the doors, and the man he protected.

They sipped their tea and after a while the judge broke the silence.

"I imagine you find my little garden fascinating, Richard."

Drake gave him a look. The judge continued, his expression sly.

"Maybe you will even start your own little garden." Then he smiled. "Fine. I know you have your tasks to do, and you are not here to chat about gardening. I suspect I know the subject, and I admit that I have prattled about herbs simply to delay our conversation."

"We have to discuss your security," Drake said. "I've thought about the pair from Colombia and about all the people here on the North Side. We both know who these residents are and what their backgrounds are, thanks to research by various enforcement agencies."

The judge sighed. "And I stand out as the only rational target. I agree, as I have said before."

"Really?"

"Yes, but I am not at all enthusiastic about leaving the island. It would be giving in to terrorism. My whole career, my whole being, is focused on the abolishment of that scourge from the world."

"Similar to a modern-day mission to rid the Caribbean of pirates," Drake said quietly, suddenly appreciating the breadth of the judges' goal. "It was considered impossible at the time, but the navies of the day kept at it."

"As did your early Navy against the pirates operating in the Mediterranean – out of the city of Tripoli and other ports in the North of Africa."

Drake nodded, giving the judge the opportunity to move to the next step, and thankfully, he did.

"I know you have something in mind. And that you always come with a solution to whatever problem arises."

Drake grinned at the compliment.

"Thanks, Judge Santiago. What I'm thinking is that you and your security detail would enjoy a day or two of vacation in a delightful watch tower, complete with cannons, just above the Coxon home."

"Built by the original pirate – John Coxon?"

"Yes," said Drake, admiring the judge's memory.

"I think that is a reasonable idea. When do you suggest we move?"

"Immediately."

"All right. No surprise there," the judge said wryly.

Drake continued, "I've checked with the Coxons and they have spruced the place up, added a comfortable bed with mosquito net, and a few other furnishings for you and your guards."

The judge shook his head.

"You are one of a kind, Richard, you know that?"

Asked as a question, but from the twinkle in his eye, delivered as praise.

"Thanks, Judge Santiago – for your compliment, and for agreeing."

Drake left the judge and walked to the Coxons' to confirm the visit. Getting the judge to agree to move to the safety of the tower was a major victory. Let Matazos and his assassins try their best – the judge was safe.

Drake smiled. This was going to be a good day.

CHAPTER 36

Hardly believing his luck, Webb leaped from the cover of the bushes and pounced on Sophie, wrapping her in a bear hug. His momentum and the downward slope of the mountain carried them forward and he landed on top of the squirming bitch.

She struck out at him, all elbows and fingernails, but he straddled her, rose to a kneeling position and smacked her hard three times across the face. She coughed and sucked air, her eyes vacant. He sat back. Looked both ways. They were completely alone.

He pulled off his shirt, the same one he'd worn last time, and ripped it down the middle. He twisted one of the halves into a rope then leaned close to her.

"Sophie, you little bitch, if you even breathe too loud, I'll kill you. Understand?"

Her eyes looked daggers at him. She opened her mouth, and before she could say anything, he pressed the twisted shirt across her parted lips and pressed hard.

"Now, sit up, nice and easy."

He levered himself off and kneeled in the dirt, all the while keeping her positioned in front of him with the shirt tight across her mouth.

As he rose from his knees he lost his balance on the rough ground and reached a hand down to steady himself. His shirt dropped from her mouth. Sophie screeched like a banshee and kneed him in the groin. Pain shot through his balls and he bellowed in rage.

She spun away and began to run. He thrust with his thick legs and caught her in two lightning-quick strides. Tripped her onto the dirt.

He stood above her, gasping for breath from the exertion, the pain in his nuts, the pulled stitches in his feet.

Amazingly, she sprang to her feet, hefted a heavy stick with a sharp root protruding at its base, and swung!

Webb raised a protective arm. The stick landed hard. He twisted his hand around, aiming to grab the stick, but she withdrew, the root scraping his palm.

She crouched for a second, got her bearings, and ran toward the houses. The uneven surface of the path slowed her, and Webb lunged. His arms encircled her ankles and she went down with a thud. They rolled and separated.

She squirmed sideways and kicked his face. He blocked the blow but lost valuable time. She rose to all fours. With his breath coming in labored gasps, his feet on fire, he knew this was his last chance.

She turned, threw a handful of dirt in his face. Desperately, he shook his head, cleared his vision. Webb rose to his feet, she tried to as well, but he pushed her hard. She fell and he kicked her in the ribs, squatted and turned her onto her back. Slapped her hard across the face, already mottled red from his previous blows. Her arms went limp.

He straddled her for several breaths, and then stood, grasping the front of her shirt to keep control. Her eyes looked dazed and she rose to her feet without a further fight.

He turned, looking for the half of his shirt he'd used as a gag.

She hit him! With the flats of both hands against his ears. He saw stars, felt his knees weaken. *Damned that hurt.*

But Webb held fast. Again, his football training. She wiggled like a fish on a line. But she was hooked.

He had no energy to hit her again. He dragged her to the torn cloth that had been his shirt, stooped while holding her tight. He roughly turned her around and gagged her.

Conscious of the thropping ache in his groin, he almost struck her, but remembered in time that she needed to be in good enough shape to walk back to Matazos. He turned her to face him. She looked awful. Welts rose on her cheeks and forehead. Snot drained from her nose and tears streamed from both eyes. Her expression was pure hate, lathered with fear.

Just how he liked it.

He wondered if he should fashion a leash, because she was a fast runner, and with his wounded feet she could out distance him in a heartbeat. But the other half of his shirt was too short, her clothing was totally too skimpy, and damned if he was taking off his pants.

He slapped her bruised face again. Not too hard, but enough to get her attention. She stared away, into the woods.

"Don't even think about escaping," he said. "One step and I'll pull you down and beat the crap out of you. Walk where I point you, nice and easy. I'll be one step behind. Don't worry about where we're going. Just listen and obey."

She squared her shoulders. After a while, she nodded once.

Miraculously, her blouse was still tucked in. What the hell. He turned her and un-tucked the back of the blouse. Grasped the tail as a make-shift leash, and aimed her off the track and into the bush, up the mountain. It would give him that extra edge of security.

Webb maneuvered her west, along the deer tracks. At the road, he listened then looked both ways and forced her to run across with him, into the opposite woods. They kept under cover all the way to Matazos' compound, then, as before, carefully sprinted across the road.

The journey took two hours, his feet and groin in constant pain. As Webb passed the two outside guards, all he wanted to do was stash Sophie and put himself behind an ice-cold beer.

They entered the great room, where Matazos and the Colombian assassins sat around a table. They looked thick as thieves, and Webb wished to holy hell he wasn't tangled up with them. He kept his thoughts to himself. Looked at Matazos.

"I got her."

"Along the path?" Maria asked.

"Yes," Webb said, looking at her and Juan, "The one you showed me."

There was an awkward silence.

"Thanks," Webb said to Juan. He was sure he could have found the path, but, well, yeah, maybe he never would have. "Thanks a lot."

Maria gave the slightest smile, which could have meant anything.

Juan seemed to appreciate the gesture. "*De nada*," he said with his soft voice.

Matazos rose, smooth and only mildly interested in Webb's capture of Sophie, as if Webb had just announced he'd brought home pizza for dinner. Matazos came close and examined her.

"You have beaten her?" he asked.

Webb shrugged. He didn't answer stupid questions.

"Will you take her to your boat?" Matazos asked, his tone hopeful.

"Rather stay here for a little while," Webb answered, his throat parched, feet and balls throbbing. "Ask her some questions. Overnight, no longer."

"Okay," said Matazos. "I have just the place. It's very private."

CHAPTER 37

Drake arrived at the Coxons' tower to find the family and Jenny's entire gang sweeping, carrying, and scrubbing. He came across George, lugging a propane stove.

"I thought you said the toweer was already clean," Drake said.

"Well, yeah, enough for Jenny and her friends as their clubhouse. But we need to buff it up a little for the judge."

"And make sure he can get a hot meal," Maren said, taking the stove and placing it on a long table, beside a selection of pots, pans and utensils. Jenny and her friends began arranging canned goods and gallon jugs of water along the adjacent wall.

The cooking arrangements were similar to those he'd seen in island houses on the South Side, including his cottage. Nothing fancy, but sufficient for making delicious meals. Kerosene lanterns were placed strategically, ready for use. Four ventilation ports high in the walls were open for fresh air, their heavy wooden security plugs set on the floor.

Everyone was working hard, and all were smiling and chatting. But one person was missing.

"Where's Sophie?" Drake asked Maren as she dusted a pot.

"Oh, she's at John's store, helping with the morning business. She'll be back, any time now."

Michael Coxon stepped close, ashen faced.

"Mother, I took her to the head of our track before noon. I thought she was at home!"

Maren dropped her pot, crashing loudly onto the floor. Everyone turned.

"She never arrived," Maren said, her voice quivering.

George put a hand on Michael's shoulder.

"Go, son – check the path. Let's hope she is there and safe. If you don't find her, search the woods, but not too long. Come back in half an hour, whatever happens."

Michael nodded, ran through the small clearing that surrounded the tower, and disappeared into the bush. George and Drake stood close. Drake's gut tightened, his thoughts raced.

Jenny approached and asked her father, "Can we help search?"

"No," said George kindly, "there may be bad people involved in this. You all must stay here, together."

"I'll go take a look," Drake said, his tone casual. "Maybe she twisted her ankle in the woods."

But his expression, as he made eye contact with George, said he feared something far more serious than a sprained ankle.

"I know," George said quietly, no doubt remembering what Drake had told him about the branch and piece of fabric. And the implication.

Drake melted into the bush soon found the deer track, across which the branch had been placed. He moved quickly, all senses alert. He thought through the possibilities. Two hours had passed since Michael had left her at the track to the Coxons'. Had she simply gone off the trail and gotten lost or injured, or was it something more sinister?

Drake feared the latter, and he looked for tell-tale marks of Webb's passing. To make out footprints on the leafy path was impossible, and he saw no other signs indicating anyone had been that way recently.

When he reached the tree branch that was set across the path, he stooped. It appeared untouched. Perhaps good news, indicating Webb had not returned. But probably no news at all, because the man either did not come this way, or if he did, he must have decided that Drake or a Coxon had already noticed the branch, and to remove it was to confirm his return.

Ranging through the woods, he found no lost or injured Sophie. Yet he was sure she had come this way, perhaps only to explore, or maybe to take a shortcut across the loop in the trail between the road and the Coxon home.

Drake paused and uttered a silent prayer. He had a sinking feeling that Webb had somehow found her and taken her to a place where he could interrogate her at his leisure. Maybe his boat, but more likely Matazos' compound. There, he was in control of the situation – privacy and time were his.

What was Webb's plan after the interrogation? To murder her? Yes, Drake reluctantly admitted. With Sophie dead, he was safe. With her alive, there was always the chance of her revealing damning secrets to a competitor or the law, including the murder she had witnessed.

Drake realized the track from the road to the Coxons' was just two hundred yards down the mountain, so between this place and the track could have been the area of contact. He was tempted to search that area, but decided not to. He was now convinced Webb had taken Sophie to Matazos' place.

The man might be interrogating her right now, torturing answers from her. Or maybe that was done, and Sophie was already dead. Drake put that last thought out of his head. Useless to dwell on the worst case. Better to assume she was still alive. First, he must find out where she was. Next stop was Matazos' compound.

Drake decided to use the deer track. He traveled west, crossed the road, and continued under cover. At one point, he thought he saw light furrows in the path. Perhaps Webb had taken Sophie this way and she had briefly struggled, maybe attempted to escape.

When he neared Matazos' compound, he lowered himself onto his belly and crept to the edge of the bush. He looked across the road to the walls, the palm trees in the front yard, and the house compound.

All was quiet. One guard patrolled the front yard, walking among the trees and tropical plants, his sidearm evident.

The front door opened and shut, the sound clear, but the door was obscured by plants. There were muttered words. Male and female voices. A woman emerged, passed through the gate, and turned east on the road.

A woman he recognized.

CHAPTER 38

Sophie stood in Matazos' great room, along with Cliff, Jorgue Matazos, the woman she'd passed on the pier at Red Bay Marina in St. Thomas, and, next to her, a man she had never met.

Cliff acted hale and hearty, as if he'd just brought home a prize swordfish. God, what a prick he was. He slurped a cold beer.

Jorgue stood between Cliff and the mystery couple, his eyes darting from one person to the next. That Cliff brought her there was apparently a surprise to Jorgue, who must have thought Cliff would kill her in the woods or take her right to sea in his sport fisher and dump her over the side with an anchor tied around her ankles.

The couple – Jorgue had called them 'Juan' and 'Maria' – stood close to each other. They were balanced in posture, as if poised to engage in combat. Their gimlet eyes surveyed her as if she were a fish and they were wondering how to gut and fillet her for dinner. They looked by far the most dangerous people in the room. In fact, the most dangerous people she had ever met, and that included a Colombian drug lord.

What had Richard said about those two? Oh yeah, that the woman 'could have been jet lagged.' But now she looked fully alert. Damn.

For the tenth time, Sophie mentally kicked herself for not following Richard's security suggestions to the letter. But here she was, right in the middle of something that went way beyond herself and Cliff. That son of a bitch Cliff had wrapped her into whatever plan Matazos and the couple were hatching.

Sophie looked at Cliff. She had noticed his shortness of breath and how he favored his feet.

Once, along the deer track to Matazos' house, she tried to escape. But he was too quick. Kept his grip on her shirt tail, pulled her close, and grabbed her by the neck.

Jorgue pointed down a hall that seemed to lead to a kitchen, judging by clattering sounds of pots and pans. Cliff placed his empty beer glass on a table. Jorgue led the way into the hall, and Cliff pushed Sophie to follow. A door closed at the far end, and kitchen noises stopped.

The couple followed behind, and skin prickled at the back of Sophie's neck. She prayed they were coming along out of curiosity. She did not want to be part of anything connected with those two.

They all entered a bedroom. No luggage or personal effects were apparent, meaning the room was not occupied by one of Jorgue's current guests. He stooped, and pulled a rug away from a trap door. The hinged door measured about four by five feet. He lifted it, revealing a cellar.

Jorgue motioned for the couple to flip a switch on the bedroom wall, and a light illuminated the cellar, served by a set of wooden stairs. They descended into the cellar. It was the same size as the bedroom, plenty large enough for all of them. The floors and walls were poured concrete and a concrete bench extended all around. A wooden table and four chairs sat in the center of the room. Lighting came from two bare bulbs.

She sure needed a bathroom, but figured she could hold out. She didn't want this bunch to think she was scared. What that gained her she wasn't exactly sure, but she hated to be a wuss.

"My hurricane cellar," Jorgue said, to no one in particular.

Sophie looked for ventilation, and noticed a six-inch diameter pipe protruding from the ceiling in a corner of the cellar. Maybe it was a fresh air vent, maybe not.

Oddly, the woman addressed Sophie, and hearing her tone, Sophie broke out in a cold sweat.

"You will have water and food and a chance to use a bucket for your personal needs. I will visit you every few hours. Stand back from the stairs when I come down, with your hands in plain sight.

If you cause problems, your stay will become very uncomfortable. Do you understand?"

Sophie nodded, making brief eye contact just to show she was not completely cowed. But hell, against three bruisers and this hellcat, what could she say?

Cliff approached her, breathed hard, leered into her eyes and backhanded her. She stumbled backward onto one of the side benches and sat heavily. She immediately rose and looked straight at him.

He approached, very close, and said, "I will return to ask you questions about my business. Do you understand?"

Reluctantly, she nodded. Her mouth was dry as a desert. Just in case she had to say something, she sucked and moved her tongue to make saliva.

"Good," he said. "I want you to spend your spare time down here thinking of everything you overheard about my business since the day we met, including names and places."

He waited a beat, then continued. "I know what you're thinking. What if you give me incomplete information? Right, Sophie?"

"If you say so," she replied, amazed at how calm her voice sounded.

"I do say so. In the end you will talk. You will tell me everything. If you 'forget' something, Maria will cut you. First, she will cut off all your toes. Then your fingers. Your nose..."

"I get the idea."

Out of the corner of her eye, Sophie saw Maria smiling wickedly at her. Then they all left, the vile woman turned for a final evil look before she ascended into the bedroom above. They lowered the wooden door and it dropped in place with a solid thump.

No food, no water, stale air. But at least she had all her body parts firmly attached. She took a deep breath. Decided her best plan for survival was to draw out the questioning. Take her time with each answer. Ask clarifying questions. It wasn't much of a plan, but every minute counted. *Richard will discover I am gone and he will come.* Of that she was sure.

But will he come in time?

CHAPTER 39

Drake recognized the woman leaving Matazos' compound as Amy, Matazos' cook. He remained prone and hidden as she walked the paved road east and disappeared from sight. No doubt she was going home for her break.

She came from England and was married to James Maitland, a general handyman for the people who lived on the North Side. They were a quiet couple, doting on their baby boy, and didn't gossip about their employers.

Drake often shared a beer with James at Pirates Rest Bar and Grille, but knew Amy only enough to say hi. He decided to meet her at her cottage on the hill above the bay.

Drake backed up from behind the low bush, stood, and began making his way southward to town along the maze of deer tracks. He made good time, and arrived in town as Amy said her good-byes to a lady in front of John's store. He approached her and smiled.

"Hi Amy."

"Oh, hi, she said, pausing in the shade. "You must be Richard. James talks about you. Says you were in the service. The Marines, I think." She had an easy way about her, and like everyone in the islands, was never in a hurry.

He grinned. "Yep, that's me. Only Marine on the island, unless there's one among the folks living on the North Side." He stepped closer and lowered his voice. "Amy, I need to talk with you for a minute."

She tilted her head and lifted her eyes to his.

"Amy, you may also know I look out for the security of Judge Santiago."

"Oh sure. None of us are supposed to know, I guess."

"It's okay. We're all family."

She nodded, eyes curious.

"Well, also, you know about Sophie."

She smiled mischievously. "Richard, we're going to be standing here all afternoon if you keep asking me about stuff that everyone on the island already knows, inside and out. James says you're the strong and silent type, that you don't say much besides 'hi' until about three beers."

"I guess that's about right. But this needs talking about. I think Sophie is in trouble. I have to know if she's in Mr. Matazos' house."

Her eyes widened. "Oh my gosh. Mr. Matazos has a man visiting, and a young couple just arrived as well. Then this afternoon there was a new person. But I was in the kitchen and they were in the great room. I never saw the person, or heard her – or him - speak."

"That's very helpful. Do you think this person could be Sophie?"

Amy reached out and grasped Drake's arm tight. Her eyes blinked, and she whispered, "She didn't say anything, as I mentioned, but it could have been your Sophie. My word! I thought the person was another of his guests. Whoever it was, they put him or her in a guest room. But you know what? That room has a cellar. Could they have put her down there? Why do that?"

Drake felt his gut tighten. Amy didn't fully confirm his suspicions, but who else could it have been but Sophie?

Damn. With an effort, he kept his expression relaxed.

"You think it's Sophie?" she asked, her voice breaking.

"I'm afraid so. And we need to rescue her quickly."

"What can we do, Richard? Mr. Matazos has guards."

"I'll find a way."

She took a step back, staring up at his face.

Drake drew a calming breath. His mind was in combat mode. Tactical plan, risk evaluation, logistics. An idea began to form.

"Amy, I may need your help. Wait in your house, okay? I'll send word if I need you."

"But he expects me back in an hour to make dinner."

"Okay, you're right. You need to return and make dinner. But you must appear normal. Don't hurry, don't go looking for Sophie."

"All right. I'll act normal."

He gave her a reassuring pat on the shoulder. "Don't worry."

Drake sprinted to his cottage, unlocked the safe, and selected a pistol, a knife, a night vision scope, and a stun grenade. Next, he visited the boatyard. George was there, as was Jenny, a little way off, drinking a cola. They must have completed preparations at the tower.

"Hi Richard," George said. "You just run a hundred-yard dash or something?"

"Sophie's being held at Matazos' house."

George's eyes turned cold.

"How can I help?"

"I have an idea. I want your thoughts, but that's all."

"Just my thoughts?" Coxon made a fist. "How about a strong right hand?"

Drake shook his head. "No. Rescuing Sophie is my problem. I brought her here. She's my responsibility."

Coxon scowled. "No, my good friend. You can't get rid of me. I'll stick to you 'til we get her out safe and sound. Think man! On this island we all pitch in."

Drake raised his hands in mock surrender. "Okay, okay. I guess I hoped you'd say that."

As they talked, Jenny edged close. She looked at her father with tears in her eyes. "Sophie?"

George put a hand on her shoulder. "Only for a little while, sweetie. We're going to get her. Real soon."

She put an arm around his waist and blinked. After a moment she said, "You know, Daddy, me and my friends, we can help, too."

George looked at Drake and gave a ghost of a smile.

Drake said to Jenny, "Jenny, go and get your friends and come back here. Your dad will tell you what to do."

Jenny was about to run, but Drake put a hand on her shoulder. "Jenny, Miss Sophie is in Mr. Matazos' house. You and your friends must stay away from that house. Just bring your friends here. Don't do anything else, okay?"

She nodded and left at a dead run.

"What next?" asked George.

Drake explained.

CHAPTER 40

The cook, Amy, cleared the dinner dishes from Webb's place at the table. The others had already finished and now lit cigarettes.

"You can go home," Matazos told her. "Clean up tomorrow."

"Yes, Mr. Matazos."

He gave her a look, then shrugged and turned to the others – Webb, Juan, and Maria. The front door opened and closed and Webb felt the tension rise.

Maybe Matazos was at last going to explain what the hell was going on. Webb sure as shit didn't have a clue, and from the looks coming from the two killers, they didn't either. Matazos stubbed out his cigarette and looked around the table. His gaze stopped at Webb.

"Cliff, *mi amigo*, I have things to share with you."

Webb looked at his host, glanced at the couple, and then back at Matazos.

"Okay," he said, remembering with a feeling of dread that Matazos only called him '*mi amigo*' when something unpleasant was to follow. Such as fouled up plans with a potential loss of a few million dollars.

"You see," Matazos said, gesturing to the stone-faced couple. "My associates are here on the island to perform a delicate task. It is the culmination of months of careful planning."

Webb waited for him to say more. But Matazos turned silent and looked at him expectantly. Webb said what he had to say.

"I will be pleased to help in any way I can."

The couple relaxed minutely. Matazos a lot. Especially after he got up and drank a slug of scotch. His face was red when he again sat down.

"Your task," Matazos said, "is to create a diversion. This diversion will be in the form of a big fire aboard your sport fisher. It is a rental, correct?"

"Yeah."

"Good," Matazos said, and he gestured magnanimously. "You can report it as an accident. The rental company will collect insurance, and everyone will be happy. Or, you can reimburse the rental company directly, because our next project will net you enough to buy twenty sport fishers – if I am to believe what you tell me."

That got Webb's interest. The guy was offering something in return, not simply claiming the destruction of an expensive boat as repayment of the favor of ratting on Sophie's whereabouts. Matazos had been on the fence about partnering on that multi-million-dollar project, probably with the present negotiation in mind.

Webb said, "Does this mean you're formally in on the deal?"

"Yes."

They shook hands across the table.

"Now, about the fire," said Matazos. "With your okay, my men will place explosives and gasoline on board the boat."

"That's fine," Webb said.

Matazos nodded to a guard standing in the shadows near the front door. The man left, presumably to load the explosives. Matazos reached into a pocket and produced a white plastic device the size and shape of small cell phone. He opened a cover that revealed a single red button, and extended a telescoping antenna. He handed the device to Webb.

"You're holding a remote detonator," Matazos said. "It will work perfectly for lighting the fire. The button glows in the dark for night work."

"Which is what we'll be doing," Webb said almost to himself as he turned the device over in his hands, "since it seems tonight is the night."

"You are perceptive," said Matazos. "I must caution you to remain silent about all you have seen and heard on this island. As you Americans love to say, 'the shit will hit the fan' for the next ten years or so. It's high profile."

Webb was about to speak, but Matazos held up a hand.

"No. Do not guess. Do not say anything aloud. It's that sensitive."

Webb shrugged. He could have blustered a little, just for shits and grins, but Rule One in this business was 'do not piss off your associates.' Most were very sensitive about everything from their stature to their annual income.

"Good," Matazos continued, "You will leave from my pier after midnight and take your sport fisher to the mouth of the harbor on the south side of the island. There, you will shift the engines to neutral and get into the dinghy tied to your transom. You will drive a safe distance away in the dinghy, say two hundred yards, and press the button. Any closer and you're in danger from the fireball. Beyond three hundred yards and there is no reception for the signal."

"Sounds fine to me," Webb said. He closed the cover of the remote, collapsed the antenna, and put the device in his pocket.

CHAPTER 41

As his partner to rescue Sophie, Drake selected the only other man on the island with the kind of experience he needed – Jimmy Franklin. He was a medic, but he'd seen combat in Afghanistan and he often joined Drake in target practice on the west end of the island. He could have chosen George, but he needed him for another assignment.

Night had fallen an hour earlier. The sky was clear and only a sliver of the moon shone. The hiss of waves against the coast joined the chatter of insects as the only sounds in the night – not too loud but plenty useful to cover the noise of the odd scrape as they approached Matazos' compound.

As they walked the road toward the compound, Drake reviewed the situation. He was now convinced the two assassins were after the judge, probably to kidnap him, but if that didn't work, to kill him. Either way, their goal was to create leverage toward the release of the ex-president, who the judge was now trying. Sophie was an afterthought. Catching her was a high priority for Webb, but not Matazos and the assassins.

At least that was Drake's theory. He also felt that tonight was the night for the kidnapping attempt, after everyone went to sleep. Perhaps in the next hour.

When Matazos' compound lay directly ahead, Drake and Franklin turned right and entered the gap between the adjacent privacy walls of Matazos' and his neighbor's compounds.

About twenty feet separated the walls, an area in which grew field grass, bushes, and a lone palm tree. The terrain sloped

171

downward toward Matazos' compound. Halfway along the gap, Drake stood with his back to the wall of the adjoining compound and found he had an excellent view over the wall, into Matazos' backyard.

He looked through his night vision scope, seeing green-tinged images of the wall, a bit of the front yard, even a glimpse of the guard walking his beat, then disappearing around the front of the house. Patrolling the backyard another guard paced, looking left and right around the pool area, inside the pool house windows, and continueing across a manicured lawn, past lush plantings of bushes, flowers, and trees, forming a miniature jungle. He also checked the gate at the side of the wall facing the sea.

Drake carefully scanned the top of the wall and noted with satisfaction there were no intruder alarms, barbed wire, or glass shards.

However, three cameras hung from the eves of the house, covering side and backyards. He assumed they were low-light capable, and he'd have to keep behind cover as much as possible. He handed the scope to Franklin, who made his own visual reconnaissance.

"Back guard has a set route," whispered Franklin.

"Yeah, along the side of the house, along the back, the other side, then a wide circuit through the plants out past the pool."

"About four minutes?"

"Yep."

"We go over the wall, sneak in a rear window, and rescue Sophie?"

"I haven't gotten quite that far," Drake said. "Except that only I go in. You stay on watch. Signal me if there's a problem."

"A little owl hoot, maybe?"

"Should do."

They stood in silence as Drake weighed his options, which boiled down to, like Franklin said, entering through a window along the kitchen wing of the house, and preferably ending up in the bedroom where the cellar door was located.

Then open the trap door, untie Sophie, and sneak her out.

Outwitting two trained assassins, Matazos, Webb, and who knew how many additional guards in the house.

The odds did not look good.

But he did have one ace up his sleeve.

CHAPTER 42

Cliff followed Juan and Maria to the cellar. He watched Juan open the trap door, smelled the musty air drifting up. Maria stood at the head of the stairs and looked down, a cruel smile twisting her lips.

"I see you, Sophie," she said. "Show me your hands. Good, now position a chair at the foot of the stairs. No, further away, with its back to the stairs. Now sit in the chair."

Sophie did as ordered and Maria descended the stairs, holding a black leather satchel and a coil of thin climbing rope. She tied Sophie to the chair with the rope, then placed another chair in front of Sophie. She dragged the table close and set her satchel on top.

Webb glanced at Juan, who was grinning as if in anticipation. Sure, Webb thought, they hadn't killed anyone in over a day. Getting a little restless.

Juan tapped his shoulder and pointed with his head. Webb tip-toed down the stairs and sat, five feet behind Sophie.

Maria zipped open her satchel and laid out three knives, their shimmering blades of different widths, all appearing razor sharp and all well within Sophie's range of vision.

Sophie gasped, shut her eyes for a moment, then stared at Maria and said with only a slight tremble, "What do you want?"

Webb felt a feral excitement in his loins, and in that moment understood the needs of Juan and Maria, why they both bubbled with enjoyment at the unfolding drama. Webb swallowed, his mouth suddenly dry, nervous as always prior to drawing first blood, and anxious to learn new techniques.

He smelled a trace of cigarette smoke and glanced up the stairs. Juan was sitting, a cigarette hanging from his lips, as relaxed as if he were watching the preliminaries of a soccer game.

Maria, made a slight adjustment in the perfect parallel alignment of her knives and faced Sophie. Her voice sounded hollow in the concrete confines of the cellar. "You are facing your final hours of life. There will be no rescue. This is it for you. Do you understand?"

Sophie felt like vomiting. But there was nothing there, not even water. She looked into the black eyes of her tormentor and nodded. She didn't trust herself to speak. Besides, her mouth was too dry.

Maria continued, "Good. For you the problem is not whether you can save your life, but rather how you will experience the least amount of pain. And with the most of your body parts still attached to your body, which is now very pretty, but soon will be horrible to see. Now, pay attention. I'm going to ask you questions..."

Sophie moved her tongue around in her mouth, producing enough saliva to speak. "Where's Cliff? He said he was going to ask the questions."

"Oh, too bad. He cannot be here."

"I'm not talking to you," said Sophie. "How do I know who you are? How do I know Cliff gave you permission to know the answers to your questions? I want to see Cliff. I'll answer his questions."

Webb signaled to Maria to come to him so he could arrange to ask the questions. If Sophie refused to answer, the woman could have her way. Hell, how could Maria even know what to ask?

Besides, he was surprised to find he was getting cold feet. He didn't hate Sophie. Sure, he was pissed at her and wanted to beat her up, but cut off her toes and fingers and ears? That was sick. No, let him ask the questions, slap her around, and get the answers. Then leave her on the boat. Nice and clean.

But Maria didn't even give him eye contact. Instead, she stared straight at Sophie.

"No," said Maria. "You will answer my questions. We will start with your name."

"No."

Juan moved quickly down the stairs, stubbed out his cigarette on the floor, and punched Sophie hard in the stomach. She gasped and bent forward against her rope bonds. Cliff winced.

Maria calmly selected a thin-bladed knife. She turned to Sophie, who wheezed, attempting to catch her breath.

"You see," said Maria, "we are serious."

Footsteps sounded from above the cellar. Maria paused, knife in hand. Webb turned to see a wide-eyed Matazos surge into the room and stand at the top of the cellar steps.

"¡Vengan – pronto!" he shouted.

He quickly led Webb, Juan, and Maria to a small room adjacent to the great room. They crowded in, behind a burly security guard seated at a console, viewing a row of video monitors.

Matazos pointed at the center monitor. "There!"

Webb looked at what appeared to be a low-light enhanced view of the closed iron grille gate to the compound, beyond which swirled a growing crowd of agitated people. There was no audio, but he needed none, because their combined shouts easily reached the cramped security room. He couldn't make out what they were saying, and he saw no signs that might indicate why they were demonstrating.

"Why are all those people out there?" Webb asked "Everyone on the island seems to be pissed at you, Jorgue. What the hell?"

"I have no idea!" Matazos tapped the guard on the shoulder and ordered, "Contact the guard out front. Ask if he can make sense out of what they are saying – if it's a chant of some kind. Alert the back guard. Tell him to make a quick circuit and then come to the front to stand with the guard there."

"Yes, sir," the guard at the console said, and urgently spoke by walkie-talkie to the two outside guards.

Webb saw the back guard's movements on other screens, and then the two guards standing together in front of the house about ten feet inside the compound walls.

One spoke into his walkie-talkie. "What do you want us to do?"

"Hold," said the inside guard, who turned to Matazos.

"Tell them to stand where they are," Matazos said angrily, "and not to pull out their pistols. Just stay there."

The guard transmitted his orders.

Matazos, regained his composure, leaned forward, focusing on the center screen, which now showed about thirty people – men, women, and kids.

"Peasant scum," he said under his breath, "exactly the same as in my country." He frowned at the screen. "I'm looking for their leader, someone who everyone turns to for encouragement and guidance. Usually, this person stands in the second rank, safe from immediate police action, but within the crowd to communicate his desires."

"I don't see anyone like that," Webb said.

"Nor do I." Matazos stroked his chin, his expression thoughtful. "No, these people have been given instructions to come to my home and make noise."

He pounded a fist into his opposite palm. "That's it." Again, he tapped the shoulder of the guard operating the console. "Contact both sentries. Tell one to remain in front, visible to the crowd. Order the other sentry to examine the sides and the back of the house, looking for signs of intrusion."

Matazos turned to Juan and Maria. "Are you familiar with handling this type of situation, of crowd control?"

Juan shrugged. "For people such as these, the sound of a single gunshot will cause them to disburse."

Matazos scowled and spoke to the guard at the console. "These people are a diversion. An attempt to focus our attention on the front gate. The only reason could be the woman in the cellar. Someone has come for her." He leaned close to the guard. "Wake up the other two guards. Tell them to patrol *inside* the house."

Webb edged toward the door of the security room. The others crowded around the center monitor and its view of the gate and the milling, screaming islanders.

"Those people aren't coming in here," Matazos declared. "They're not going to rob or murder anyone. It has to be a distraction."

"My God," exclaimed Webb. "You're right – they want Sophie."

"Yes, no doubt," said Matazos. "I am sure they will not attack, not with all those women and children. But their appearance is inconvenient for our plan. We must get rid of them."

Webb's mind raced. What the hell was going on? How did they find out Sophie was here? In spite of what Matazos said, were they planning to storm the house to rescue her? Against armed guards? No, no way. Maybe it was a diversion. Sure, to give someone else the opportunity to sneak in and grab her. Who could be fool enough to do that, in a walled compound with armed guards?

That damned Marine!

If he got in, or if the mob got in, they'd set her free. He'd never get his hands on her again. She'd be out there on her own, a loose cannon, a constant danger to him from what she could tell his competitors or the law. That was unacceptable.

He rushed down the hall and down the stairs into the hurricane cellar. He pulled out his sheath knife. Sophie turned her head, eyes wide with fright.

Webb realized she believed he was planning to kill her. He paused, thought for a second. Well, why not? Because then there'd be a body in Metazos' house when the mob stormed in. Worse, he would never know whether she had passed on any of the secrets she had overheard, or, especially, whether she had actually witnessed the interrogation in the garage.

He smiled, looked her in the eye, and spoke quietly. "Sophie, it's okay. I'm here to take you out of this place. You'll be okay. We just need to get out, quickly."

She gave him a disbelieving look. He couldn't blame her, considering all that had happened, especially the fight in the bush. He let her consider her options – Maria or him? It took her only three seconds. Bright girl.

She motioned with her head and asked, "What's that noise?"

"Nothing. Some sort of yelling between neighbors after a party. They're out in the street making a scene."

He sliced her bonds and helped her stand.

She rubbed circulation into her arms. "I don't know if I can run. My legs are all pins and needles. The rope was too tight. Cut off circulation."

He grabbed her arm and aimed her up the steps. "No choice, sweetie. We get out in the next minute or Matazos' two killers will be back and chop you into hamburger."

She made a gagging sound, and worked her legs just fine. Almost beat him up the stairs.

"Where now?" she asked.

"Great room," he said, guiding her down the hall, glancing at the open door to the guard room thirty feet away, sweating bullets one of those guys would see them. Or one of the inside guards. Shit! They'd be dressed and on the prowl any second.

CHAPTER 43

Drake waited for the guard to move to the opposite side of the backyard, then scaled the compound wall and landed lightly on the other side. He sprinted across the lawn to a palm tree, its trunk and numerous bushes shielding him from the guard. He prayed no one spotted him on a security monitor.

The night remained quiet, except for the usual insect sounds and a dog barking briefly in the next compound.

From out in the front of the house came a yell, then another, joined by a dozen more. The sounds increased in volume, drowning out the insects. He thought he heard George's whoop amid the din. The dog next door growled and barked like crazy.

There was the guard, nearly invisible in his dark blue uniform, standing on the grass to the right of the pool and its flagstone patio. Frozen, obviously puzzled by all the racket coming from the front of the house. He put his walkie-talkie to his ear, nodded, spoke quickly, and ran straight toward Drake.

Drake dropped flat on the ground and squirmed beneath a nearby bush. He pressed his cheek flat against the grass. Felt the vibrations of the guard's pounding boots. The guard passed within three feet, made a hasty circuit of the entire yard, then sprinted toward the noise.

So, the diversion worked. The racket up front was amazingly loud in the tropical night, encouraging Drake as he slipped across the yard. He skirted the pool and the pool house and hid behind a wide bush. Checked for guards or dogs between him and the windows of the right side of the house – the side that included the kitchen and the room with the hurricane cellar. All appeared clear.

A door slammed shut. Drake slid his head to the side of the bush, to see.

Two shadowy figures paused outside French doors at the back of Matazos' house and stepped onto the pool patio. Light from inside the house illuminated their faces. It was Sophie, and Webb was gripping her arm!

As they crossed the patio, Webb shouted above the din, "I'm taking you to a safe place until this ruckus blows over. Now, run!"

Sophie obeyed, and they dashed away from the house, Webb still holding onto her.

"You're hurting my arm."

"Just keep moving, around the side of the pool house."

Change of plan, Drake thought.

Lights at the base of a dozen plants and trees dimly illuminated a surly Webb and frightened Sophie. They moved beyond the patio toward him, weaving around foliage, their steps barely audible above the shouting in front of the house.

Webb continued to goad Sophie forward, directing her past the pool house, onto the lawn that sloped toward the sea. Drake drew his pistol. He let them get twenty feet onto the grass, past his hiding place and, hopefully, out of sight of the security cameras. He leaped at Webb from behind, gripped Webb's left shoulder and pressed the muzzle of his pistol against his muscular neck.

Webb froze.

"Let her go," Drake whispered fiercely.

Muttering a curse, Webb released his grip. Sophie backed away from him, massaging her arm.

"Richard!" she said, her voice sounding desperate.

"Stay there," Drake said. "Don't get anywhere near him."

She took another step away.

To Webb, Drake ordered, "Down on your knees."

Webb did so, slowly, twisting his head from side to side, as if searching for an opportunity to turn the tables.

A shout came from the front of the house.

A command?

Pounding feet crossed the patio, toward where they stood.

Drake cold-cocked Webb with the butt of his pistol. Webb slumped and Drake grabbed Sophie's hand. He aimed toward the east wall, where Franklin waited.

A guard appeared out of the gloom. He was big, and breathed evenly, despite his fifty-yard dash from the front. Before Drake could turn and raise his pistol, the guard pressed his own pistol against Drake's back.

The guard snarled, "Drop your weapon."

Drake paused for a split second. The pistol pressed harder.

"Or I shoot," the guard hissed. "Makes no difference to me."

Drake dropped his pistol.

At the guard's command, he lay on the ground and let the man attach plastic ties around his wrists and ankles. Drake kept alert for any opportunity to escape, but none came his way. The man was a pro. So were their communications – spotting him in the back yard on the security camera, ordering the guard in front to make the intercept. Definitely pros.

The guard scooped up Drake's pistol and turned to Sophie.

"Do not think of escape," he hissed. "The compound walls are high, and your man is tied up firmly" He gestured at the crumpled Webb. "I will pick up the *señor* and we will together support him and take him inside."

The Guard glared down at Drake.

"I will be back soon. I hope it is with orders to kill you."

Webb groaned as the guard lifted him. Sophie gave Drake a tense look, but moved close to Webb and assisted the guard, lugging the unconscious man toward the house. Drake lay helpless on the grass as the others entered the house.

One thing he knew for sure – that guard was not going to leave him alone for long, even if he was tied up.

CHAPTER 44

Webb blinked his eyes. He seemed to be propped up in a chair, in the great room of the island house. But hadn't he just left here with Sophie?

The lighting was way too bright. He lifted one arm to shade his eyes. He blinked and made out the fuzzy figures of a man and a woman. Sophie and one of Matazos' guards.

"Do you remember anything?" asked the man.

"Give me a glass of water," Webb said, mostly to gain time to gather his wits. Damn, someone must have knocked him out. He touched the back of his head. His hand came away wet with blood.

Sophie handed him a glass of water. He craved whiskey, but something told him now was not the time. The room slowly came into focus.

She looked scared shitless, mouth open, glazed eyes. Well, that made sense. Probably torture time again. Too bad. Shame to cut that cute face.

Unfortunately, she wasn't the only one in danger. Webb realized he was up to his ass in some kind of international vendetta. Could get wasted by half a dozen pissed-off international police agencies. Or the cartel, if it went south. He gritted his teeth against the throbbing pain in his head. He carefully placed his hands on the armrests of the chair and levered himself to his feet.

"Careful, *señor*," the guard said, "you have taken a hard blow."

Webb waved him away. He heard shouting from outside the house. Oh, right, he'd tried to take Sophie to safety from the mob of islanders. He staggered over to the security room, crowded with

Matazos, the couple, and the seated guard with his eyes on the monitors. The air was ripe with body odor and tension. The yelling from outside sounded louder than he remembered.

All eyes turned to him.

"What the hell?" screamed Matazos. "I thought you had gone down the hall to take a piss, and you show up on my security monitor." He gestured at the screen and stepped close to Webb. "You took the girl and were going to run away? To where? Why?"

Webb tried to ignore the shrieking pain in his head and refused to cower. "I needed to keep her from that mob. I have a sat phone and the remote trigger, and I knew your people had loaded the explosives. I planned to lay off the harbor and wait for your call, just as we planned. But a man, a local, jumped me before I could get my woman to the boat."

"*¡Jesús, María y José!*" Matazos screamed in his face.

His spit sprayed Webb's cheeks. Webb kept mum, his expression neutral. Respectful. Matazos was at his limit. The pressure of the job had gotten to him more than he'd let on, and the mob tipped him over the edge.

Webb raised his hands slowly, his voice calm. "You are right, *mi amigo*, and I am wrong. I should have had faith in your security team holding off the mob. The peasants will tire and leave, eventually."

"Yes," said Matazos.

Webb nodded. His head wound throbbed. What a mess.

"Well," declared Matazos, "what is done is done."

He looked at the guard who had retrieved Webb and Sophie. Now standing with a firm grip on the girl's arm.

"You have done your job well."

The guard stood at attention, eyes straight ahead. Nodded slightly at the compliment. Waited for further orders.

"Who was this man?" Matazos asked.

"The Americano," the guard said. "I think he is the man named Richard Drake."

Matazos and Webb looked at each other and grinned.

"I'll have his balls," Webb vowed.

Matazos gestured impatiently. "Do that on your own time, my friend."

To the outside guard he said. "Bring him to me. We will ask him questions later. For now, I want him out of the action."

"And the woman?" the guard asked.

"Leave her here. You go out and bring back that gringo."

"If he attempts to escape?"

"Alive. I want him alive. None of your 'escape' bullshit."

The guard left at a run. Webb gripped Sophie's arm, again noticed her glazed eyes, and he silently chuckled. Good, the bitch was suffering. Worrying about the knives.

The guard at the console pointed at the center monitor.

"Look! The people out front are leaving."

Webb and Matazos watched, puzzled expressions on their faces. In seconds, the road in front of the compound emptied of people. Not a soul.

"They're all gone," the guard breathed in astonishment.

"Yeah," said Matazos, his face grim.

Webb waited. This was a moment of truth. Matazos was under unbelievable pressure. Had to pull the rabbit out of the hat. With the entire island awake and roaming about, the element of surprise was gone. The guy could turn paranoid. It happened a year ago in Colombia. Shot four men in cold blood. Webb shivered in the small room.

CHAPTER 45

Drake lay perfectly still on the grass, listening. He sorted through the sounds. Night insects. Waves crashing in the distance. An owl's call.

The shouting from in front had stopped.

An owl's call?

Drake hooted in response, which didn't sound just right because he couldn't cup his hands over his mouth. But he heard the response, felt approaching footsteps.

"Cavalry's here," a man whispered.

Franklin. He must have been waiting under cover, because he hooted almost as soon at the French door closed. Now he knelt and sliced Drake's bonds. Helped Drake to his feet.

"They can see us," Drake said urgently.

"No shit, *amigo*. I vote we get the hell out of Dodge City."

"Roger that," Drake said, casting a glance at the house and thankful the French doors remained firmly closed with no one visible inside.

They sprinted to the wall. Franklin gave him a leg up, and Drake reached back to help his friend roll up and over the top.

Drake pointed toward the road in front of the compound and began running, Franklin at his side. "We find George, sort things out."

They worked their way through the fringes of the crowd, careful to keep foliage between themselves and the house and its low-light cameras.

They found George and he clapped them both on the shoulder.

But his huge grin disappeared as he looked around. "Where's Sophie?"

CHAPTER 46

Webb's head still throbbed worse than a son of a bitch, but his mind was clear. He stood silently in the security room. Watched and listened, confident of an opportunity arising that he could turn to his advantage.

The guard at the console stared intently at the row of video monitors that showed the two guards again on silent patrol. The killer who called himself Juan glared at Matazos and broke the silence, his voice grim.

"You have failed in your part of the job."

Matazos looked at him without emotion, certainly not fear. Their eyes locked. Maria cleared her throat, looking from one to the other.

"Do we wait until tomorrow night?" she asked.

Juan broke eye contact, ostensibly to light a cigarette.

"I could complete my interrogation," she said hopefully.

Neither man spoke. Webb had seen this kind of impasse before, always with nasty incriminations, often ending with knives and bullets. He wondered what the hell Matazos could do in response to Juan's challenge.

For sure, the two killers had orders to murder everyone with knowledge of the job if things went wrong. Webb glanced at Juan, his face a blank, eyes hard. With the element of surprise lost, Juan must be wondering if the time had come to cut his losses and get off the island.

Even though only Matazos knew the incriminating details, Webb felt certain that Juan and Maria planned to murder everyone

– Matazos, himself, Sophie, and the guards. Then they would steal the sport fisher, speed to a British island and take the next plane out. Hell, maybe that was their plan anyway – kill the judge and the witnesses, then escape in the boat. They sure couldn't get a helo at this time of night.

The silence seemed to last a year, though in reality only a minute may have passed. Too bad that asshole Drake had ambushed him. He should have been at sea and rid of these scumbags. But he wasn't. He kept his face relaxed, and remembered to breathe.

Sophie slumped against the wall.

"Stand up," commanded Webb.

She spoke softly. "Sorry, Cliff. I haven't eaten or had any water since breakfast."

He stared. Yeah, she looked wasted. Face a sickly shade of gray, eyes dull. He started to speak, but Matazos gestured for silence.

"Don't you see?" he announced. "That distraction from the island mob is to our advantage! The island is now off balance. Their routine is ruined for the night. Who will notice movement? Anything out of the ordinary? The islanders tried to rescue the woman and failed. They may try something else, but not tonight. Tonight, they will sleep."

"Until there's a boat fire just outside the harbor?" ventured Webb.

"Exactly," said Matazos, scanning their faces.

Juan dropped his sullen mask, apparently drawn in by Matazos' logic. He stubbed out his cigarette.

Webb had to admire Matazos. He'd turned the situation around. Made it look easy.

Matazos faced the killers. "Juan and Maria, you will carry out your silent work with your usual efficiency. You know the layout, the challenges. We have spoken in great detail. I am confident in your success."

Juan's eyes flashed, obviously not appreciating flattery from this man.

Webb smiled inwardly. This was a break in the ranks. First, because Juan openly displayed that he did not care for Matazos assuming authority over him, and second – most important – because he made his feelings known.

Men like Juan did not form their own opinions. They took on the opinions of those to whom they were loyal. In this case, Juan's Colombian cartel boss. The boss didn't trust Matazos, and he had shared his opinions with Juan. Matazos was on the outs, pure and simple. He was a man not worthy of Juan's respect.

This knowledge presented Webb with an opportunity to rid himself of this middle man, Matazos. Not now, but over weeks and months, Webb must ally himself with the boss, eventually moving up in the hierarchy, and replacing Matazos. More power and more wealth for Webb. At last, a good reason for this whole damned trip.

Webb was pulled from his thoughts by a look from Matazos.

"You will take Sophie and Drake in your boat."

Webb nodded, happy to get rid of the pair of them in the fire.

The French door slammed open. The backyard guard appeared, sweaty, eyes wild. He looked at Matazos. "He is gone, *señor*! I have searched the entire backyard. No one is there."

Webb swore, but Matazos raised a silencing hand.

"No, do not worry. He was but a side show."

Matazos looked at the couple, who nodded grimly.

"We are ready," said Juan.

Matazos faced Webb. "You know what to do. Take Sophie with you. Interrogate her if you want. I don't care. But you must be in front of the harbor in…"

"Thirty minutes from now, precisely," said Juan.

"Good," said Matazos. "Go. Do your job. Do not wait for a phone call." He gave Webb a quick *abrazo*. "We will meet again soon, my friend, in Colombia. And we will toast the events of this night."

CHAPTER 47

Drake winced at the disappointment in George's eyes. He knew the blame fell on him, their leader in the failed rescue attempt. The islanders had trusted his judgment, his expertise. But he refused to mope, remembering an oft-quoted saying in Marine Recon – 'No plan survives contact with the enemy.'

"It's a setback, George," Drake admitted. "She's still held by Cliff in Matazos' house. But I know what I need to do." He turned to Franklin. "You did fine back there. Saved me, got me out of a bad fix. Give me your pistol. Take my night scope and join the judge's guys at the tower. Keep your eyes open for two Latinos, a man and a woman. They were born and raised in the jungle and are world-class guerillas."

Franklin nodded, they transferred gear, and Franklin trotted down the darkened road.

George put a hand on Drake's shoulder.

"I know you will succeed," George said in his grave way. "But before you go, I must give you a message from the judge. He said he is completely safe in the tower with his men. Michael is there as well. They are well armed, and they have night vision scopes. The guards are fully trained." He raised a hand. "I know, they are not Marines."

Drake shrugged. "They'll do."

"That was the judge's point. Plus, he knew we might not be able to rescue Sophie on the first try. He gave me a message for you – 'Tell Richard we do not want him here with us. Not until Sophie is safe.' That's what he said."

Drake was at a loss for words. The judge took the decision into his own hands, relieved him of his responsibility and allowing him to focus on saving Sophie.

The judge's decision was not rash, Drake knew. The man wasn't foolish. He appreciated the importance of remaining free and unharmed. Not only for his personal safety but for the integrity of the process of law, which he represented. He must appreciate that the assassins' mission was in shambles. They had lost the element of surprise, which put the judge's security team on alert and burned up operational time. Dawn was not far off.

More to the judge's advantage, he had moved from his compound. The assassins had doubtless studied the layout there, as well as the logical positions of guards, and the best routes of approach and withdrawal. All this was useless to them now.

The judge's new location could take many daylight hours to discover and the ground was unfamiliar. Also, wheels were in motion to alert and mobilize police and Coast Guard, and possibly special forces.

Still, they might dare an attack, especially because such a move was unexpected. Maybe Webb had discovered the tower, maybe they had reconnoitered and monitored the judge's move. Drake shook his head – too many 'what-ifs'.

The main point was that, even if they did attack, the judge was well protected and not in need of Drake.

George was looking at him, giving him time to think.

Drake nodded at last. "He's one hell of a man."

"You are as well," said George. "Now go and rescue our girl."

Drake turned to go, but paused. "What about you and your family?"

"We've thought of that. I've suggested that everyone treat tonight as a hurricane. All doors and windows will be buttoned tight with storm shutters in place. I'm sure the island will be entirely safe – even safer than the usual nightly security against wandering Jumbees."

"And Jenny?"

"You ask too many questions. She is with friends in town. The kids just look at it as a sleepover. She and her little gang are with one of the fishermen's families. They are safe. Now, go."

"Thanks," Drake said.

Drake thought through his plan as he retraced his steps toward Matazos' compound. One house short, he turned right, toward the sea, and worked his way through foliage to where he knew Matazos had a pier.

Drake figured there was a good chance that Webb was headed to his sport fisher with Sophie, aiming to leave the island and avoid being part of the assassination or kidnapping. That could indicate that his presence on the island just happened to coincide with the arrival of the assassins. Webb was therefore not a part of their plan. He had gotten what he came for, and was on his way, leaving Matazos and the assassins to carry out their plan or withdraw.

Based on this thinking, Drake carefully traced his way along the coast, between prickly bushes and treacherous rocks. Ahead, behind a point of land came the rumble of diesels.

He quickened his pace. Slipped on a rock and caught himself then turned a bend.

Ten feet below and fifty feet distant lay Matazos' pier, alongside which was the sport fisher, rocking in the Atlantic swells. Sophie must be tied up inside.

In the darkness, a figure moved about the deck, stepped onto the pier and released lines forward and aft.

Drake maneuvered close, sticking to shadows, conscious of the dim light of the moon. He squatted behind a bush just short of the pier.

The person on the pier – Webb, for sure – walked aft, glanced up, turned, and scanned land and sea. He stepped aboard the boat, now drifting about a foot from the pier, its engines idling. Ready for sea. He gripped the rails of the ladder to the flying bridge, set his foot on the first rung, and began climbing.

CHAPTER 48

The rungs of the ladder to the flying bridge stung Webb's feet, but he forced himself up, anxious to separate himself from the deadly situation brewing in Matazos' compound.

What a screwed up job. He estimated the chance of success at no more than fifty percent. The island mob, the asshole Marine, and an unbalanced Matazos. All ingredients for failure, especially Matazos. Webb could smell his panic. The guy was in danger of shitting his pants every time Juan looked at him.

The job was way over Matazos' and the two killers' heads. Obviously, their target was Judge Santiago, the only person on the island of any political importance. The guy was protected by the Marine. For sure, he had his own protection as well, all hunkered behind his compound wall with who-knew-what weaponry. Plus, they could call in reinforcements.

This was a job for which they certainly had no training, no experience. To go from jungle fighting to kidnapping or assassinating an internationally-known figure was a huge jump. This wasn't the jungle. There were no clever ways to draw out your enemy or ambush him. And they had no back-up. They didn't even outnumber the enemy.

If they succeeded in getting Santiago, the international community would go berserk. Within twenty-four hours, law enforcement would have identified Juan and Maria and linked them to their boss, the Colombian drug lord. They already knew who Matazos was. They'd form a permanent team to track these guys, for years if necessary.

Matazos and the others would become like lepers. No one would want anything to do with them, fearing they'd get contaminated with their blame. Like World War II Nazis on the run. The Israelis never gave up. Same here. Webb sweated at the thought of being hunted down. He wasn't a praying man, but now he uttered a silent prayer that the assassination – or kidnapping, or whatever the hell they were up to – never got going.

Webb padded across the deck of the flying bridge to the control console. He settled in at the controls, took the weight off his feet, and scanned his instruments. Fuel about three quarters, engine RPMs at idle, oil pressure looked fine. He listened to the rumble of the twin MAN V12s. They would do the job tonight and get him the hell away from shit-hole St. Mark.

Oh yeah, he'd promised Matazos a distraction. Webb felt for the lump of the actuator in his pocket. Swallowed hard. Decided he was not yet free of Matazos. Best to go through with the fire, then make for Tortola in the dinghy. He'd get there early in the morning, about when the airport opened. Have his Learjet 70 hop over from St. Thomas and pick him up, then fly back to the States.

He looked down at the pier to be sure all the lines were loose. Checked out to sea for boat traffic. Didn't see a single light this early in the morning, with dawn an hour off.

CHAPTER 49

Drake waited as Webb took his seat up on the flying bridge. When Webb faced toward the sea and put the engines in gear, Drake sprinted the final few yards along the rocky shore, across the pier, and lightly stepped onto the gently rolling sport fisher. He heard nothing beyond the rumble of the engines, and felt their vibration through the soles of his boots as the sport fisher left the pier behind.

He edged past an arrangement of cans on the afterdeck, lashed in place. Was tempted to look closely, but he moved on. First things first. He edged forward and peered through a window into the cabin. Interior lighting was sufficient for him to see the galley, tables, and bench seating. A passageway led from the main compartment to the front of the boat.

He saw no one inside, and he considered. The assassins or one of Matazos' guards could be crouched below the window or behind the galley bar in ambush. He decided that was unlikely because he'd kept to the shadows and was only visible during his five-second sprint to the boat. Possibly someone was asleep in a stateroom up forward. He hoped to hell Sophie was that someone – not Matazos or the couple.

Drake opened the door and slid inside. Shut the door. It was much quieter here and he listened. Heard Webb shifting his position directly overhead on the flying bridge. Heard the hum of air conditioning. The slosh of water against the hull as the boat left the pier behind and headed into the open sea.

He crept forward, through the cabin toward the passageway, methodically noting the seats, the navigational instruments, the galley, and a head. All looked to be in order, no sign of struggle. Or of other men aboard – no weapons or clothing lying about. Which made sense. Matazos, his guards, and the couple had their own mission, to assassinate or kidnap Santiago.

He entered the passageway, eased down four stairs. The boat's motion became rougher, the engines louder, and then she heeled to port in a sharp turn. Webb had entered the deep ocean, increased speed, and was headed west.

The first door was to his left. He braced himself against the boat's motion, gripped his pistol in his right hand, chest high, and turned the knob. He gently pushed the door inward.

A stateroom, unoccupied. He stepped to the other side of the passageway and opened the door.

CHAPTER 50

Webb throttled up to ten, then fifteen knots and made a wide left turn toward the western end of the island. Back aft, behind the sport fisher, the dingy tagged along, centered in the flat part of the sport fisher's wake, just visible in the nearly moonless night.

He checked his watch – twenty-one minutes to go. Cutting it close. He boosted the speed to twenty knots. He thought of Sophie, tied up on a bunk in the master stateroom. Very comfortable, probably wondering just a little why she was tied up instead of whipping him up a little breadkase. After all, he had told her they were escaping.

Well, because there was no food in the fridge for one thing. Also, it would be awkward to explain that she had to remain on the boat during the fire. He chuckled. Man, he sure dodged the rocks and shoals on this deal.

He rounded the west end of St. Mark and pointed the bow due east. The seas were marginally calmer with the island blocking the long Atlantic swells.

He remembered that the Caribbean islands were peppered with rocks near the surface, capable of gutting the hull of a boat. They may or may be visible at low tide, but with the nearly five-foot draft of the sport fisher, they posed a real danger. As he had learned recently the hard way. He needed the chart, which was below at the navigation station.

Webb set the autopilot to four knots with an easterly heading, rose, and hobbled aft to the ladder. He hummed a little tune as he descended to the aft deck, in spite of the stinging pain in his feet, because he knew he'd won. He'd be back home for dinner.

On deck, he walked forward and entered the cabin, bracing himself against the boat's motion. He stepped toward the navigation station, to the left of the door.

Noticed movement out of the corner of his eye.

CHAPTER 51

Drake found Sophie inside the second stateroom, gagged and tied to the bed. He quickly entered, and shut and locked the door.

Sophie stared at him with wide eyes. He put a finger to his lips for silence, sat on the bed, and untied her gag, which looked like half of a man's sweaty undershirt.

She lay still, tears flowing down her cheeks, as he cut her bonds at wrists and ankles. She had been tied with thin line, leaving angry red welts.

She sat up and he hugged her tight and whispered, "You're safe now."

She wept, swallowed, and hugged him back for a minute, then kissed his cheek. "Where is he?"

"On the flying bridge, driving the boat. I think we're headed around the west tip of the island."

She massaged her wrists, sobbed once, and looked him in the eye. "I thought I was going to die." She shuddered. "I *knew* I was going to die. Cliff had that look – he was unstoppable. At first, he let me believe he had forgiven me for running away, and was going to let me go, but when he got me on the boat he turned mean. He said I knew too much, demanded to know who I'd told about what I had learned at the estate.

"He never asked about the torture and murder of that man in the garage. I think he hoped I had not seen it. After he was done asking questions, he tied me up. When I saw the door open just now, I was sure it was him coming to kill me. God, I was scared."

Drake felt her chest heaving as she gulped air, so he held her close. Slowly her breathing settled.

He found himself jumpy as hell because of the close call – if he'd missed getting aboard, Webb would have murdered her and dumped her over the side. He banished the thought.

He held her at arm's length and looked into her eyes. She appeared so vulnerable. He hated Webb for doing this to the sweet and caring woman she was. The woman who was becoming precious to him. The woman the whole island adored.

He hugged her again and drew a deep breath. Purged his mind of emotion. Prepared himself for what lay ahead – deadly combat with Webb.

Consciously, he shut his eyes and breathed, slowly, evenly. He was well aware of his surroundings, the warmth of Sophie tucked close to his chest, the slosh of the ocean against the hull, the tangy smell of diesel and mold, the vibrations from the mighty engines.

But in his mind's eye, he conjured a blackness, a void. He continued to breathe, focused on that vision, for two minutes. The pounding of his heart turned slow and regular. He was ready.

The boat's motion changed and then her speed, now down to a crawl. They must have rounded the west end of St. Mark and were now pointed east into the prevailing seas. Strange – why not continue south to St. Thomas?

The answer popped into his head. Webb was heading east because St. Thomas would soon be closed tight by a ring of security. The two assassins would make their move and get out as quickly as possible, before that ring could be established. Maybe to St. Thomas, maybe to the British Virgins, where the ring would take longer to close.

By early morning, the word would be out. Someone, probably George, would call Graham on a sat phone. Police, Coast Guard, and who knew what other outfit would lock up St. Thomas Airport, check every boat between St. Mark and St. Thomas, and descend in force upon St. Mark.

Webb was buying more time by taking the British Virgin Islands route. Get a flight out of the airport at Tortola, maybe even on his own jet, if he had one.

Drake looked at Sophie and asked quietly, "Is Cliff the only other person on board?"

She nodded, her face gaining color.

"Good," he said. "Do you know what's piled on the after deck?"

"No, it was there when we arrived from Jorgue Matazos' compound. I thought it might be supplies of some kind, and was curious. I asked Cliff, but he didn't answer. He rushed me into the cabin and said we had to leave right away."

Drake put his hands on her shoulders.

"Sophie, I've got to take care of Cliff."

"Kill him?" she asked with a shaky voice.

"Maybe."

"Whatever you do, be safe." She kissed him quickly on the lips.

"I'll be okay," he said, forcing a smile. "You stay here, even if you hear fighting. Lock the stateroom door and then lock yourself in the head. That will gain time in case he pushes me out of the way. Whatever happens, wait until you hear my voice at the stateroom door."

She glanced at the door and nodded.

Drake touched her shoulder realizing that nodding was all she could do. She had greeted him with her story. Now she needed time with people she loved and trusted – the folks on St. Mark. She'd been through too much in too little time. Her whole world was turned upside down when she arrived, but in the last day she'd looked death in the eye.

He slipped into the passageway, intending to check the pile on the after deck. There was also what looked like a portable radio with its antenna raised. That was not encouraging.

After solving those mysteries, he thought, as he worked his way along the short passageway to the main cabin, he planned to continue up to the flying bridge and deal with Webb.

But when he stepped into main cabin, he found Webb standing at the navigation station.

Webb turned, glared and took a fighting stance, fists raised.

Drake reached behind his back, grabbed the pistol tucked into his belt and aimed at Webb's gut. "Your choice," Drake drawled. "You'll never make it. I suggest you lie down on deck with your hands behind…"

In that split second, the boat struck a steep wave and jounced violently up and back. Drake lost his balance, and Webb lunged, eating up the six feet that separated them in the blink of an eye.

Webb struck hard with arms flailing. "I'll break you in half and feed you to the sharks."

Drake's pistol clattered to the deck. Drake punched a right to Webb's abdomen and a left to his chin. Drake saw a head-butt coming and whipped to the side, avoiding the deadly blow. He kicked hard into Webb's right knee and stomped on his right foot with his hiking boot. Webb wore boating shoes and swore at the pain.

There was no room to maneuver and they traded vicious punches to stomach and chest and head. Drake took a backhand to the face and felt blood streaming from his nose. One of Webb's eyes had swollen nearly shut.

Drake ended up with his back to the door to the after deck. Webb faced him.

Breathing hard, Webb backed a step and jerked open a galley drawer. Keeping his eyes on Drake, he reached in and his right hand emerged with a wicked-looking carving knife.

Drake kept his hands half-raised in front of him, ready. He focused on the knife, and moved to the port side, opposite the galley, giving himself slightly more room to maneuver or retreat out the door to the aft deck.

Webb's eyes burned. He adjusted his grip on the knife, spread his legs to absorb the roll and pitch of the vessel.

Out of the corner of his eye, Drake saw motion in the passageway. The door to the master stateroom opened furtively. Sophie slipped out, face drawn, wielding a heavy flashlight.

Drake locked eyes with Webb, goading the man to attack, forcing him to concentrate on him, to remain unaware of the movement behind in the darkened passageway. Drake risked a glance about him for a weapon to block the coming knife thrust. Nothing at hand. He swallowed hard.

Drake stepped to the right. Webb adjusted. Drake took another step right. Then back and left.

Webb mirrored each feint, never closer, never farther away. He smirked. "You're dead meat."

Drake remained silent, just inside the door to the after deck. Behind Webb, Sophie pressed herself against the passageway bulkhead, nearly invisible in the shadows. And then she edged forward, slowly raising the flashlight.

Webb tensed for the charge and opened his mouth as if to yell. But nothing came out.

Sophie stared as Webb slumped like a sack of potatoes at her feet. The flashlight shone red with blood. Her tormentor twitched once and then lay still.

"There's plenty of rope in the stateroom," she said in a surprisingly calm voice. "The thin kind that's impossible to untie."

"But leaves marks."

"Something like that."

Her eyes darted from Cliff, to the right, to the left, and back at the fallen man. Drake felt she was close to losing it. Doubtless, this was the first killer she had cold-cocked.

Drake moved close to Sophie, put his hands on her shoulders, looked into her eyes. "Sophie, you did it. You faced your fear and did what had to be done."

She sobbed once. Nodded. Tried to smile, but gave a little chuckle instead. She returned to the stateroom, came back holding out a ball of thin line. Drake found the knife on deck and cut lengths of line, each about three feet long.

Together, they knelt and pulled Webb's thick arms behind his back. Tied his wrists and then his ankles. Drake rose and found his pistol, which he stuck back in his belt. He looked at Sophie and grinned. "Thanks for saving my life."

She smiled and her eyes sparkled. "Happy to help."

"Come on, let's check back aft."

Outside, Drake found eight red-painted gas cans arranged around a central cone. On top of the cone was mounted what could only be a transmitter-detonator, its antenna extending upward. There was an indicator light on top of the device. Not illuminated, which was likely a good sign. He decided the cone was filled with explosive, easily detonated, and designed to sink the boat and trigger the gasoline, which would create a giant fireball.

"Transmitter-detonator and gasoline," Drake said, looking up at a wide-eyed Sophie. "Would you mind searching his pockets?"

"Sure. What am I looking for?"

"A plastic or metal box, about the size of a cell phone. And if you see buttons or switches, don't touch them."

She returned and handed him the remote. He'd seen such devices before, but they were painted desert-tan and about half the size.

"Is this what you use to set it off?" she asked.

"Yes." He opened the cover, saw the detonation command button, and snapped it shut. He looked at the sea and the islands beyond. They were cruising at a leisurely four or five knots, coming even with St. Mark Harbor to their left, no doubt on auto pilot. No other boats were visible. The sky remained dark, except for a hint of gray to the east.

"What?" Sophie asked.

"I'm thinking," he said as he handed the device back to her. "It looks like Webb was supposed to create a diversion with this, probably right about where we'll be in five minutes, opposite the harbor. While everyone on the island is looking at the ball of fire and wondering what to do next, those two assassins are free to kidnap or kill the judge."

"But he can't, because he's tied up."

"Maybe. Remember who he's working for."

"Matazos – another crook."

"Yep."

"So, what are you thinking?"

"Just a nasty suspicion."

"So we should leave?"

"I'm thinking that's a good idea. Follow me."

Drake strode to the stern, pulled the dinghy to the transom, and scrambled aboard. He turned and helped Sophie. Then he started the motor, released the tow line, and pointed the bow toward the harbor.

After less than a minute, he heard the crack of a pistol shot.

"Damn," said Sophie.

"I guess he found the knife. My bad. Should have thrown it overboard. And a pistol."

Drake looked back toward the sport fisher, which rolled in the swells, dead in the water. Webb must have switched the autopilot off. Didn't want to overshoot the harbor.

Webb waved the pistol.

"You made a serious mistake, Drake. You should never have tangled with me. Should have given me that bitch when I asked you politely. Now it's too late for both of you."

Drake said nothing. Kept the motor revved, gained distance between them. But too slowly, he knew.

Webb braced himself against the transom, steadied the pistol with both hands, and fired again.

CHAPTER 52

Three more pistol shots rang out, all wide, whipping harmlessly into the sea. Drake still needed to get them farther from the coming gasoline fireball, but at least they were out of pistol range. He looked over his shoulder. Strange – Webb was gone.

"Do you have the actuator?" Drake asked.

"Yes." But her smile turned to an expression of horror as she patted her pockets. "Oh God, no! It must have dropped out when I boarded the dinghy."

Before Drake could respond, Sophie pointed back at the sport fisher, her eyes wide. Drake turned. Webb stood on the after deck, armed with a rifle.

What the hell?

Webb braced himself, put the rifle to his shoulder and aimed. Drake judged the distance as being all too close for a rifle shot on land. But at sea, with both boats rocking? Maybe they had a chance.

Webb shot. Once, twice, the bullets zipped into the water on either side of the dinghy.

Another shot – the bullet slammed into the outboard motor with a metallic thunk. Smoke poured out, black and acrid. Worse, Drake smelled gasoline. He shut the motor off.

Their forward momentum faded, leaving them wallowing, defenseless, a hundred yards from the sport fisher.

"Too bad," Webb yelled, pointing the rifle at them, finger on the trigger. "I've got you sighted in. Just a little offset to the right, to allow for the breeze. Next shot will hit one of you for sure. Easy targets. But you don't have to die. There's oars in the dinghy. Come back and I'll let you both live."

"You'd kill us anyway," Drake said, casting about for options.

Maybe jump overboard and keep the dinghy between themselves and Webb? No, he'd run them over. Or he'd maneuver the sport fisher alongside and shoot them at point-blank range. Yeah, that was more likely. He'd get close, wound them. Watch them suffer. Keep shooting, drawing blood for sharks. And if the sharks didn't come, he'd finish them off with kill shots.

Should they return to the sport fisher and await an opportunity to overcome him? No, even with Sophie as an ally, Webb was too canny. There would be no opportunity.

"I won't kill you," he said, his voice clearly heard above the gentle sloshing of the boats in the morning swells. "I had a change of heart. Just give me the transmitter, I'll get in the dinghy with you, and I'll swing close to shore. You can swim in. Simple as that. See, I believe what Sophie told me. She had no reason to lie."

"But he's lying," Sophie whispered urgently. "He was going to kill me and throw me overboard. Otherwise, why would he tie me up? There's no reason for him to change his mind."

Drake nodded. He leaned down and felt around. Found the oars with their oarlocks attached. He switched seats with Sophie so he was on the center seat, she back aft. Set the oarlocks and rowed, strong and even, toward land.

"You son of a bitch!" shrieked Webb.

CHAPTER 53

Sophie slipped off the seat and sat in the clammy water in the bilge, making herself as small a target as possible. She twisted to look at Webb, certain his next shot would be aimed at her. She had an awful feeling in the pit of her stomach. There next to her was the dead motor, which he had just hit. All he had to do was raise his aim.

She looked for a moment at Drake, straining at the oars, and then back at Webb, his rifle ready, visible in the gray dawn, pointed right at her. She lowered her head to the seat, trying to hide behind the skinny motor. She shut her eyes, muttered a prayer, and drew her final breath.

But he paused. She heard a faint beeping from the sport fisher, saw a blinking red light.

"Richard, isn't that the light on top of the detonator?"

"It is," he said, pulling the oars.

"But the remote is lost, right? Did he find it? Why – ?"

"That's a five-second warning," he said, grunting with exertion. "The signal's been sent. By Matazos."

She had a split-second view of Webb his face a mask of horrified surprise. Hearing a clatter of oars, she turned to see Drake suddenly rise to his feet, and pull her up and over the side of the dinghy, capsizing the little boat in the process.

Treading water, facing her, he commanded, "Take a deep breath and stay underwater for thirty seconds. Now!"

He gulped, his eyes burrowing into hers, and dove out of sight. She followed, realizing in horrible detail what was happening. The beeping, the flashing light, meant that the pile of gas was a heartbeat away from blowing into a fireball.

She swam down to where the water pressured into her ears, then squeezed her nostrils shut and popped her ears into equilibrium. Then dove deeper, perhaps thirty feet.

Above her, the water flashed a bright, iridescent orange, remaining so for long seconds. She shut her eyes. Shuddered at the thought of being caught in that broiling heat and flame.

The orange faded out, but she stayed down. Richard said 'thirty seconds' and she planned to remain for the full duration. She suspected the very top of the water was hot, but that the energy of the blast also roiled the water.

The hot and cooler water from several feet down would mix and reach a temperature safe for a person. Was their time below sufficient for that mixing and cooling? She didn't know. She decided to surface with her arms splashing, to force the water to mix and cool.

At thirty-one seconds, she muttered a prayer and surfaced, splashed about until she was sure the water on her arms was safe. Seh looked about for Richard.

He surfaced, a shadow in the darkness.

"Sophie," he said, not too loud.

"Here," she said, and swam toward his voice.

They embraced, and she felt herself shaking from the danger – both from Cliff and from the fireball.

"Are you okay?" he asked.

"I guess so." She felt her hair and her face, moved her legs. "Yeah, everything is okay. Hard to believe we even survived that fire. It looked horrible from underwater."

"We're lucky. It could have been all explosives instead of mostly gas."

Sophie looked toward the boat, its entire aft section in ruins, the fire continuing to burn forward, fueled by the fiberglass structure and the interior outfit. The wind shifted, carrying a tart stench of the burning mix of materials.

Drake was guiding them toward shore, but the current pulled toward the west.

"Will we make it?" she asked, swimming at his side.

He was silent for a long time, then said, "We may be in the water for a while, Sophie. The current is pretty strong. If we take it slow and easy, conserve our strength, we'll be fine."

Which didn't sound completely convincing, but Sophie decided to believe him, and they swam in companionable silence. Though she was now thirsty and hungry and the water seemed colder than before. She agreed – they must keep moving to keep up their body heat, and to get closer to land.

Time seemed to drag, and their world became one of water lapping against their heads, and their methodical movement of arms and legs. They didn't talk, but she felt like they were close, sharing danger and surviving, so far.

She watched the sun rise, the clouds turn pink and orange, then white and fluffy for the new day. Funny, she'd never taken time to do that before.

She felt, rather than heard, an odd vibration in the water. She looked around, but the swells blocked her view beyond a few yards. She shut her eyes for a moment, suddenly dead tired. She'd been up for twenty-four hours, give or take, most of that in a state of terror. Kidnapped, beaten, threatened with torture and disfigurement, pushed through the underbrush, scratched by bushes and branches, tied and gagged, shot at, and witnessing a deadly fireball.

She felt it again – the vibration, a vague tickle along her legs and trunk.

Then, nothing, and then again.

"Richard…"

"Yes, I feel it. Maybe a motor."

Finally, lifted on the crest of a swell, she saw it. Richard did as well, and they both pointed. She couldn't help weeping and she didn't care, and they gave each other a hug.

It was a boat, riding over the swells.

"Help! Over here!" She yelled, and then Richard took his turn.

They rose again, saw she two people in the boat, heads up, looking over the sea, faces serious, intent.

She yelled with all her strength.

Another trough. Another crest. And there they were. Very near, bobbing in the swells, the air stinky with motor fumes. A wooden fishing boat. A man sat back aft, tending an outboard motor.

Their eyes met and his tanned, wrinkled face broke into a grin. The most beautiful grin she had ever seen.

Then Jenny popped into view at the bow of the boat, hopping up and down, waving her arms.

"Sophie! Sophie!"

And then, "Mr. Richard? Mr. Richard! Sophie!"

The boat chugged alongside, bobbing in the swells.

Sophie clung to the side of the wooden boat, strong and curved. The fisherman shut off the outboard. He clambered forward, nearly knocked off his balance by a euphoric Jenny.

"Are you okay?" he asked.

"We're fine," Richard said. "We dove underwater during the fire."

The fisherman reached down for Sophie. He gripped her upper arms and lifted her, gently and high, avoiding the rough wooden gunwale. He sat her on a seat that spanned the width of the boat, and grinned, his teeth white in the morning sun.

He turned and helped Drake aboard and guided him to sit next to Sophie. Then Jenny arrived with two blankets. The air was surprisingly cool, and the blanket felt good over Sophie's shoulders.

Sophie was vaguely aware of the boat's pitch and roll, very different from their stillness in the water. She vaguely watched their rescuer return to his seat aft and start the motor.

She looked at Richard, who smiled back, and at Jenny, facing them on the next seat forward in the boat, full of happiness and excitement.

The boat moved easily through the waves, thanks to all those graceful curves in her hull. She smiled at the thought that George and his boatyard crew had probably made it.

Sophie reached across, and held Drake's hand, and then turned to him, her voice serious. "He died, didn't he?" she asked.

"I don't see how he could have gotten off in time," Drake said thoughtfully. "Yes, he's gone. You're safe, Sophie. You can live your life."

"And stay with us!" exclaimed a beaming Jenny, who bounced up and gave Sophie a hug around the neck. "Oh, Miss Sophie, your hair is so wet!" She giggled and sat down again.

Sophie gazed at Jenny and they shared the moment, as she shared the moment with Richard. Jenny turned toward shore, her eyes on the small, quiet crowd lining the pier. They were still too far away, even for Jenny's strong voice, but she stood and waved. A few people waved back. The rest waited patiently.

Sophie soaked up the morning sun. She reached over and smoothed Richard's hair. There it was – they were both together and with friends. They'd be all right. They had won.

She kissed him on the lips, and tears stung her eyes. She let them flow. Tears of joy.

CHAPTER 54

Drake felt like he was on top of the world, sitting next to Sophie, his arm around her waist. Her kiss made it all feel real.

Cliff was nothing more than a bad memory. Drake savored the moment, though as the pier grew close, he thought of the judge, who made Sophie's rescue possible. Drake knew he must go to the judge and be with him until the assassins no longer posed a threat. Hopefully, they had never found the judge's safe place in the tower, or if they did, then were frustrated by its stout walls, defended by the judge's guards and George.

At any rate, Drake must check immediately, and he suddenly became impatient to be ashore.

Fifty feet from shore, Jenny stood tall in the bow and yelled through cupped hands, "Miss Jenny and Mr. Richard are s-a-a-a-fe."

Now Richard saw the smiles, and he knew he must be among these people. He could not run immediately, no matter the urgency. These were his family, and he found himself ready to feel their love, their energy.

The boat bumped against the pier, and dozens of elated, babbling islanders surged forward, grinning, helping Sophie and Drake onto the pier, listening to the fisherman and Jenny recount their discovery of them, swimming, being drawn to the west by the current, and scooped into the boat.

Drake became entangled in the throng, sometimes next to Sophie or Jenny or the fisherman, sometimes adrift among the other smiling folks. It brought strong memories of that time with Jenny, pulled from the sea, and he wiped a tear from his eye.

Which is when George's fourteen year-old son, Michael, appeared at the run, breathless and unsmiling.

CHAPTER 55

Drake gave Michael his full attention, not prodding, but letting him catch his breath, remarking to himself that the young man must have broken a speed record to get here. The boy was only fourteen, but wore the serious and determined face of a man.

Releasing a final deep breath, Michael said one word – "Fire."

At first, Drake and the others were puzzled. Michael was in the tower – did he mean that he saw the fire on the sport fisher from there?

"What do you mean, Michael?" Drake asked, raising his voice above the din of the puzzled crowd.

Michael swallowed hard and continued. Everyone realized he had not even heard of, much less witnessed, the boat fire. This news of his was entirely different. The Islanders grew silent, all eyes on Michael. Fire on the island was a grave danger, and he spoke of fire in a tone of dread.

"We smelled smoke," he said, "and it got into the tower and it got worse. From the platform on top we saw grass and bushes burning inside the cleared circle. They put it there and set it on fire."

"In the security circle around the tower?" Drake asked.

Michael nodded, and he bent down, with his hands on his knees, still exhausted by his rush to share the news and bring help. Drake signaled for quiet. Several knots of people stood away and whispered among themselves. Jimmy, one of the island's firemen, and Sophie remained, their attention riveted on Michael.

Drake set a hand on Michael's shoulder, his gut lurched from the thought of fire on the island, and the danger to the judge and the others in the tower, including his best friend.

"Okay, Michael, tell us what happened."

"The fire, like I said. Not too many flames but lots of smoke. We had to plug the ventilation ports. Still, the smoke is coming in from cracks."

Jimmy said, "Sounds like some military smoke there along with the bushes and grass."

"Michael," Drake said, "Did you see flames outside the cleared area around the tower? Were trees on fire?"

Michael shook his head. "No, only on the ground, like grass and low bushes."

"It's the Colombian enforcers, the two assassins," Drake said. "They've figured out that the judge is inside the tower and they're trying to smoke him out."

"Everyone is fine so far," Michael said. "The smoke inside rises, so if people sit on the floor, it's okay."

"But – " said Jimmy, looking at Drake.

"You're right. The smoke also blocks visibility. People in the tower are blind to an attack across the cleared area. The assassins can attack when and where they please, even sneak to the top of the tower if they rig a make-shift ladder or grapple."

Everyone looked at Drake and he said, "Let's get on up there. We need a car to get to the path. That'll save us ten minutes."

A man trotted off and a moment later returned with a weather-beaten Jeep.

"Will this do?"

"Amen," said Jimmy with a smile.

Everyone jumped in, and hung on.

"Wait," said Drake. "Can you run me by my place?"

"Sure."

Drake sprinted inside his cottage and gathered pistols for himself, Jimmy, and, following a stern look from Sophie, her as well. He passed around extra magazines. He kept three hand grenades for himself.

He and the others hung on while the Jeep careened up the steep road. At the entrance to the path, Drake and the others got off and Drake turned to the driver.

"Can you stay here and wait, in case we need you later?"

"I'll wait all day if you want."

"Good." Drake clapped him on the shoulder. "But you leave the Jeep. Take the keys and get into the woods so you can just see the Jeep. Make sure you can move further away if need be."

The man melted into the bush, invisible, and they entered the track. Michael set a fast pace, arriving at the Coxon home in under ten minutes. There were no dogs – they were with the kids at a house back in town.

Drake was breathing hard and felt like something the cat dragged in, wondering if there were at least one square inch of his body that didn't hurt. Sophie was out of breath but looked okay, if he didn't look too hard for the bruises, starting to color a dark purple. Jimmy was fine, and Michael had gotten his second wind.

Drake began to sort out his options against the assassins as he aimed to bypass the main house and move uphill, to where the tower was located.

Michael interrupted his thoughts. "Follow me. " He he scampered up the front porch steps to the main house.

CHAPTER 56

Webb was tempted to shoot the fisherman out of hand because he was a witness.

The old guy maneuvered his wooden boat toward Jorgue's dock. Sure, the man had pulled him out of the water, and had agreed to take him halfway around the island instead of straight to town, which would have been a hell of a lot quicker.

They neared the dock, and Webb jumped off with the bow line, tied off to a cleat, then did the same at the stern.

"I'll be right back with the gas," he told the fisherman, now standing, stretching his legs.

Webb climbed the steps toward the house. Sure, Matazos would give him a pistol and he could shoot the fisherman. But Webb was a practical man. There was a time and place for killing and torture, but only to advance his reputation and therefore the business.

Otherwise, that sort of thing resulted in unnecessary complications. The body for one. Witnesses for another. And finally, all the evidence. Better in this case to thank the fisherman, give him gas so he could return home, and let him be on his way.

Jorgue was a different story, Webb thought as he walked across the lawn and around the pool. Now there was a candidate for murder and torture. That double-crosser had detonated the explosives and damned near killed him. The blinking light had barely caught Webb's eye, and he dove into the water, down deep, without a split second to lose. Damn near thing.

But again, practicality raised its head. Gotta keep Jorgue alive. See the operation from his point of view and agree it all made sense. Pain in the ass to his pride, but there it was. Besides, with the sport fisher cooked and probably sunk by now, Webb needed a ride out of whatever firestorm Jorgue and the two assassins had up their sleeves.

Webb paused and talked to the backyard guard, said he needed to see *Señor* Matazos.

The guard called in the request. "He will come right away."

Webb took a seat on a pool chair. The guard placed himself between Webb and the French doors.

In less than a minute, Matazos appeared, shaven, hair combed, dressed in khaki shorts and colorful island shirt. But his eyes looked bleary. The man must have remained awake through the night, on hand to help solve problems encountered by the assassins. Matazos approached with a concerned expression. He spread his arms, Webb rose for a tight *abrazo*.

Matazos backed away, holding Webb by the shoulders. "I was worried about you."

Webb looked at his lying eyes. But he nodded anyway and shrugged like it was no big deal. "You gave me a warning with the flashing light. It was up to me to jump quickly. Sort of took me by surprise. Figured it would only blow if I keyed it locally."

"You're right," Matazos said, smiling, "but when I saw you right where you needed to be and no fire, I knew you had some trouble brewing. I heard the shots, as I stood up there on the promontory. Looked like you had your hands full. We needed the distraction, so I sent the signal. I knew you'd get off the boat."

That last part was a lie for sure, Webb thought. *Well, we'll see who comes out on top after I work the politics with your narco boss.*

"And now you are here," Matazos said. "You look fine. Do you have injuries? Shall I call my doctor friend?"

Webb gestured. "No need. I dove underwater and was shielded from the fire. The bow section still floated and burned, but it's gone by now."

"Good," said Matazos. "The cook will be here any minute, *mi amigo*. Feel free to take a shower, get into clean clothes. I will have someone call you and we can enjoy an early breakfast."

"Thanks, Jorgue, but I still need to take care of Sophie."

"Oh?" Matazos said, scowling, "I thought that was first on your agenda. She still lives?"

"Yeah, another fisherman pulled her and Drake out. The seas were choppy, but I caught glimpses before we reached the west end of the island."

"Drake as well? How did he – "

Webb gestured. "Long story. But they're both out there. I don't give a rat's ass about Drake, but I need to find Sophie, quick as possible, because when your two folks get done with whatever it is they're doing, the police are going to swarm the island like angry hornets."

"Yes, that is clear. I have made arrangements. Within an hour, a helo will take us off. We will catch a private jet on St. Thomas before the alarm reaches that island, and will soon be in international air space, headed for Colombia."

Matazos let that sink in for a second, and before Webb could ask, he said, "You are welcome to join us. In fact, I strongly advise you to do so. You will be linked to us, no matter that you are not a part of the plan."

"Very kind of you, Jorgue," appreciative, in spite of his feelings about the man. Jorgue could have said there was no room on the helo, but there it was. His motivation was simple – he wanted in on the next deal they'd been discussing.

"On this Sophie problem," Webb said, "I'll need to borrow a pistol."

"Yes."

"And I need to know where she is."

Matazos' eyebrows raised in question, then his face brightened.

"Ah, yes. Because where the Marine goes, Sophie goes. And the Marine will go to where the judge is located."

"Santiago? He's their target?"

"Yes, I can tell you. Even now, they may have succeeded, and in hours this will be on the news all over the world."

"To assassinate him?"

Matazos shook his head. "Preferably to kidnap, but if that is not possible, yes, assassinate. But to your question, because I believe I understand that you will skip breakfast."

"That's the plan."

"Okay then. They are at the tower you saw on Google Earth. They have scouted it and have seen preparations had been made, such as clearing all bushes in a space around the tower, and women coming and going with kitchen things. He is certainly there, along with his guards."

Webb's expression must have shown doubt, because Matazos continued.

"Also, Juan and Maria checked the judge's compound and found it deserted. There have been no helos visiting the island since their arrival, so the judge is still on the island. He would not hide in town or with any of the others on the North Side because only the judge's compound has security features. My compound is the only other."

"And you think he's holed up in the tower?"

"It's the only logical place. That is where you will find Juan and Maria. Drake will go there to help protect the judge."

"How are Juan and Maria going to attack?"

Metazos shrugged. "It is their problem. And Cliff – do not waste time interrogating her. I can hold the helo for only ten minutes after Juan and Maria board, not a moment more."

CHAPTER 57

Drake followed Michael, with Jimmy and Sophie close behind. They entered the shaded great room to find Michael pulling away a rectangular section of the grass matting that covered the floor. He looked up as he lifted a hinged wooden hatch. He stood, holding the hatch.

Drake peered down to what had to be a hurricane cellar, lit by a flickering kerosene lamp. He led the way down a set of stairs, asking as he descended, "Is there a passage to the tower?"

"Yes," Michael said, pride in his tone.

Sophie was the last to descend the stairs, visibly shaking, her face drawn. Drake reached took her hand. "What's wrong?"

She came to him and clung tightly. "In Jorgue's house," she said with a trembling voice, "I was imprisoned in a cellar like this, all afternoon. Then, that woman from Colombia, Maria, tied me to a chair and was..."

Drake held her, listened to her sob once, then sniffle, and swallow. She let her arms drop to her side and stepped back. Still close enough for Drake to see face eyes in the dim light of the lantern. Gone were the sharp lines of worry, replaced by arched eyebrows and a look of determination.

"She was going to torture me to death." She gestured with a fist. "That's behind me. She will not touch me tonight. Not ever." She looked around at her three friends. "Thanks to you."

One by one, she touched their shoulders and looked them in the eye. "And thanks to the people of this island." The men nodded gravely.

After a moment, Michael climed the stairs and fiddled with the carpet and the hatch. "The matting will look normal in case anyone comes snooping."

He motioned for Jimmy to stand to one side, away from a door in the north wall of the cellar, about four feet high, made of hand-hewn boards. He gestured for Jimmy to take the kerosene lantern and grasped a second one set just inside the dark tunnel.

The cool, dusty feeling of the cellar was accentuated in the tunnel, a stone-faced structure with a low arch that caused everyone to stoop.

Michael's voice echoed hollowly as he said, "This was an emergency escape route during the early days, when pirates still roamed the islands. Dad says he hasn't been down here in years, and he had trouble finding the hatch in the tower. It was buried for security, and we all dug for about half an hour before we found it."

Drake brushed against the rough stones, rougher than the walls of the main house. The pad and scrape of footsteps upset ancient dust that tickled his nose.

He asked, "What's the situation in the tower?"

Michael said, "Lots of smoke, mostly outside, making it so we can't see, but also leaking inside, looking like a thick cloud."

"But people can breathe?"

"The judge is having problems. Everyone is sitting on the floor and that helped, because the smoke rises in a cloud."

They trod forward, Drake organizing his thoughts, wanting to hear from the judge's security guards before forming a plan. The floor sloped upward after the tunnel emerged from under the house, and Drake felt his legs working. He remembered the steeply slanting mountainside, and realized they were paralleling that. Easier to move the wounded this way rather than have to negotiate stairs or a ladder at the tower. He admired the original Coxon, a canny and tough guy, judging from George's stories.

After ten minutes, a light shone ahead and soon they reached the hatch into the tower. Smoke had wound its way into the tunnel, and Drake sniffed.

"Like, we thought, Jimmy," he said.

"Yeah," Jimmy said, "part fire, part chemicals. Lucky it's not tear gas."

"I figure they plan on combat inside the tower and don't want the bother of gas masks."

"Roger that."

Michael climbed into the tower and Drake followed. As the others joined them, Drake surveyed the interior. There was no physical damage, either from flames or munitions, which was good news.

He shifted his thoughts to what was going on outside. Were there other fighters in addition to the two assassins? In the time he was away, someone could have landed by boat or helo. No, that didn't make sense. They would have all arrived together. As an integrated unit they could then reconnoiter and lay detailed plans.

Drake concluded that only two people faced them, accustomed to working together by the sound of the intel Walters had received from the Colombian authorities. They could be married, could be brother and sister.

At any rate, they were veterans from Colombia's guerilla war. Walters labeled them as enforcers or assassins. That type worked best on their own with no one to answer to. Did their own recon, worried about their own logistics, depended only on each other.

One of the security guards, the somber inside man, approached Drake.

"Welcome, Señor Drake. Thank you for coming to our little *fiesta*."

They shook hands and felt the firm clasp of a European, not the gentle Latino grip. The guard made firm eye contact. His lips were compressed, indicating tension. But he had made light of their situation, a '*fiesta*,' displaying courage. The guard gestured at the floor, and they both sat, with Jimmy joining them.

"The breathing is easier here," the guard remarked.

By the far wall, the judge sat calmly, his back straight, head up, with a handkerchief to his face. He removed the cloth for a moment and inclined his head to Drake slightly in greeting. Drake responded, but stayed put, with safety and not courtesy on his mind.

"What's our situation?" Drake asked.

"*Señor* George and my associate are on the platform above, moving from place to place, keeping an eye out for an attack from any quarter. Five minutes ago, my associate told me that the smoke still comes. We are certain it is not only from burning brush and grass, but also from smoke grenades."

Drake nodded toward Jimmy and said to the guard, "That's our thought, too."

The guard continued. "There is no visibility around the tower except at the very top. The entire perimeter to the woods is obscured. Someone could ascend on a ladder or place a charge on the tower and we would never see them."

"Could they grip the gaps between the rocks and climb?" Jimmy asked.

"Maybe, depending on their skill. They have shot several times, using pistols. They have not used anything heavier, such as RPGs. We believe the shots were to keep our heads down, and that was about twenty minutes ago, after the fire and grenades smoked up the outside."

"You've blocked the air vents?" Drake asked.

"Yes, right away, but smoke comes through cracks in the mortar." After a pause, the guard said, "I think we should evacuate the judge. He has been coughing and he is not a young man."

"I agree," Drake said. "I think you and your partner should take him out through the tunnel. Sophie and Michael as well."

"Good. We agree," the guard said. "But I am concerned for his safety outside the tower. What will happen if the attackers look inside and discover the judge is no longer here? This is the problem, *señor*."

"I have a plan," Drake said.

CHAPTER 58

Sophie had been less than thrilled about hiking in semi-darkness through the claustrophobic tunnel with its creepy spider webs. She wondered why men seemed to love such places.

Richard, in front of her, had a freaking spring to his step, in spite of his injuries from the explosion. She was glad when they had finally climbed out of the tunnel, hopefully never to see it again.

Now, inside the smoky tower, Michael sat a little away from the others, his face somber. Jimmy kneeled close to Richard and one of the judge's Spanish guards. The judge, by the wall, looked fatigued and tense. Thinking he might like company, she joined him.

He sketched a smile behind the handkerchief that he pressed to his nose.

"Judge Santiago," she said, "I'm Sophie Cooper."

They shook hands. His palm was sweaty. His eyes, watery from the smoke, showed – what? Resolve, she decided.

"Yes," he said in a kind way, "I thought you were Sophie. I hear from Richard that you are an athlete."

A simple conversational opener, she realized, but something else came into sharp focus – from the way he said 'Richard' and from the body language of the judge and the guard. They welcomed Richard to their side. They showed no stiffness, no anger that he had been absent during the initial attack on the tower, no feeling that he had deserted the man he was paid to protect.

She suddenly understood. The judge had given his permission – perhaps more than that – for Richard to save Sophie rather than remain with him and his guards. She felt a wave of gratitude.

"Judge," she began.

He made a dismissive gesture.

"No need," he said.

She admired him. Under attack by trained killers, yet so generous and humble.

"Now, Sophie, you must tell me about yourself. Surely your life is more interesting than that of a dusty judge. From your tan, and the way you move, you must be an athlete, as Richard said."

"I'm pretty good at swimming." She smiled.

"Yes, I understand. And you are a sailor as well."

"Richard told you?"

"Yes. The whole island is in your debt."

She frowned. "That's what people keep telling me, but I see it the other way around. Everyone has accepted me as if I am part of a big family. I've never felt so at home."

"Perhaps you will decide to stay?"

She blinked, wondering how she could be talking so freely with this man, an international judge. "I'm working for John in his store, and, well, once this is over…I don't know."

His eyes twinkled. "There is no hurry, Sophie. Do you have a university degree? You sound like an educated woman."

"Yes – "

Guns fired. Bullets ricocheted off stone. A handful of mortar squirted from a seam between two rocks in the wall. The white dust fell onto Sophie's t-shirt, the one given to her by a woman in town. She brushed it away. Heard more shots, then an agonized groan.

Richard and the guard rushed up the tower ladder and disappeared into the smoke. The hatch to the platform opened.

CHAPTER 59

Webb was sweating like a stuck pig by the time he reached the deer track that ran above the suspected Coxon home. He strode the path as fast as the foliage allowed, wanting to get to the Sophie problem solved as quickly as possible.

This was his so-called best shot for finding Sophie. But he wondered. Had Matazos lied to him, as he had so often in the past? A lie of omission perhaps? The best kind. The one you could back out of.

No, he decided. Matazos wanted in on the next job, and the one after that. Because, whether they trusted each other or not, they each brought to the table his own contacts, resources, and skills. Which were mutually beneficial. Sure, theirs was a partnership of convenience, but it was lucrative and not to be lightly thrown away. Webb concluded that Matazos had probably told him the truth about the assassins and their mission, and where they were headed – to the tower up the mountain from the Coxon home.

Webb continued forward, hunched down to avoid branches that hung too high for deer, but at face level for him. A flock of green parakeets fluttered toward the east, far overhead. Where the morning air was fresh – not hot and heavy.

His feet ached. Crotch still throbbed. God, the shit he had to endure in this life.

He passed the branch he had placed across the track, and he paused. Listened. Only the usual drips and bumps of the forest, a place much like the scrub of Florida but denser and without pine trees.

Before Webb got too close to the tower, he veered off the path and trudged uphill. He debated whether to make his presence known to the assassins, and decided not to. Their attention was focused toward the east. To approach such people from behind, no matter how noisy he made himself, risked surprising them and receiving a quick gut shot in greeting.

But he still needed to find the tower and assess the surrounding foliage and terrain. Only after knowing the layout, he could predict the attack and the defense, and from there develop his strategy.

Matazos never said, but he implied that Juan and Maria preferred small arms and knives for combat. They liked to fight up close and personal. Stealth was their specialty, and that was likely their strategy to take the tower. But Webb was curious. How did they intend to get close to the tower? And would they scale its walls or attack through the door? Each option would in turn present options for Webb.

Webb realized he would likely have to remain hidden and watchful until the fighting commenced. To predict was easy enough, but to predict correctly, following engagement with the enemy, was impossible. He was confident of an opening for his purpose and understood the need for patience.

He sniffed the air. Smoke!

Webb stopped, looked around, and there to the east, where he believed the tower was located, he detected the faintest wisp of gray, wending among the trees and bushes. He looked all around. Yep, only there.

Webb smiled. Gotta give the assassins credit. They were smoking out the judge and his guards. Maybe Drake and Sophie as well.

Fire – what a weapon. Everyone feared fire. And smoke – a foolproof way to become invisible. A blanket of smoke completely erases the ability of defenders to locate an approaching enemy.

He followed the smoke, which slowly increased in density and spread to either side of his route. After a minute, he changed direction, diagonally to his right, aiming to position himself directly downhill of the tower. Just close enough.

He was off the trail now, and the smoke surrounded him, equally dense on all sides. The only orienting element was the slope of the mountain.

He paused to catch his breath. Wished he had water. But once again, he had neglected to bring supplies. No food or water. His hunting buddies would laugh their asses off.

He heard shots, uphill and slightly to the right – pistols, judging from the sharp reports.

Smiling grimly, he moved in that direction, his thirst forgotten.

CHAPTER 60

The moment Drake emerged onto the platform, he saw George was down, blood seeping from a wound in his left shoulder.

Another shot rang out, the bullet striking the low parapet. Sheared stone skittered across the platform. The guard already on the platform gave Drake an odd look when he saw that Drake wore the other guard's clothes. He spoke briefly to his associate, who'd arrived on the platform with Drake. They then separated and shifted from gap to gap along the crenelated wall, checking for the expected attack, their movements cool, methodical.

Drake crawled to his friend's side. Blood was seeping, not pumping, which meant no major blood vessel was cut. That was about all Drake could tell. But he knew his friend was definitely out of action.

George spoke between gritted teeth, "I poked my head out too far I guess, trying to check if they were scaling the tower."

"Can you move?" Drake asked.

"Yeah, I can slide over to the hatch. Right arm's fine. Feel like an idiot."

"Can happen to anyone," Drake said, helping George position himself at the hatch. He turned the wounded man's feet toward the top rungs of the ladder. "Did you see them?"

"Couple of times we saw movement. Only for a second. Do you think they have anything heavier than pistols? Plastic explosive? They could blast the door and we'd never see it coming."

George had his foot on the ladder now, right hand holding a rung, left arm hanging free, blood oozing.

"We think they're only using pistols and knives," Drake said, "with the smoke screening them."

Drake watched George descend into the smoky interior, pictured Jimmy and Michael helping him. Fortunately, Jimmy had his medical kit with him.

The two guards continued to shift position, watching. Drake waved at the guard who'd first been on the platform. By now, his partner would have filled him in on the plan. Having gotten his attention, Drake gestured toward the hatch.

The guard looked at his partner, received a nod, slithered across the platform, and down through the opening. Drake pictured him exchanging clothing with Jimmy. He hoped George would still be able to play his part in the plan.

Another shot twanged onto rock. Drake hoped to hell there were only two people out there, that they only had small arms, and that the smoke was going to clear in the coming few minutes.

Jimmy emerged from the hatch, dressed as a guard. He tossed Drake a lopsided grin and thumbed the fabric of the shirt, as if to say, 'nice touch, don't you think?' Drake shook his head in mock dismay at his friend's cocky humor.

Jimmy tapped the remaining guard on the shoulder and the guard departed, replaced a minute later by Michael, poking his head through the hatch.

"We're going. Dad's okay – he's staying and he said he'll do whatever you say." Michael looked scared and excited and about to say something else, but seemed to decide not to. He disappeared down the ladder.

"Just us now, partner," Jimmy drawled.

"Yep, plus George."

"George the pirate," murmured Jimmy.

CHAPTER 61

Sophie shuddered as she descended into the black maw of the tunnel, feeling like she was jumping out of the frying pan into the fire. She almost preferred the tower and guessed she had more faith in the structure than the men had.

Michael led the way with his lantern, the judge was next, and she took up the rear, carrying the second lantern. Amazingly, the downhill trip was more difficult than the trek uphill to the tower. It was like descending a mountain trail, except for the tunnel wall rocks poking her shoulders, the slippery grit on the floor, the low ceiling. Oh yeah, and the spider webs.

When they reached the door to the hurricane cellar, Michael turned with his finger to his lips. He doused his lantern and gestured for Sophie to do the same.

Freaking pitch black.

"Haunted house in Disney World," she breathed, not believing how calm her voice sounded.

The judge chuckled.

"Shhh," from Michael.

A hinge squeaked and then went silent. Then squeaked, longer this time as she pictured Michael peeking into the hurricane cellar, checking for intruders.

"We can go into the cellar," he whispered. "After you enter, move to the right and stand still. I'll check the hatch to the great room."

He didn't mention the possibility of people with drawn guns waiting in the great room. She said a prayer.

Michael pushed upward, and a sliver of light appeared around the edge of the trap door. Sophie's mind veered disconcertingly to that last cellar she had occupied. Tied to a chair. Staring at glistening steel knives.

"All okay," he said. "I'll go up and be sure. If I don't come back soon, return to the tower, like we talked about. Use your hands to guide yourselves – you'll be fine."

"Okay," whispered Sophie.

After five long minutes, the trap door opened an inch.

"It's clear," he said in a quiet voice, then he opened the trap door fully, flooding the cellar with light and a hint of fresh air.

The judge, and then Sophie, emerged. The light in the great room seemed way too bright. She squinted back into the cellar and couldn't even see the bottom of the stairs in the gloom. She blinked. Drew a full breath of fresh air.

"To the kitchen?" she asked.

"Yes," Michael said. "But first, we shut the storm shutters."

Sophie remembered their discussion in the tower. The houses and the kitchen must all look like they were locked up tight and deserted. There were no actual locks of course, only pivot-bars to hold the shutters from the outside of one door, and from the inside for windows and other doors. Defense against hurricanes, Jumbees (island ghosts), and of course, wandering killers.

After closing the shutters, they gathered in the dark kitchen. Michael lit a candle.

"Saves kerosene," he remarked. "We'll have to put it out at night or if anyone comes snooping around."

"I wish the dogs were here," Sophie said.

"Me too," Michael said, "but Dad told me they'd bark, and give us away."

"Yeah," Sophie said. "I'm sure he's right."

They sat on chairs at the small table and listened. Few sounds filtered through the thick wooden shutters. Sophie heard the judge's breathing. Michael cracked his knuckles, then admonished himself in a whisper to be quiet.

Sophie recalled the judge's resolute last words to his two stone-faced guards, "Go! Help these people. Take your orders from Drake until this is over. I realize the risk and I accept."

CHAPTER 62

Drake carefully lifted the wooden bar from the metal fittings on either side of the tower door. He set the bar aside and opened the door an inch.

Outside, a dirty gray cloud filled the air, forming a visually impenetrable mass. Bad news for Drake's plan.

No, there was a break, for a moment, as a tendril of morning breeze parted the cloud. There was another, offering a momentary peek at blue sky.

Jimmy tapped his shoulder. "Thirty minutes since they left in the tunnel. Ten minutes to the house, ten to check it out. I think they're safe."

Or caught, Drake thought, but he said, "Good. Shut the trap door and cover it with sand."

"Already done."

Drake turned to the guards. "Ready?"

They nodded.

Drake looked at Jimmy in the guard's uniform, at a bandaged George, dressed in the judge's trousers and white shirt.

"Okay, gentlemen, here we go."

They slipped out, the last man silently shutting the door.

The guards dropped to the ground and crawled on their bellies down the mountain. Their goal for this first leg was fifty feet – about fifteen meters.

Drake, followed by George, and then Jimmy, crouched in the cloud of smoke. They waited a minute for the guards to gain distance, then walked furtively around the tower and to the east, across the cleared perimeter, into the bush. Drake carefully parted branches as the three men moved through the woods.

Drake examined for the tenth time the logic of his plan. It contained elements of risk, but remaining in the tower was even riskier. The assassins had probed the tower, found it structurally sound, and they'd probed the courage of the defenders on top of the platform. Again, no weaknesses. From the woods, they could observe those on watch and must have judged that they were on constant alert.

Which left either the use of plastic explosive on the door or scaling the tower with a grapple or makeshift ladder. Likely, they had no explosive but Drake did not know for sure. He did know those two assassins were masters of stealth attack. Supposedly, time was on the defender's side, but so far, the enemy seemed to have all the time in the world. As he pushed forward, Drake swallowed his doubts and focused on strategy.

As they moved further from the tower, the smoke dissipated, replaced by morning sun, its heat descending through the trees. The air smelled clean and salty. Drake paused, heard crashing waves ahead.

They continued forward, George looking a little loopy from the morphine Jimmy had given him after dressing his wound. As the group's rear guard, Jimmy eyed their backtrail.

The trees thinned as they approached the east shore of the island, and the sound of pounding surf increased. Then, only wind-bent bushes remained, their roots grasping rocky ground. Here and there lay driftwood, thrown from the sea by past hurricanes.

They paused at the edge of a precipice, with the blue sea beyond and black, wave-washed rocks fifty feet below.

"End of the line," said Drake. He looked at Jimmy, just catching up. "Any sign of them?"

"Not physically, but I got the itch, like someone was watching me, you know?"

"Yeah, I know." He surveyed the barren eastern end of the island, brushed his wind-blown hair, made his decisions.

"We'll take position there and there," he said in a low voice, pointing to two bushes about forty feet apart, close to the edge of the precipice. Like all the other bushes, they were about knee high and desiccated, hardly qualifying for cover, barely better than nothing. Drake gestured and said quietly, "George, you can put yourself between us, but closer to the precipice. Wouldn't want you in our fields of fire."

Silently, Drake and Jimmy lowered themselves onto their bellies, eyes toward where the tower lay, backs to the sea.

"George," Drake whispered. "Can you see the edge okay?"

"Yup, all along the edge. No one's gonna sneak over."

At least during daytime, Drake thought, again wondering how long the assassins were planning to stay. Someone must have reported the fire at sea. Also, Walters should be hustling police, maybe special forces. He thought of the judge, of Sophie. Well, Sophie first, and his lips twitched.

At least Webb was dead.

CHAPTER 63

Webb was puzzled – through a momentary break in the smoke, two uniformed men and a person he assumed was Judge Santiago walked away from the tower toward the east end of the island.

What the hell? Had the assassins made life too hot in the tower? What a dumb move those three guys were making by deserting the structure. All they'd had to do was stay inside those tall stone walls. Now they were out in the open. The assassins could sneak up on the guards like silent ghosts, then they could kidnap the judge. Didn't the guards realize that?

But where was Drake? How about Sophie? Webb had believed they'd all be together. He thought he'd seen them in the other fishing boat after the explosion. But the light was poor – maybe they died in the fire. Were the guards and the judge the only people left?

What the hell? Not fifty feet from him, a bush moved. He shifted position, found a break in the foliage. A man was crawling on his belly. Drake! Alive. And, Jesus, there was another man. Was Sophie alive, too? Probably, but she was nowhere to be seen.

Then the whole picture clicked into focus in his mind. The judge and his guards were the target – bait to draw out the assassins. Drake and his partner would be on the flank of the judge and his guards. The assassins were good, but to remain invisible in the sparse foliage close to the sea from two different vantage points was impossible. Someone – the guards or Drake and his buddy – would spot their movement and kill them.

Webb scowled. Should he warn the assassins? Hell no – those pompous bastards didn't deserve a warning. Let them figure it out for themselves.

He knelt, counted to two hundred to be sure Drake and his partner were on their way, then he turned downhill.

Because a thought had occurred to him.

CHAPTER 64

They'd been in the kitchen for less than an hour when footsteps sounded on the porch of the main house. Sophie's blood froze.

Her eyes darted to the judge, to Michael. Their expressions of fear confirmed it. Someone was out there.

Sounds came to her of someone releasing the locking bar on the front door, of hinges too long without oil. The footsteps faded, meaning the intruder was inside the house on the grass matting.

God – could it be Cliff? That was something he'd do, walk into a place he had no business being. But he had been killed in the fire. How about the assassins? No, they'd be silent if they came around. This person was making noise.

The footsteps sounded again on the porch.

Sophie looked at Michael. "That's someone looking for me or Judge Santiago. He won't care about you. Hide! Find a cupboard and crawl in. After he takes us, you run for help. Not to the tower. Run straight to town. Start with John at his store. He'll know what to do."

Michael's expression turned from fear, to doubt, to resolution. Sophie let out a breath. Give him credit for courage – must be the Coxon pirate blood in his veins.

He opened and closed doors below a long counter. Found one he liked and began carefully removing big pots, placing them on the counter, neatly arranged as if that was where they were kept.

There was a tapping on the kitchen windows, the door. Followed by a splash on each window.

The tang of gasoline entered the kitchen. Sophie's heart stopped. Michael climbed inside the cupboard. Sophie looked into the judge's eyes.

A voice from the grave sounded through the door. "Sophie, I know you're in there. Everyone left the tower, even the judge. I saw his guards lead him toward the east end of the island. Your boyfriend and another guy are up there too, trying to trap the assassins. So that leaves you. They wouldn't leave you in the tower and they wouldn't risk you getting caught walking to town. Nope, they'd tell you to shelter right here."

"Go away!" Sophie yelled. "The police will be here very soon. Richard called them when we landed. They've probably already arrived by helo."

"Not a chance, Sophie. Guess what? I found the gas that the Coxons use for their lawnmower. It's all gone now, because I splashed it on the wooden storm shutters. I'm counting to three. I have a lit kerosene lantern. At six it will be too late. I won't let you leave. You'll die in the fire. One…"

Sophie shook her head with dread. She was tempted to tell the judge to hide, but…

"Two…"

"Okay," she said. "Okay, come in. I'm unarmed."

"No, Sophie, you come out. Hands up."

She motioned for the judge to get on the floor behind the table. He did so. Looked at her and they nodded. *Good-bye.*

Outside, the sun was bright. Cliff stood ten feet from the door, a pistol in his right hand, aimed at her belly.

"Right over there," he said, pointing, "lie down on your stomach, hands behind your back."

She lay down in the warm sand.

"You have that little look, Sophie, like you're lying to me. Why would you lie? What is there to lie about?"

Keeping the pistol aimed at her, he carefully entered the kitchen. Peered in. And whooped in delight.

"Judge Santiago! Come on out, judge."

Webb stepped away from the door, shifting his aim between Sophie and the judge. The judge stepped out, eyes blinking in the bright sun.

"Gosh, judge, you don't look as fierce as your picture, do you?"

CHAPTER 65

Drake heard the merest whisper of cloth against dry brush as the judge's two guards crept to their positions to his left.

He visualized one looking north and east, covering his flank, and the other scanning back and behind for a possible surprise attack. Drake rested his right hand in front of him, grasped his pistol – finger outside the trigger guard, safety off, cocked.

They were all ready.

Maybe the assassins saw 'the judge and his two guards,' maybe not. If they had, they would arrive in the next hour. Maybe much sooner. Certainly no longer – their clock was ticking.

They could have withdrawn already, out of prudence. But Drake felt that was unlikely. *He* sure wouldn't have quit if he were in their shoes, not with possible success so close.

The surf pounded far below, and the air grew still. A seagull cawed. George shifted his position, stifling a groan. Jimmy and the two guards made no noise and lay perfectly still.

Drake had heard the stories about military-trained snipers, a version of assassins. They learned to stalk their prey with almost no cover. They lavished infinite patience on every movement of an arm or leg and advanced at such a slow pace they appeared stationary.

Were Juan and Maria that skilled, that patient? No doubt they could sneak up on someone in the jungle of Colombia and slit a throat without their victim ever knowing he was in peril. But how about here, with the bushes only knee high? Were they thrown off their game by such unfamiliar terrain?

Drake tried to blink away his doubt, and his fatigue from a sleepless, hazardous night. He maintained his vigilance, scanning ahead and to the side, barely moving his head, overlapping the field of view of Jimmy to his right, and the nearest guard to his left.

A cicada stirred in the woods, sharp and scratchy. Parakeets zipped overhead. His left foot itched.

Abruptly, he stopped scanning and shut his eyes. Drew a slow, long breath. He felt eyes on him. How could that be? No matter. Eyes, watching. Not far, ahead and to the right. Now gone. Now back, brushing past his position.

He avoided the temptation to look directly at the source because that would alert a sensitive enemy. He pointed his eyes to one side, close but not exactly aimed at the searching eyes. He saw it – a spot very close that had been bare a minute ago but now appeared dense and shadowed.

A bead of sweat formed on his brow. Again, he shut his eyes and breathed, opened his eyes. Checked the shadow. Slightly changed, less of a shadow now. Same bearing. Which meant he – or she – had spotted him and was advancing.

Drake maintained his breathing. Slow, controlled. But he couldn't control his racing heart or the beads of sweat trickling down his forehead and into his eyes. He slipped his finger inside the trigger guard of his pistol.

The shadow formed against a stand of grass, six inches high. The attacker's vision scanned him once, twice. Range five feet.

Drake felt the trigger with his finger, applied ever so slight pressure. Pictured his arms and legs ready for action, ready to spring. Damned sweat in his right eye. He blinked away the sting.

The grass moved an inch to the side.

Four feet from him the assassin's face appeared, soot-blacked.

Drake raised to his knees, right arm extended, finger contracted once, twice, three times. Cordite stench in the air.

The body spasmed once.

Drake fell flat, backed up from his former position, ignored the stones poking his body. Moved four feet to the left. Smelled the coppery stench of blood, heard the first flies buzz hungrily to the corpse.

Resumed his scan.

One down.

To his left a scuffle. Silently, Drake turned. The guards were on their feet, pistols pointed down. A figure rose, threw a knife. One guard grunted in pain. Both guards fired three shots. The figure – Maria in jungle fatigues – folded into an angular heap.

Drake rose, signaled the guards and Jimmy to kneel and cover him as he checked Juan and Maria for pulses. None. Remaining on his feet, he scanned the area for other attackers, moved forward five paces, scanned again.

He motioned to the others, and they all moved in a line across the land in front of their positions, pistols at the ready, inspecting for potential enemies.

After two minutes, Drake raised a hand, signaling a halt. They were alone.

CHAPTER 66

Sophie pushed through the all-to-familiar woods on the faint deer track, the judge and Cliff behind her. The judge was breathing hard but maintained his pace. Webb limped, as if his feet hurt.

They'd travelled for about fifteen minutes. Thankfully, Webb had not searched the kitchen and hadn't burned it down. It would have been like him to destroy the kitchen, even the main house, out of spite. But he beamed like a little boy in a toy store, at his victory of capturing not only herself but the judge as well.

Sophie guessed they were heading to Matazos' compound. Maybe he'd secured a get-away boat, maybe ordered a helo to take his team off the island. Richard, Jimmy, and the guards were fighting the assassins. Maybe that had already happened and she prayed that Richard's side had won.

But, even if they had won, they didn't know that Webb had survived the fire. Richard would feel no urgency to go to the Coxon kitchen because he thought she, the judge, and Michael were safe.

The police and Coast Guard were nowhere to be seen. She felt helpless frustration surge over her body, weakness in her arms and legs, the pinprick of tears behind her eyes. Sophie slogged ahead.

She tried to shake off the feeling of doom. She'd gotten through that awful squall and the fireball. She could get through this, even though her thoughts felt mechanical, forced, because all the cards were stacked against her.

What would Richard do? He'd keep looking for opportunities. He'd never give up. Okay, to start with, she decided not to try to escape on her own. She'd stay with the judge. Maybe they could escape together, maybe not, but they were staying together.

But Sophie felt her choice was fully justified, if only because she owed the judge her life. If Richard had remained on the island as part of the judge's security detail, instead of rescuing her from Webb's boat, the judge might still be free. Make that *probably* be free. The judge had willingly taken that risk. She was deeply in his debt.

She decided her best bet was to surprise Webb – disarm him and knock him out. Easily said, but he maintained a wary distance. She trudged onward.

The ground grew steep and rocky. Through a break in the foliage, she saw a clearing a hundred yards ahead. She recognized the grassy area behind the place Richard called the promontory, high above the crashing waves. She heard the hiss and crash of the waves to her left, pictured them far below the edge of the cliff.

An idea came to her.

CHAPTER 67

Drake gathered the others around him. The two guards looked serious, Jimmy grinned, and George appeared subdued.

"Good work," Drake said. "They were skilled opponents."

Jimmy, noticing the guard holding a hand over his wound, strode to the man and unshouldered his medical kit. He snipped the sleeve of the man's shirt to get a better view and the man said something in Spanish.

The other guard told Jimmy, "He says it's a good thing the shirt is not his own or he would have to buy a new one."

"Hmm," said Jimmy, looking closely at the wound, "Lucky for me too. It's Richard's shirt."

Drake shook his head. "I guess I'll bill the judge."

Everyone chuckled.

"The knife grazed your arm," Jimmy said, swabbing the wound with antiseptic.

The guard nodded.

"Gracias. Mejor no estuvo a la derecha, a la corazón."

His partner translated, "He said, better not to the left, to his heart."

"Roger that," Jimmy drawled, tying on a field dressing. "There. Good as new, *amigo.*"

"Gracias."

Drake took a deep breath. "We better check on the judge, Sophie, and Michael."

George led the way.

When the house appeared, they spread out and approached carefully.

Drake sidled up to the door, sniffed what smelled like gasoline, and carefully peered inside.

"Clear," he said.

The guards searched the other buildings and declared them empty. At a rustle of trees, they all turned.

An ashen-faced Michael ran into the yard between the buildings.

"A man splashed gas on the shutters," Michael gasped, "He yelled for us to come out or he'd set us on fire. Sophie told me to hide. She said the man was only after her and the judge, and she was right. He took them prisoner and never looked inside the kitchen. I waited until they were gone. Just started on my way to tell John in town when I heard you coming."

"Who was it?" asked Drake, puzzled. They'd just killed the two assassins, and Webb died in the boat fire. Was it Matazos?

"Sophie called the guy 'Cliff,'" Michael replied.

Damn. So Webb had escaped the fire.

"Matazos doesn't have another boat at his pier," Drake said thoughtfully. "They must be on the way to the helo pad."

The others nodded. Drake turned to Michael, standing next to his father, the older man's arm tight around his shoulders.

George said, "You've done very well, Michael. We're going after them. We'll take the Jeep." He looked at George. "Can you two get to John, ask him to call the police in St. Thomas? I'll call Graham Walters as well." Drake looked at the wounded guard. "Do you want to go with them?"

The guard nodded in understanding. "*No. Voy con ustedes.*"

"He's coming with us," said the other guard.

Drake smiled. "I got it. Good. We can use you."

They trotted down the track toward the road. On the way, Drake called Walters, who said the police were on their way to the island, and also to guard the airport on St. Thomas.

Drake figured Webb was traveling along deer tracks to stay out of sight. That would slow him down.

"We'll intercept them at the promontory," Drake said. "If we wait until they reach the helo pad, we'll have Matazos against us as well."

"Do we have time?" asked the wounded guard.

"Just barely, even with the Jeep."

CHAPTER 68

Sophie caught the judge's eye as Webb continued marching them toward the promontory clearing. *When I shout,* she mouthed, *run! Understand?*

He frowned, but then gave a brief nod.

A few steps further on, she spun on her heels, looked the judge square in the eye, pointed away from the path. "Now!" she yelled at the top of her lungs.

The judge, his eyes hazed with fatigue, caught her urgency, turned and flew headlong into the woods to his right. Sophie bounded to the left.

"Damn you two to hell!" Webb shrieked.

Sophie surged ahead, pushing limbs aside, dodging bushes, pumping her legs up the steep ground toward the clearing. She knew she could gain valuable distance by running across the grass and get outside the range of Webb's pistol. With the judge running in the opposite direction, at least one of them had a chance of escaping. If she succeeded, she could lose herself in the woods and work her way to town and wait for the police.

She was off the deer track and rushing through the woods. Branches whipped her face. She ducked and twisted, avoided the large trees and bushes, but she had to maintain speed and ran over the small foliage.

Behind her a pistol fired, followed immediately by splintering impacts on a tree five feet to her left. She faked to the left for two paces, then returned to her original uphill track, gulping air. More shots, and near misses, then more gunfire. No doubt aimed at the judge.

She heard a yell and groan and muttered a prayer. *Dear God, let it only be a wound.* She hoped she hadn't gotten the old man killed. She continued to run and dodge, and suddenly sprang out of the woods onto the grassy clearing.

Sophie forced her legs to keep moving as she sprinted across the grass. She looked behind her, saw where the deer track entered the field – thankfully now empty of Cliff.

But he would soon appear. She looked right and saw four men emerge from the bush, all breathing hard, eyes searching. She kept running, but looked closely. Two of the men were dressed in uniforms, two in civilian clothing.

Oddly, one of the uniformed men looked like Richard, and she remembered the ruse of switching clothes. It *was* Richard!

She veered toward the four, waving her arms to get their attention, warn them of Cliff close by. "Richard! Richard!"

His face burst into a smile and he ran the remaining distance to her. They embraced and she felt tears streaming down her cheeks. She pulled back, panic in her chest.

"Webb is alive! He found us in the kitchen and he's just shot the judge."

"We heard the shots," said one of the guards, gesturing toward the bush. "Where did this take place?"

"There," Sophie said, pointing toward the deer track. "About a hundred yards down the track and to the left."

"How badly hurt is he?" Jimmy asked, looking back at her as he and the two guards sprinted away.

"I didn't see. Only heard him yell," Sophie said.

She felt Richard's arm around her shoulders as they stood alone on the promontory clearing.

"You are one spunky lady," he said, wiping a tear from his eye. He gave her a quick hug, and then stepped back. "So, Cliff is still out there," he said, gesturing with his pistol.

"How about the assassins? Where are they?" She asked.

"We got them," Richard said as he scanned the woods to either side of the track. "They're both dead."

Sophie felt relief for only a moment. She, too, scanned the woods and shivered in the morning sun. Cliff was in there. She knew the guards and Jimmy were more than a match for Cliff, but now he was desperate. He had become the hunted, and was even more dangerous than before.

There was brief motion to the side of the path and out stepped Webb, pistol aimed at Sophie. He stood fifty feet away, perhaps less – well within pistol range.

CHAPTER 69

Drake stepped to Sophie's side and accessed the grim situation. He and Webb were armed and capable, but Webb's crazed expression gave him a terrible edge.

In his next breath, he was going to kill.

No matter whether Drake shot first.

"Put the gun down," commanded Webb.

Drake bent and placed his pistol on the grass, stood straight, hands raised.

Webb stepped to within ten feet of Drake and Sophie, wearing a smug expression. "Richard Drake. All dressed up like a guard. I've got to admit, you had me fooled back there at the tower. I guess you fooled the assassins too, switching outfits. You even had a fake judge. Too bad, really. I hoped they would've cut you to pieces by now. I guess I need to kill you myself."

Drake felt like an idiot, but he banished the thought, kept his mind alert. The situation was pretty grim, he admitted. The guards and Jimmy would never get back in time. Webb had ten feet of distance, plenty to shoot Sophie and then him before he, Drake, could rush the man.

"I think I'll kill you first," Webb said. "You've screwed up my plans big time and I owe you for cold-cocking me by the pool."

Webb raised his pistol, aimed for Drake's chest. Drake looked him in the eye and Webb squeezed the trigger.

Nothing happened.

Drake tensed, ready to spring.

Webb cocked the pistol, released the slide, pulled the trigger. Drake saw the man strain, as if pulling the trigger harder was the solution. Must've been a jamb, Drake thought.

He sprang forward, hoping to get to Webb before he cleared the jamb. Webb swung his pistol like a club, Drake only partially blocking a hard blow to his left shoulder.

"You're toast," Webb growled, pounding Drake with fist and pistol.

Drake's guard was up. He deflected much of Webb's attack, managed a quick punch to Webb's gut and heard a satisfying wheeze.

Webb quickly recovered, dropped the pistol and swung a roundhouse to Drake's jaw, another to his chest. Drake blocked, then counterpunched the man's gut and face, aware that he was pushing Webb toward the edge of the promontory.

Drake, noticing Webb's limp, stepped close, slammed a boot on top of Webb's right foot and stepped back, feinted and clobbered the left foot.

Webb's face contorted in pain and rage.

Drake smiled to himself. *Angry people don't think straight.* He charged again, kicked the man's shins. Tried for a crippling side blow to the knee but Webb turned away at the last moment. Drake charged with a left and right, to chin and chest.

Webb fought back, held his ground.

Drake pushed harder, got Webb to step backwards. Drake drew a quick breath and lunged with all his strength.

A surprised Webb backed another pace and now stood less than a dozen feet from the crumbling edge. Drake looked him in the eye, pulling all the man's attention, all his rage, to him.

Webb obliged, attacking with a windmill of lefts and rights. Drake took an awful blow to his chest. He sidestepped, which put Webb off balance, and charged, head down, his fists punching. Webb backpedaled, desperate to regain his balance.

At the edge, Webb must have felt the spongy earth. He looked behind himself, realized he had no place to go, and glanced at Drake, his expression of fury replaced by wide-eyed fear.

Drake shoved with his final reserves and Webb tottered back, thrust his arms forward, fingers grasping for Drake, but finding only air.

Webb's back foot pedaled in the void, his front foot remained in place, and the man's body pivoted, arms spinning in desperation. His front foot lifted and Webb tipped back and fell in a long arc.

Three seconds later, Drake heard a sickening crack. He peered over the edge. Saw Webb's contorted body, sprawled on black, wave-washed rocks.

CHAPTER 70

The judge's compound appeared on the right of the road, and Drake sauntered through the open gate, looking forward to joining the party – the judge's way of thanking everyone on the island for their help. Lights shone brightly, with dusk gone and night upon them.

A different guard stood at the gate with George Coxon. Coxon gave Drake a bear hug with his good arm, then stood back, grinning.

"Look at you! Wearing clean clothes for a change."

"Yeah," Drake drawled. "Figured it was about time."

"And me," said Jimmy Franklin, stepping out of the shadows, holding a bottle of Heineken. "All dressed up for a party."

"And me," said Sophie, smiling broadly.

"How about me?" asked Jenny. "I found you guys." She beamed at Sophie. "Just like you found me."

Drake laughed, elated to be home with a whole island full of family. They walked toward the front door of the judge's house. After a few steps, George lagged behind and Drake turned.

"Come on, George," he said, "Join the party – you earned it."

"I'll be right there. I'm sort of a visual ID checker for the guard. Only the islanders are invited."

"Is there anyone else on St. Mark except the usual folks?"

Coxon grinned and nodded toward the guard. "Not really, but the security folks want to be extra careful till the dust settles."

The party was out back, and Drake, with Sophie at his side, spent the first twenty minutes thanking the judge and accepting congratulations from everyone.

He looked for the two regular guards, standing watchfully at the edge of the crowd, and thanked them for their part in rescuing the judge and Sophie.

After pleasantries, Drake said, "You know, there's one thing that puzzles me."

"What is that?" the inside guard asked.

"Webb tried to kill me. He pulled the trigger, but his pistol didn't fire. The slide wasn't locked. If he was out of bullets, the slide would lock back, right? It was a Glock – I thought they did that."

"Well, I looked, and the magazine was empty, so, yes this is a mystery." The guard shrugged and patted Drake on the shoulder.

"You were lucky, *señor*. If the slide had been back, he would have known the magazine was empty, and he would have reloaded." The guard gave a rare smile to Sophie and then faced Drake.

"Perhaps *la señorita* is your lucky charm. But you know, many things can cause a slide not to function, like a weak hold on the grip, bad ammo, even a crack in the magazine."

They talked for a while longer and then Drake and Sophie moved among the islanders. After a while, Drake excused himself and joined a man he'd seen hovering at the edge of the gathering. He extended his hand.

"Hi, Graham. Glad you could make it."

"Thanks," Walters said, shaking hands with his friend. "You look like shit."

"Yeah. Spent a little time in the water, some in the bush. Got a little dehydrated." He lifted his beer. "Getting back on track, though."

"Just dehydration? You don't suppose we're getting old, do you?"

"Naw. Hell, we're still here, aren't we?"

They went silent for a minute, scanning the crowd. Then Walters spoke.

"Starting yesterday when you guys were wandering all over the island shooting people and throwing them off the promontory, St. Mark's had a minor invasion by the FBI, police from Spain, officials from the international court in the Netherlands, and me from home-town St. Thomas. Amazingly, we all worked together okay. I think your judge had something to do with that. He's quiet-spoken and has all that old-world courtesy, but he's got a spine of steel."

"Yeah, I've seen that quality in him more than once."

"Anyway," Walters said, "everyone went back to fill out their reports, so I'm the only one left visiting, courtesy of the judge."

"The judge?"

"Yeah, he let me ride the helo over this evening with all the goodies for the cook-out. George provided a pig to roast, and the locals brought their specialties, but the judge flew over cold beer, wine, ice cream for the kids, and some good eats. Anyway, he invited me."

"Well, thanks for coming. Means a lot to me."

"Wouldn't miss it. Gotta admit, I was worried for a while there, getting the first calls from John, you almost roasted by a fireball and all. But, hell, I knew a Marine like you would pull through okay."

Drake shook his head, but smiled. He knew what his friend really meant.

"What happened to Matazos?" Drake asked.

"He was snagged in St. Thomas. I guess he figured he'd gotten off St. Mark early enough. Booked a morning flight to San Juan. But your call, and John's, gave us all the time we needed to be on hand at the airport for his arrival. He gave up peacefully."

"What'll happen to him?"

"Three countries want to extradite him, and the Feds want him as well. We sent him to Puerto Rico for holding while everyone figures it all out."

They talked for a while longer. The party was winding down for most people, accustomed to getting up early in the morning.

Sophie walked over, and after introductions a small talk, Walters politely excused himself. Drake put an arm around her shoulders.

She snuggled close. "I hope I didn't cause too much trouble," she said.

"Well, it was sort of a perfect storm with the Colombian enforcers and Cliff showing up at the same time, all loaded for bear. But no, you didn't cause any trouble. You got caught in the crossfire."

"And nearly killed," she said with a shudder.

"I'm sorry I couldn't get to you before Cliff shut you away in Matazos' house. Would've saved a lot of trouble."

"I'm glad you tried. I knew you would. And you kept trying. Is that a Marine thing?"

"*Semper Fi*. No one left on the field. And the truth is that everyone on this island sticks together. We all saved each other."

"You're right," she said. "We all stuck together."

She sipped a Spanish wine that came over in the helo. He took a pull on his Heineken.

"What'll you do now?" he asked.

"Well, I'll help John in his store for a while. For the long term, I've got to do some thinking."

"Take your time – it's a big decision. Could take, oh, maybe a couple of years?"

"You're sweet, James."

"Yeah."

"Sometimes."

He reached up to muss her hair, but she blocked him and grinned. They gazed at the judge's manicured back yard, listened to the crashing surf.

"It's getting late," he said, "can I walk you home?"

"I'd like that a lot."

They thanked the judge, said their good-byes, and walked hand in hand down the road toward the Coxons'.

Bugs sang, the stars twinkled.

When they reached the trail to the house, Sophie paused.

"I was planning to walk you to the door," Drake said.

"Thanks, but there was something I was thinking." She squeezed his hand. "I know the island is safe again, but I was wondering if I could – well, stay with you tonight."

"Sure, but…"

She stepped close, put her hands around his waist, and looked up at him, pretty in the moonlight.

"I know you only have one bed and I certainly wouldn't want you to sleep on the floor."

Drake caught the mischievous glint in her eyes.

She took both of his hands and said softly, "I think that will work out okay, don't you? That is…"

He pulled her close and kissed her, enjoying the feel of her in his arms, and the feel of her arms around him.

ABOUT THE AUTHOR

Jonathan Ross spent his boyhood summers in the countryside of St. Thomas, when the island residents lived much like folks on St. Mark – without electricity, catching rain for their water, and relying on Tortola sloops to ferry people, livestock, and small cars from island to island. He saw charcoal being made the old way, climbed rocks along the rough coast, stepped on sea urchins, and watched shooting stars on dark Caribbean nights. You may visit him at Facebook.com/ jonathanrossnovels and at jonathanrossnovels.com.

Made in the USA
Monee, IL
03 July 2020